In the Onyx Lobby

By Carolyn Wells

Originally published in 1920

In the Onyx Lobby

© 2011 Resurrected Press
www.ResurrectedPress.com

Published by Resurrected Press

This classic book was handcrafted by Resurrected Press. Resurrected Press is dedicated to bringing high quality classic books back to the readers who enjoy them. These are not scanned versions of the originals, but, rather, quality checked and edited books meant to be enjoyed!

Please visit ResurrectedPress.com to view our entire catalogue!

ISBN 13: 978-1-937022-09-9

Printed in the United States of America

FOREWORD

Carolyn Wells began her career as a humorist, and this shows in *In the Onyx Lobby*. While murder is a serious subject, in the twenties and thirties, the detection of the same need be anything but. With a back story involving the romantic entanglement of two young lovers who's mother and aunt have been involved in a decades long feud and a plot that revolves around the secret recipe for British buns, it has all the makings of one of the "screw ball" comedic films of the era.

Set in Manhattan at a fashionable apartment building between Columbus Circle and Times Square, it provides the American counterpart to the British country house party mystery. There is the same closed circle of suspects consisting of the residents and staff of the building, the bumbling police officers that insist on following the wrong clues, and finally the appearance of the private detective to arrive at the solution in the last chapter. There is plenty of misdirection, with everyone suspecting someone else and throwing around aspersions and allegations.

Wells was always more interested in the interaction of her characters than in offering an accurate and serious portrayal of crime and detection. In many ways, *In the Onyx Lobby* can be considered a "mystery of manners" rather than a detective story, not that that makes her work any less enjoyable. Her crimes often had an "impossible" solution, but it was the process, and the comments it allowed her to make on the side, rather than the actual detection which were important.

Carolyn Wells was a popular and important figure in the history of American detective fiction. She is less well known today than she once was, and deserves to be more widely read. Her works are always entertaining.

For that reason, Resurrected Press is happy to offer this new edition of *In the Onyx Lobby*.

About the Author

Carolyn Wells, June 18, 1862 - March 26, 1942 was an American writer and poet. She was best known for her books of poetry and humor until around 1910 she read one of Anna Katherine Green's mysteries and took up the genre. Many of her mysteries featured the detective Fleming Stone. She was married to Hadwin Houghton, heir to the Houghton-Mifflin publishing company. She was a collector of poetry by other authors, and, upon her death, she bequeathed her collection of the works of Walt Witman to the Library of Congress.

Greg Fowlkes
Editor-In-Chief
Resurrected Press
www.ResurrectedPress.com

TABLE OF CONTENTS

CHAPTER 1: SUCH A FEUD! 1

CHAPTER 2: A TRICKY GAME 13

CHAPTER 3: THE SCRAWLED MESSAGE 25

CHAPTER 4: THE BUSY POLICE 37

CHAPTER 5: WHO WERE THE WOMEN? 49

CHAPTER 6: THE LITTLE DINNER 61

CHAPTER 7: ENLIGHTENING INTERVIEWS 73

CHAPTER 8: JULIE BAXTER 85

CHAPTER 9: THE LIBRARY SET 97

CHAPTER 10: SEEK THE WOMEN 109

CHAPTER 11: THE OLD FEUD 121

CHAPTER 12: ONE WOMAN AND ANOTHER 133

CHAPTER 13: MOTIVES 145

CHAPTER 14: PENNY WISE 157

CHAPTER 15: AND ZIZI 169

CHAPTER 16: TESTIMONY 181

CHAPTER 17: A WOMAN SCORNED 193

CHAPTER 18: FITTED TO A T 205

CHAPTER 1: SUCH A FEUD!

"Well, by the Great Catamaran! I think it's the most footle business I ever heard of! A regulation, clinker-built, angle-iron, sunk-hinge family feud, carried on by two women! Women! conducting a feud! They might as well conduct a bakery!"

"I daresay they could do even that! Women have been known to bake—with a fair degree of success!"

"Of course, of course,—but baking and conducting a bakery are not identical propositions. Women are all right, in their place,—which, by the way, is not necessarily in the home,—but a family feud, of all things, calls for masculine management and skill."

Sir Herbert Binney stood by the massive mantelpiece in the ornate living-room of the Prall apartment. The Campanile Apartment House came into being with the century, and though its type was now superseded by the plain, flat stucco of the newer buildings, yet it haughtily flaunted its elaborate facade and its deeply embrasured windows with the pride of an elder day. Its onyx lobby, lined with massive pillars, had once been the talk of the neighborhood, and the black and white tessellated floor of the wide entrance hall was as black and as white as ever.

The location, between the Circle and the Square,—which is to say, between Columbus Circle and Times Square, in the City of New York,—had ceased to be regarded as the pick of the householders, though still called the heart of the city. People who lived there were continually explaining the reason for their stay, or moving across town.

But lots of worthwhile people yet tarried, and among them were none more so than certain dwellers in The Campanile.

Miss Letitia Prall, lessee of the mantelpiece already referred to, was a spinster, who, on dress parade, possessed dignity and poise quite commensurate with the quality of her home.

But in the shelter of her own fireside, she allowed herself latitude of speech and even loss of temper when she felt the occasion justified it. And any reference to or participation in the famous feud was such justification.

Her opponent in the deadly strife was one Mrs Everett, also an occupant of The Campanile, and equally earnest in prolonging the life and energy of the quarrel.

Sir Herbert Binney, an Englishman, knighted since the war, had come to America in the interests of its own business, no less an enterprise than the establishment of an American branch of the great and well-known "Binney's Buns."

Celebrated in England, he hoped and expected to make the admirable buns equally popular over here, and trusted to his engaging personality as well as his mercantile acumen to accomplish this purpose.

Not exactly related to Miss Prall, Sir Herbert was connected by the marriage of a relative. That is, his stepbrother's son, one Richard Bates, was also the son of Miss Prall's sister. This young gentleman, who, by the way, lived with his Aunt Letitia, was another reason for Sir Herbert's presence in New York. He had thought that if this nephew showed the right sort of efficiency he could be set to manage the American branch, or, at least, have a hand in the management.

And so, Binney of "Binney's Buns" had established himself in one of the smaller suites of The Campanile, had had his living-room repapered to his taste, had made arrangements for his proper service, and was comfortably domiciled.

The fly in his ointment was that young Bates didn't take at all kindly to the Bun proposition. For the chap was of an inventive turn, and had already secured patents for some minor accessories and improvements connected with aeroplanes. Without parents or fortune of his own, Richard Bates was dependent, so far, on the generosity of his Aunt Prall, which, though judicious, was sufficient for his bodily welfare. But Bates was ambitious, and desired large sums with which to carry on his inventions, certain that they, in turn, would repay a thousandfold.

As the only legal heir of both aunt and uncle, and with utmost faith in his own powers of success, Richard requested, almost, indeed, demanded advance on his inheritance, sufficient at least to put over his present great piece of work, which was expected to prove of decided value in aeronautic plans.

But such advances were positively refused; by Miss Prall, because Richard declined to accede to an accompanying condition, and by Uncle Binney, because he wanted his nephew for his Buns.

The recipe for the famous buns was of an age and tradition that made it a historical document in England, and, as yet unattained in this country, it was sought for by bakers and bunners of repute. But it was not for sale. Sir Herbert Binney would establish Binney's Buns in America, and all good Americans could eat thereof, but sell the recipe to some rival bakeshop he would not. This state of things had made necessary much parley and many important meetings of Baking Powers. Among these were the great Crippen's Cake Company, the Vail Bread Concern, the Popular Popovers and others of sufficient importance to get a hearing.

Genial and good-natured, Sir Herbert met them all, discussed their offers and reserved decision. He did not say, even to himself, that he was waiting on the will of one young man,—but, practically, that was the truth. If Bates would give up his fool inventing, and take hold of the Buns in earnest, Sir Herbert would put him through with bells on, would make him heir of the Buns and all the great English properties that the Buns possessed, and would do all in his power to make the life of young Bates a bed of choicest roses.

But Richard Bates had all the obstinacy and stubbornness of the born inventor. He knew he couldn't devote to Bun business a brain teeming with new notions for the furtherance of scientific attainment. And he was too honest and honorable to accept the Bun proposition and then turn to aeronautics on the side. Nor was a side issue of sufficient importance to satisfy his hunger for his own chosen work. He knew he could put up the goods that he had in mind, if he could only get the presently needed money for his experiments and models. If he could but make either uncle or aunt agree to his views, he could, later, select his own roses for his bed of life.

But Sir Herbert was as obstinate as his nephew and Miss Letitia Prall more so than either of them.

Her unflinching and persistent adherence to her decisions was clearly shown in the matter of the long continued feud. Not every woman could meet an opponent frequently and casually for twenty years or so, and pursue an even tenor of enmity.

In the same social circles, Miss Prall and Mrs Everett attended the same teas, luncheons and bridge parties, yet never deviated one jot or one tittle from their original inimical attitude.

Never, or at least, very rarely, were there sharp words in the presence of others, but there were scathing silences, slighting inattentions and even venomous looks that could not pass unseen.

In fact, they carried on their feud after what would doubtless be conceded by connoisseurs the most approved methods.

And, indeed, after twenty years' experience it would be strange if the two ladies had not attained proficiency in the pursuit of quarreling as a fine art. Not always had they lived under the same roof. The Feud had begun when they were denizens of a small country town, and, fostered in that nourishing atmosphere, had attained its proportions gradually but steadily.

When circumstances took them to the city to live, and, as if afraid the unsociability of town life might interfere with their hobby, the Feudists acquired homes in two of the most desirable apartments of The Campanile.

Miss Prall, tall, spare and with the unmistakable earmarks of spinsterhood, directed her menage with the efficiency and capability of a general. She was nicknamed among her friends, the Grenadier, and her strong character and aggressive manner made the description an apt one.

Her one weakness was her adored nephew. As an orphaned infant, left to Miss Letitia a bequest from the dying mother, he had been immediately adopted into the child-hungry heart of the old maid and had held and strengthened his position throughout the years until, at twenty-five, he was the apple of one of her eyes, even as her precious feud was the apple of the other.

But hers was no doting, misguided affection. Miss Prall had brought up her nephew, as she did everything else, with wisdom and sound judgment.

To her training the young Richard owed many of his most admirable traits and much of his force of character. No man could have more successfully instilled into a boy's heart the fundamental requisites for true manliness, and only on rare occasions had his aunt's doting heart triumphed over her wise head in the matter of reproof or punishment.

And now, this upstart uncle, as Miss Prall considered him, had come over here from England, with all sorts of plans to take her boy from his chosen and desirable life work and set him to making buns!

Buns,—Binney's Buns! for her gifted inventive genius!

This impending disaster together with a new and regrettable development affecting the Feud had thrown

Miss Prall into a state of nervous agitation quite foreign to her usual condition of calm superiority.

"Masculine management and skill!" she repeated, with a fine scorn; "because not every woman is fitted by nature and circumstances to conduct affairs of importance it does not follow that there are not some feminine spirits with all the force and power of the other sex!"

"By gad, madam, that is true," and Sir Herbert watched the Grenadier as she sat upright in her arm-chair, her fine head erect and her straight shoulders well back. "I apologize for my seeming slight to your quarrelsome abilities, and I concede your will and strength to fight your own battles. In fact, my sympathies are for your antagonist."

"Huh!" and Miss Prall looked at him sharply; for he had been known to express satirical sentiments under guise of suavity. "Don't waste your solicitude on her! She, too, is able to look out for herself."

"It would seem so, since she has taken part for twenty years in what is still a drawn battle."

"Let up, Oldsters," laughed young Bates, coming breezily into the room. "You know the main facts of the historic Feud, Uncle Herbert, and, take it from me, sir, no amount of argument or advice on your part will help, or in any way affect it. Aunt Letty will eat up your talk, and then floor you with——"

"Floor me! I think not! Binney, of Binney's Buns, is not of the floorable variety."

"You say that because you haven't yet really met Auntie Let in the arena. Binney's Buns would cut no better figure than,—let us say, Crippen's Cakes."

"Crippen's Cakes! Do you know Crippen?"

"Does she!" and Richard Bates grinned; "why, the Cake Crippen is one of Aunt Letitia's old beaux,—might have been my uncle, if——"

"Hush, Richard!" said the aunt.

"If he hadn't also shined up to Mrs Everett, the rival faction." Richard went on, with open relish of his aunt's discomfiture.

"Hush, Richard!" she said, again, and this time some veiled hint apparently was efficacious, for he changed the subject.

"I say, Uncle Herb, what about the Follies to-night? I've got a couple of seats,—and I know your tastes——"

"Front row?"

"No; couldn't corral those,—but good ones, in the fourth."

"Nay, nay, Pauline. I don't see well enough to sit so far back. Use those yourself, Richard,—take your aunt, here! But I'll find a seat in the front row,—in some front row, if I have to buy their bloomin' theater to get it!"

"Good for you, Sir Herbert!" exclaimed Miss Prall, who admired determination wherever she met it. "I'll go with *you*. I like the front row, too."

"Sorry, madam, but I'm not taking guests." He winked at Richard.

"Naturally not," Miss Letitia sniffed. "I know why you want to go alone,—I know why you want the front row! You're going to attract a chorus girl, and invite her to supper with you."

"Marvelous, Holmes, marvelous!" Sir Herbert exclaimed, with mock amazement. "I am surprised at your clairvoyance, ma'am, but deeply pained that you should know of and be so familiar with such goings on. Do you learn of that sort of thing from your nephew? Really, Richard, I'm amazed at you!"

"Nonsense, Uncle Bin, I passed through that stage long ago. I used to girl around in my callow days, but I got fed up with it, and now life holds more worthwhile temptations. It's an old story to auntie, too. Why she used to chaperon my giddiest parties,—bless her!"

Sir Herbert's sharp eyes looked from one of his companions to the other.

"You're a pair," he opined, "both tarred with the same brush."

"And the brush?" asked Miss Prall, belligerently.

"Modern sophistication and the present-day fad of belittling everything that is interesting or pleasurable."

"That mental phase is the inevitable result of worldly experience," said the lady, with a cynical smile. "How is it that you preserve such youthful interest?"

"Well—" and the Englishman looked a little quizzical, "you see, the girls are still young."

"Very young," assented Bates, gravely. "There's a new bunch of Squabs at the Gaynight Revue that'll do you up! Better buy that place out, Unkie!"

"Perhaps; but now, young Richard, let's discuss some more imminent, if not more important, questions. Say, Buns, for instance."

"Nothing doing. I've said my last word on the Bun subject, and if you persist in recurring to it, you'll only get that last word over again,—repeated, reiterated, recapitulated and,—if necessary,—reenforced!"

"With some good, strong epithets, I suppose," remarked his uncle, calmly. "I don't blame you, Rick, for being bored by my persistency, but you see I haven't yet given up all hope of making you see reason. Why I do——"

"Well, when you do—what?"

"Time enough to answer that question when it's time to ask it. Instead, let me recount the advantages I can offer you——"

"Oh, Lord!—pardon my interrupting,—but that recounting is an old story, you know. Those advantages are as familiar to my wearied mind as my own name,—or at least as yours,—and your precious Buns——"

"Stop, sir! Don't you speak slightingly of Binney's Buns! They were eaten before you were born and will be eaten after you are dead and forgotten."

"Not forgotten if I put my invention over!"

"You'll never do it. Your success is problematical. The Buns are an assured fact. They were eaten before the war,—they will be eaten again now that the war is over. They are eaten in England,—they will be eaten in America. If not with the help of your interest and energy, then with that of some one else. Think well, my boy, before you throw away fame and fortune——"

"To acquire fame and fortune!"

"To strive for it and fail—for that is what you will do! You're riding for a fall, and you're going to get it!"

"Not if I can prevent it," Miss Prall interposed, in her low yet incisive tones. "I'm ready to back Ricky's prospects to the uttermost, if only—"

"If only what? What is this condition you impose on the lad? And why keep it so secret? Tell me, nephew, I'll let you in on the Buns in spite of any blot on your scutcheon. What is it that troubles your aunt?"

"What always troubles her? What has spoiled and embittered her whole life? Hardened her heart? Corroded her soul? What, but her old ridiculous, absurd, contemptible, damnable Feud!"

"There, there, my boy, remember your aunt is a lady, and such expressions are not permissible before her——"

"Pish! Tush!" snorted Miss Prall, who would not have herself objected to that descriptive verb, since it gives the very impression she wanted to convey, "If I did not permit such expressions Richard would not use them, rest assured of that."

Bates smiled and lighted a fresh cigarette. These tilts between his elders greatly amused him, they seemed so futile and inane, yet of such desperate interest to the participants.

"Then that's all right," Sir Herbert conceded. "Now, Richard, for the last time, I offer you the chance to fall in with my wishes, to consent to my fondest desire, and attach yourself to my great, my really stupendous enterprise. I want, with my whole soul, to keep Binney's Buns in the family,—I want a worthy partner and successor, and one of my own blood kin,—but, I can't force you into this agreement,—I can only urge you, with all the powers of my persuasion, to see it rightly, and to realize that your refusal will harm you more than any one else."

"I'll take a chance on that, Uncle Bin." Bates gave him a cheery smile that irritated by its very carelessness.

"You'll lose, sir! You'll see the day that you'll wish you had taken up with my offers. You'll regret, when it's too late——"

"Why, what's your alternative plan?"

"Aha! Interested, are you? Well, young sir, my alternative plan is to find somebody with more common sense and good judgment than your rattle-pated, pig-headed self! That's my alternative plan."

"Got anybody in view?"

"And if I have?"

"Go to it! Take my blessing, and stand not on the order of your going to it,—but skittle! You can't go too fast to suit me!"

"You're an impudent and disrespectful young rascal! Your bringing-up is sadly at fault if it allows you to speak thus to your elders!"

"Oh, come off, Uncle Binney! You may be older than I in actual years, but you've got to hand it to me on the score of temperamental senescence! Why, you're a very kid in your enthusiasm for the halls of dazzling light and all that in them is! So, and, by the way, old top, I mean no real disrespect, but I consider it a compliment to your youth and beauty to recognize it in a feeling of camaraderie and good-fellowship. Are we on?"

"Yes, that's all right, son, but can't your good-fellowship extend itself to the Buns?"

"Nixy. Nevaire! Cut out all Bun talk, and I'm your friend and pardner. Bun, and you Bun alone!"

A long, steady gaze between the eyes of the young man and the old seemed to convince each of the immutability of this decision, and, with a deep sigh, the Bun promoter changed the subject.

"This Gayheart Review, now, Richard,——" he began.

"Don't consider the question settled, Sir Herbert," said Miss Letitia Prall, with a note of anxiety in her voice, quite unusual to it. "Give me a chance to talk to Ricky alone, and I feel almost certain I can influence his views."

"A little late in the day, ma'am," Binney returned, shortly. "I have an alternative plan, but if I wait much longer to make use of it, the opportunity may be lost. Unless Richard changes his mind to-day, he needn't change it at all,—so far as I am concerned."

"Going to organize a Bakery of ex-chorus girls?" asked Bates, flippantly. "Going to persuade them to throw in their fortunes with yours?"

A merry, even affectionate smile robbed this speech of all unpleasant effect, and Sir Herbert smiled back.

"Not that," he returned; "I'd be ill fitted to attend to a bakery business with a horde of enchanting damsels cavorting around the shop! No, chorus girls are all right in their place,—which is not in the home, nor yet in a business office."

"That's true, and I take off my hat to you, Uncle, as a real live business man, with his undivided attention on his work,—in business hours,—and outside of those, his doings are nobody's business."

"With your leanings toward the fair sex, it's a wonder you never married," observed Miss Prall, inquisitively.

"My leanings toward them in no way implies their leanings toward me," returned the bachelor, his eyes twinkling. "And, moreover, a regard for one of the fair sex that would imply a thought of marriage with her, would be another matter entirely from a liking for the little stars of the chorus. To me they are not even individuals, they are merely necessary parts of an entertaining picture. I care no more for them, personally, than for the orchestra that makes music for their dancing feet, or for the stage manager who produces the setting for their engaging gracefulness."

"That's so, Uncle," Bates agreed; "you're a stage Johnny, all right, but you're no Lothario."

"Thank you, Son, such discriminating praise from Sir Hubert Stanley, makes me more than ever regret not having his association in my business affairs."

"Don't be too sure that you won't have him," Miss Prall temporized; "when does his time for decision expire?"

"To-night," said Sir Herbert, briefly, and at that, with a gesture of bored impatience, Bates got up and went out.

Chapter 2: A Tricky Game

The Prall apartment was on the eighth floor, but Richard Bates passed by the elevator and went down the stairs. Only one flight, however, and on the seventh floor, he walked along the hall, whistling in a subdued key. The air was an old song, a one-time favorite, "Won't you come out and play wiz me?" and the faint notes grew stronger as he passed a certain door. Then he went on, but soon turned, retraced his steps, and went up again the one flight of stairs. Pausing at the elevator, he pushed the down button and was soon in the car and smiling on the demure young woman in uniform who ran it.

"This car of yours, Daisy," he remarked, "is like the church of Saint Peter at Rome, it has an atmosphere of its own. But if the church had this atmosphere there'd be mighty few worshipers! How can you stand it? Doesn't it make you ill?"

"Ill?" and the girl rolled weary eyes at him; "I'm dead! You can bring the flowers when you're ready, Gridley!"

"Poor child," and Bates looked compassionately at the white face, that even a vanity case failed to keep in blooming condition, so moisty warm was the stuffy elevator. "It's wicked to shut you up in such a cage——"

"Oh, I'm all right," she responded, hurriedly, as her bell sounded a sharp, impatient ring. "I'm not complaining. But people are so trying on a day like this. That's Mr. Binney's ring."

"How do you know. Do you know everybody's touch?"

"Not everybody's,—but lots of them. Mr. Binney, he hates elevator girls——"

"Oh, come now,—my uncle is a great admirer of all women——"

"Not if they work. He talks a good deal, you know,—
talks all the time,—and he's everlastingly knocking girls
who do the work he thinks men ought to do."

"But it's none of his business,—in this house!"

"Mr. Binney is particularly and especially interested
in what's none of his business!"

The girl spoke so bitterly that Bates looked at her in
surprise.

But he was at the ground floor, and as he left the
elevator he forgot all else in anticipation of a certain
coming delight.

He strolled the length of the great onyx lobby, its
sides a succession of broad mirrors between enormous
onyx columns with massive gilded capitals. Tall palms
were at intervals, alternating with crimson velvet sofas
and on one of these, near the vestibule, Bates sat down to
wait for the delight.

And in the course of time, she came, tripping along
the black and white diamonds of the marble floor, her
high heels tapping quickly, her lithe gracefulness
hurrying to keep the tryst.

Dorcas Everett was of the type oftenest seen among
the well-to-do young girls of New York, but she was one of
the best examples of that type.

Wise, sparkling eyes, soft, rounded chin held alertly
up, dark, curly hair arranged in a pleasant modification
of the latest fashion, her attire was of the most careful
tailor-made variety, and her little feathered toque was
put on at just the right angle and was most engagingly
becoming.

She said no word but gave a happy smile as Bates
rose and eagerly joined her and together they passed out
through the imposing portal.

"It's awful," she murmured, as they walked across to
Fifth Avenue. "I said I wouldn't do it again, you know,
and then—when I heard your whistle,—I just couldn't
help it! But don't do it any more—will you? You promised
you wouldn't."

"Oh, I didn't promise, dear; I said I'd *try* not to. And I did try, but—it seems I failed."

"Bad boy! Very bad Rikki-tikki-tavi. But what are we going to do?"

"First of all, where are we going? Tea Room? Some place where I can talk to you."

"No; it's too stuffy to-day to be indoors. Let's walk up to the Park and go in."

"All right. Now, Dorrie, we trust face this thing. We can't go on meeting secretly,—neither of us likes it,——"

"I should say not! I hate it a thousand times worse'n you do. But Rick, mother is more obstinate than ever. She says if I see you again, or speak to you, she'll pack up and move out of New York. Think of that!"

"I can't think of it! It is unthinkable! Now, Dorcas, darling, there's only one thing to do. You must marry me——"

"Hush that nonsense! I don't propose——"

"Naturally not! I'm doing the proposing——"

"Don't think because you make me laugh you're going to bamboozle me into consent! I decline, refuse and renounce you, if you're going to take that tack. I shall never marry you without the consent of my mother and your aunt, and you know it!"

"I do know it, Dork, and that's what breaks me all up. Confound that old Feud! But, I say, Uncle Binney is on our side. I sounded him and he approves of my marrying at once,—doesn't care who the girl is,—and will make me his heir and all that,——"

"If you give up your inventing and go into his Bunny business."

"Yes; that's his game. Shall I do it?"

"No! A thousand times no. I don't want to marry a bakery!"

"And anyway, it wouldn't help the Feud——"

"No; nothing will help that. It would seem that we could move the hearts of those two women, but my mother is hard as adamant."

"And my aunt is hard as nails. After all these years they're not going to be moved by a pair of broken young hearts."

"No; mother says that because I'm so young, my heart will heal up in plenty of time to break over somebody else."

"Pleasant thought!"

"Oh, mother doesn't try to be pleasant about it. She makes my life a burden by harping on my undutifulness and all that,—and when she isn't bally-ragging me, Kate is."

"Kate! A servant!"

"But Kate doesn't look upon herself as a servant, exactly. She's lady's maid now,—to mother and me,—but she was my nurse, you know, and she thinks she sort of owns me. Anyway, she acts so."

"And she stands for the feud?"

"Rath-er! She believes in the feud and all its works. And she's a spy, too. If she hadn't believed my yarn that I was headed for Janet's to-day, she'd been downstairs trailing me!"

"Clever Dork, to outwit her!"

"That's nothing—I'm clever enough to hoodwink her and mother, too, but I don't want to. I hate it, Rick; I hate anything underhanded or deceitful. Only my love for you made me come out here to-day."

The big, dark eyes looked wistfully into Bates' blue ones. The troubled look on Dorcas' dear little face stirred the depths of his soul, and his heart struggled between his appreciation of her high-mindedness and his yearning love.

"I want you, Dorrie," he said, simply; "I want you terribly,—desperately,—and I—I admit it—would be willing to take you on any terms. I'd run away with you in a minute, if you'd go! To be sure, I honor your truthfulness and all that,—but, oh, little girl, can't you put me ahead of your mother?"

"I don't know,——"

"You're hesitating! You've thought about it! Oh, Dork, will you?"

"There, there, don't go so fast! No, I won't! But, tell me this: Would your uncle stand for it,—and let you go on with your own work?"

"Oh, no! It's Buns or nothing with him and me. But I'm his heir, if he should drop off suddenly, I'd have his whole fortune——"

"Dead men's shoes! Oh, Ricky, for shame?"

"Not at all. If he can make a will, I can talk about it. And he told me he has made a will in my favor,—but he's going to change it if I don't adopt his Buns."

"What nonsense,—even to think about it. Let him change it, then, for you'll never be a Bun man!"

"I wonder if it would help matters if you met Uncle Binney?"

"Let's try it. Though I'm sure I should call him Uncle Bunny! Does he like girls?"

"Adores them,—that is, some sorts. He likes nice girls properly. He likes naughty girls,—perhaps improperly. But the girls in the house,—the elevator kids and the telephone girls, he just hates."

"Hates?"

"They irritate him somehow. He thinks all such positions should be filled by men or boys. He says the war is over, and he wants all the girls taken off those jobs."

"How unjust and unreasonable."

"Uncle Herbert has both of those admirable qualities. But he'd adore you,—unless he found out you disapprove of the Buns, and then he'd turn and rend you!"

"I don't disapprove of them,—except for you."

"That's what I mean,—for me."

"Then I guess I'd better not meet Friend Bunny."

"Oh, Dorcas, I don't know what to do! There's no light from any direction. There's no hope from your mother, my aunt or Sir Herbert. If you won't cut and run with me,— and if you're in earnest about not meeting me secretly any more,—what *can* we do?"

"Nothing, Rick,—nothing at all."

Dorcas spoke very seriously,—even sadly, and Bates realized how much in earnest she was. They were in the Park now, and by tacit consent they sat down on a bench near the Mall.

Their eyes met dumbly. Though Bates was only twenty-five and Dorcas twenty-two, they were both older than their years, and were of fine temper and innate strength of character.

They had known one another as children in their little home town, and later, as the feud developed and gained strength, the young people had been sent away to schools. Later, the war took Richard from home, and only very recently had propinquity brought about the interest that soon ripened to love. And a deeper, more lasting love than is often found between two young hearts. Both took it very seriously, and each thoroughly realized the tragedy of the attitude of their respective guardians.

"Good gracious, Richard, I shall go straight home and tell your aunt!"

This speech was from the stern-faced woman who paused in front of the pair on the bench.

"Good gracious, Eliza, go straight ahead and do so!"

Bates' eyes shot fire and his face flushed with anger.

Eliza Gurney was his aunt's companion, indeed, her tame cat, her chattel, and partly from charity, partly because of need of her services, Miss Prall kept Eliza with her constantly.

Of a fawning, parasitic nature, the companion made the best of her opportunities, and, without being an avowed spy, she kept watch on Richard's movements as far as she conveniently could. And in this instance, suspecting his intent, she had followed the young couple at a discreet distance, and now faced them with an accusing eye.

"No, don't," pleaded Dorcas, as Miss Gurney turned to follow up Richard's suggestion. "Oh, dear Miss Gurney, help us, won't you? We're in such a hopeless tangle. You were young once, and——"

Dorric could scarcely have chosen a worse argument,—for that her youth had slipped away from her, was Miss Gurney's worst fear.

"I am forbidden to speak to this girl, Richard," Miss Gurney said, with pursed lips and heightened color. She addressed herself carefully to Bates and ignored the presence of Dorcas. "You are, too, as you well know, and though you have so far forgotten yourself as to disobey your aunt, I've no intention of committing a like sin."

"Fudge, Eliza, don't go back on me like that. You used to be my friend,—have you forsaken me entirely?"

"If you've forsaken your aunt,—not unless. Leave this girl instantly and go home with me, and there'll be no question of 'forsaking.'"

"Forsake Miss Everett! Not while this machine is to me! Go home yourself, Eliza; be a tattletale, if you want to, but get out of here!"

Bates became furious because of a malevolent gleam in Miss Gurney's eye as she looked at Dorcas.

"I'll go, Richard,—and I shall not only tell your aunt what I have seen, but I shall feel it my duty to acquaint Mrs Everett with the facts."

"Don't you dare!" cried Dorcas, springing up, and facing the unpleasant faced one with uncontrollable indignation. "What I do, I tell my mother myself,—I don't have the news carried to her by her enemy's spy!"

"Hoity-toity, miss, you're a chip off the old block, I see!"

"And you're a trustworthy soul, to be talking to me when you're forbidden to do so!"

The triumph in Dorcas' tone was quite as galling to Eliza Gurney as her own chagrin at having broken her word. But, once in the moil, she saw no reason for backing out, and proceeded to pick an open quarrel.

"I can explain my speech with you to Miss Prall's satisfaction," she went on, acidly, "and I'll inform you,

Miss Everett, that you've spoiled Mr. Bates' life by this clandestine affair of yours. I happen to know that his uncle, Sir Herbert Binney, was just about to make him his heir, but he will change his mind when he hears of this escapade."

"Oh, clear out, Eliza," stormed Bates; "you've given us enough of that drivel, now hook it! Hear me?"

Miss Gurney stared at him. "Your companionship with this young woman has corrupted your good manners," she began, quite undeterred by his wrath.

Whereupon Bates took her firmly by the shoulder, spun her round, and said, "Go!" in such a tone that she fairly scurried away.

"I vanquished her," he said, a little ruefully, "but I'm afraid it's a frying pan and fire arrangement. She'll tell Aunt Letitia, and either aunt or Eliza herself will go at once to your mother with the tale,——"

"Well, I'd really rather they'd be told. I had to tell mother,—for truly, Rick, I can't live in an atmosphere of deceit. I may be a crank or a craven, but much as I love you, I can't stand keeping it a secret."

"I know it, dear, and I don't like it a bit better than you do, only to tell is to be separated,—at once, and maybe, forever."

"No!" cried Dorcas, looking at his serious face. "Not forever!"

"Yes; even you don't realize the lengths to which those two women will go. I hate to speak so of your mother, I hate to speak so of my aunt,—but I know they'll move out of town, one or both, and they'll go to the ends of the earth to keep us apart."

"But they've always lived near each other,—for years, in the same building."

"Yes; that was so they could quarrel and annoy and tantalize each other. But now the necessity of separating us two will be their paramount motive, and you'll see;— they'll do it!"

"Then—then——"

"Then let's get married, and go off by ourselves? Darling, if we only could! And I'll go into the Buns, in a minute, if you say so. Much as I hate to give up my own work, I'd not hesitate, except for your sake——"

"No, I don't want to marry a bakery man! And, I've too much ambition for you to let you throw your talent away! Yet, we couldn't live on nothing a year! And, until your inventions are farther along, you can't realize anything on them."

"Bless me, what a little business woman it is! Well, we've both common sense enough not to make fools of ourselves,—but oh, Dork, I do want you so! And if it were not for that foolish, ridiculous feud, we could be so happy!"

"It isn't exactly the feud,—I mean, of course it is that, but it's back of that,—it's the determined, never-give-up *natures* of the two women. I don't know which is more obstinate, mother or Miss Prall, but I know,—oh, Ricky, I know neither of them will ever surrender!"

"Of course they won't,—I know that, too. So, must we give up?"

"What choice have we? What alternative?"

"None." Bates' face was blankly hopeless. "But, Dork, dear, I can't live without you! Can't you look ahead to—to something?"

"Don't see anything to look ahead to. We might say we'll wait for each other,—I'm willing,—and something tells me you are! But,—that's an unsatisfactory arrangement——"

"It's all of that! Oh, hang it all, Dork, I'll go into some respectable business and earn a living. I'll give up my plans and——"

"If you do that, you may as well go in for Buns."

"Buns! I thought you scorned the idea!"

"Principally because I want you to be an inventor. But if you give up your life work,—oh, Rick, what could you do?"

"Nothing much at first. I'd have to take a clerk-ship or something and work up."

"I'm willing to share poverty with you,—in theory,— but you don't realize what the reality would mean to us. Not only because we're both accustomed to having everything we want, but more especially because in these days it's too dangerous. Suppose we lived on the tiniest possible income, and then you fell ill,—or I did,—or you lost your position,—or anything that interrupted our livelihood,—then, we'd have to go back to mother or to your aunt,—and—dost like the picture?"

"I dost not! It's out of the question. I love you too much, and too truly to take such desperate chances. I think, after all, Dork, the Buns are our one best bet!"

"Binny's Buns! 'Get a Bun!' Oh, Rikki, couldn't hold up my head!"

"I know it,—you little inborn aristocrat! And I feel the same way about it. Well, we've got to go home and face the music, I suppose."

"Yes, and we've got to go now. I'll get more and worse scolding for every minute I stay here."

"Also, if Eliza tells your mother, she'll be sending Kate for you."

"Yes, or coming herself. Come along, let's start."

The walk home was saddened by the thought that it was the last. Able to face the situation, both knew there was no hope that they should be allowed to continue their acquaintance, and knew that now it was discovered, they would very soon be as widely separated as the efforts of their elders could arrange.

Their pace slowed down as they neared The Campanile.

"Dear old place," said Dorcas, as the house came into their ken.

"Dear old nothing," returned Bates. "I think it's an eyesore, don't you? That bunch of Mexican onyx ought to be taken away to make kings' sarcophagi!"

"What a thought! Yes, it's hideous,—but I didn't mean its appearance. Its dear to me because we've lived here together, and I've a premonition that before long widely separated roofs will cover our heads."

"I'll conquer somehow!" Bates declared. "I haven't made many protestations, but I tell you, Dork, I'm coming out on top of this heap!"

"What are you going to do? Something desperate?"

"Maybe so,—maybe only something queer. But get you, I shall and I will! You're intended for my mate by an Omniscient Fate, and I'm going to find some way to help said Fate along. She seems to be sidetracked for the moment."

"I wish I had more faith in your Fate helping. Oh, don't look like that! I've faith enough in *you*,—but helping Fate is a tricky game."

"All right, I'm willing to play a tricky game, then!"

"You are, son! Against whom?"

And the pair entering the wide doorway, met Sir Herbert Binney coming out.

"Oh, hello, Uncle," cried Bates, grasping the situation with both hands. "Let me present you to Miss Everett; Dorcas, this is my uncle."

"How do you do, Uncle Bunny?" said Dorcas, quite unwitting that, in her surprised embarrassment, she had used the very word she had feared she would utter!

And an unfortunate mistake it proved. The smiling face of the Englishman grew red and wrathful, assuming, as he did, and not without cause, that the young woman intended to guy him.

"Daughter of your own mother, hey?" he said to her. "Ready with a sharp tongue for any occasion!"

Apology was useless, all that quick-witted Dorcas could think of was to carry it off as a jest.

"No, sir," she said, with an adorable glance of coquetry at the angry face, "but I have an unbreakable habit of using nicknames,—and as I've heard of you from Ricky, and I almost feel as if I knew you,—I, why, I just naturally called you Bunny for a pet name."

"Oho, you did! Well, I can't believe that. I think you're making fun of my trade! And that's the one thing I won't stand! Perhaps when your precious Ricky depends on those same buns for his daily food, you won't feel so scornful of them!"

"I never dreamed you were ashamed of them, sir," and Dorcas gave up the idea of peacemaking and became irritating.

"Nor am I!" he blazed. "You are an impertinent chit, and I bid you good-day!"

"Now you *have* done it!" said Bates.

CHAPTER 3: THE SCRAWLED MESSAGE

But, as it turned out, Dorcas hadn't "done it" at all. Bates on reaching his aunt's apartment found no one at home. But very soon Sir Herbert Binney appeared.

"Look here, Richard," he began, "I've taken a fancy to that little girl of yours——"

"She isn't mine."

"You'd like her to be?"

"Very much; in conditions that would please us both."

"Meaning Bunless conditions. I can't offer you those, but I do say now, and, for the last time, if you will take hold of my Bun proposition, I'll give you any salary you want, any interest in the business you ask, and make you my sole heir. I've already done the last, but unless you fall in with my plans now, I'm going to make another will and your name will be among the missing."

"But, Uncle Herbert——"

"I've no time for discussion, my boy; I've to dress for dinner,—I'm going out,—but this thing must be settled now, as far as you're concerned. You've had time enough to think it over, you've had time to discuss it with that pretty little girl of yours,—my, but her eyes flashed as she called me Uncle Bunny! It was a slip,—I saw that, and I pretended to be annoyed, but I liked her all the better for her sauciness. Well, Richard,—yes or no?"

"Can't you give me another twenty-four hours?"

"Not twenty-four minutes! You've hemmed and hawed over this thing as long as I'll stand it! No. You know all the details, all the advantages that I offer you. You know I mean what I say and I'll stand by every word. I'm going to meet the head of a big American concern to-night, and if you turn me down, I shall probably make a deal with him. I'd rather keep my business and my fortune in the

family, but if you say no, out you go! So, as a countryman
of yours expressed it to-day, you can put up or shut up!"

"All right, sir,—I'll shut up!" and Richard Bates
turned on his heel, while Sir Herbert Binney went out of
the apartment and slammed the door behind him.

Almost immediately Miss Gurney came in.

"My stars, Ricky!" she exclaimed, "I met Sir Binney
Bun in the hall and he looked as if somebody had broken
his heart! Has his pet chorus girl given him the mitten?"

"No; I gave it to him. He wants me to sell his precious
pies over a counter,—and I can't see myself doing it."

"I should say not! It's a mystery to me how the
aristocracy of England go into trade, and if it's a big
enough deal, they think it's all right. If it's tea or bread or
soap, it doesn't matter, so they sell enough of it. Well,
young man, what about your escapade in the Park? Shall
I tell your aunt?"

"You said you intended to,—do as you like."

"I won't tell her, if——"

"Oh, you'd better tell me—what is it?"

The cool, incisive tones of Miss Prall interrupted the
speakers and Richard's aunt calmly gazed at him and
then at Miss Gurney, as she came into the room, seated
herself, and began drawing off her gloves.

"I'll tell you myself, Aunt Letitia," said Bates. "I'm old
enough not to be bossed and ballyragged by you two
women! Forgive me, Aunt Letty, but, truly, Eliza makes
me so mad——"

"Go out, Eliza," said Miss Prall, and Eliza went.

"Now, Ricky boy, what is it? About Sir Herbert of
course. And I'll stand by you,—if you don't want to go into
his business, you shan't——"

"It isn't that at all, Aunt Letitia. Or, at least, that is in
the air, too,—up in the air, in fact,—but what Eliza is
going to tell you,—and I prefer to tell you myself,—is that
I'm in love with——"

"Oh, Richard, I am so glad! You dear boy. I've felt for a long time that if you were interested in one girl—some sweet young girl,—you'd have a sort of anchor and——"

"Yes, but wait a minute,—you don't know who she is."

"And I don't care! I mean, I know you'd love only a dear, innocent nature,—but tell me all about her."

Miss Prall's plain face was lighted with happy smiles of interest and eager anticipation, and she drew her chair nearer her nephew as she waited for him to speak.

Bates looked at her, dreading to shatter her hopes,—as he knew his next words must do.

"Well, to begin with,—she is Dorcas Everett."

Miss Prall's eyes opened in a wide, unbelieving stare, her face paled slowly, her very lips seemed to grow white, so intense and concentrated was her anger.

"No!" she said, at last, in a low tense voice, "you don't mean that. Richard! you can't mean it,—after all I've done for you, after all I've hoped for you,—and,—I've loved you so——"

"Now, auntie, listen; just you forget and forgive all this old feud business,—for my sake,—and Dorcas'; be noble, rise above your old, petty quarrel with Mrs Everett, and give us your bond of peace as a wedding present."

His pleading tones, his hopeful smile held Miss Prall's attention for a moment, and then she blazed forth:

"Richard Bates, I cannot believe it. Ingrate! Snake in the grass! To deceive me,—to carry on an affair like this, for you must have done so,—under my very nose, and keep it all so sly! Dorcas Everett! daughter of my enemy,—my long time foe,—the most despicable woman in the world! And, knowing all about it, you deliberately cultivate the acquaintance of her daughter and secretly go on to the point of wanting to marry her! I can't believe it! It's too monstrous! Were there no other girls in the world,—in your life,—that you must choose that one? You can't have been so diabolical as to have done it purposely to break my heart!"

"Oh, no, Auntie, I didn't do that! I chanced to meet Dorcas,—one day at Janet Fayre's,—and, somehow, we both fell in love at once!"

"Stop! don't tell me another word! Get out, Eliza!" as Miss Gurney reappeared at the door. "I told you to get out! Now, stay out! Get away from me, Richard; you can't help any by trying to fawn around me! You don't know what you've done,—I grant you that! You don't know— you can't know,—how you've crucified me!"

Springing up from her chair, Miss Prall darted from the room, and out into the hall. Down one flight of stairs she ran, and furiously pealed the bell of Mrs Everett's apartment on the floor below.

The maid who opened the door was startled at the visitor's appearance, but the angry caller asked for no one; she pushed her way past the servant, and faced Mrs Everett in her own reception room.

"Do you know what's going on, Adeline Everett? Do you know that your daughter is—is interested in my nephew? Answer me that!"

"I don't know it, and I don't believe it," returned Mrs Everett, a plump, blonde matron, whose touched-up golden hair was allowed to show no gray, and whose faintly pink cheeks were solicitously cared for.

"Ask her!" quivered Letitia Prall's angry voice, and she clenched her long thin fingers in ill-controlled rage.

"I will; she's in the next room. Come in here, Dorcas. Tell Miss Prall she is mistaken,—presumptuously mistaken."

The haughty stare with which the hostess regarded her guest continued until Dorcas, coming in, said, with a pretty blush and smile, "I'm afraid she isn't mistaken, Mother."

"Just what do you mean?" Mrs Everett asked, icily, transferring her gaze to her daughter.

Very sweet and appealing Dorcas looked as she realized the crucial moment had arrived. Now she must take her stand for all time. Her big, dark eyes turned from one furious face to the other as the two women waited her response. Her face paled a little as she saw their attitude, their implacable wrath, their hatred of each other, and their momentarily suspended judgment of herself. Yet she stood her ground. With a pretty dignity, she spoke quietly and in a calm, steady voice:

"I heard what Miss Prall said," she began, "I couldn't help it, as I was so near, and all I can say is, that it is true. I am not only interested in Richard Bates, but I love him. He loves me,—and we hope—oh, mumsie,—be kind!—we hope you two will make up your quarrel for our sakes!"

"Go to your room, Dorcas," her mother said, and in those words the girl read her doom. She knew her mother well, and she saw beyond all shadow of doubt that there was no leniency to be hoped for. She sensed in her mother's expression as she pronounced the short sentence, an absolute and immutable decision. She might as well plead for the moon, as for her mother's permission to be interested in Letitia Prall's nephew.

"Wait a minute," countermanded Miss Prall. "Answer me this, Dorcas. Are you and my nephew engaged? Has it come to that?"

"Yes," the girl answered, thinking quickly, and deciding it best to force the issue.

"Hush!" commanded her mother; "go to your room!"

Mrs Everett fairly pushed her daughter through the door, closed it, and then said: "There is little need of further remark on this subject. We might have known it would come,—at least we might have feared it. One of us must leave this house. Will you go or shall I?"

"You take no thought of the young people's heart-break?"

"I do not! Dorcas will get over it; I don't care whether your nephew does or not. I can take care of my child, and that's all that interests me."

"You think you can,—but perhaps you do not know the depth of their attachment or the strength of their wills."

"It is not for you, an unmarried woman, to instruct me in the ways of young lovers! I repeat, Letitia Prall, I can take care of my daughter. Her welfare in no way concerns you. I am only thankful we discovered this state of things before it is too late. Good Heavens! You don't suppose it is too late, do you?"

"What do you mean?"

"You don't suppose those young idiots are—married!"

"Of course not! My Richard is above such clandestine ways!"

"Your Richard isn't above anything! My Dorcas is, but—he might have persuaded her—oh, well, I'll attend to Dorcas. There is no need for you to tarry longer."

The exaggerated courtesy of her manner goaded Miss Prall to rudeness.

"I shall stay as long as I like," she returned, stubbornly sitting still. "There is more to be said, Adeline Everett. There is more to be done. I want your assurance that you will move away,—it doesn't suit my plans to leave this house,—and that you will take your forward and designing daughter far enough to keep her from maneuvering to ensnare my nephew."

"I shall be only too glad to take my daughter away from the vicinity of your crack-brained charge! What has Dick Bates ever done? He has never earned a dollar for himself!"

"He doesn't need to. He is a genius; he will yet astonish the world with his inventions. You know me well enough to know that I speak truth. Moreover, he is his uncle's sole heir!"

"Binney, the Bun man!"

"Yes, Sir Herbert Binney, proprietor of ·the famous Binney's Buns. But, look here, Adeline," the absorption in her nephew's interest blotted out for the moment her scorn of the other woman, "Uncle Binney favors the match."

"What match?" Mrs Everett was honestly blank.

"Between Richard and Dorcas."

"Why, he doesn't know Dorcas."

"He has seen her, and anyway, he'd approve of any nice girl that Rick cared for. You see, Sir Herbert wanted the boy to marry and settle down and become the American branch of Binney's Buns."

"My daughter the wife of a baker! No, thank you! You know me, Letitia Prall, well enough to know my ambitions for Dorcas. She shall marry the man I choose for her,—and he will not be a baker! Nor," and her face was drawn with sudden anger, "nor will he be Richard Bates!"

"Indeed he will not!" and Miss Prall rose and flounced out of the place.

In his own small but attractive apartment, Sir Herbert Binney was dressing for dinner. Always a careful dresser, he was unusually particular this evening. His man, Peters, thought he had never seen his master so fussed over the minor details of his apparel. Also, Sir Herbert was preoccupied. Usually he chatted cheerily, but to-night he was thoughtful, almost moody.

"A cab, sir?" said Peters, half afraid that he'd be snapped at for asking an unnecessary question, yet not quite certain that a cab was desired.

"Yes," was the absent-minded response, and Peters passed on the word by telephone to the doorman below.

Then, satisfactorily turned out, Sir Herbert left his rooms and touched the elevator bell.

Once in the car, and seeing the pretty elevator girl, his mood brightened.

"Good evening, Daisy," he said, "give me one kiss for good luck. This is my busy day."

He carelessly put an arm round her, and kissed her lightly on the lips, even as he spoke. The girl was taken by surprise, and anger surged up in her soul.

"You coward!" she cried, wrenching herself free with difficulty and mindful of her elevator gear. "Take shame to yourself, sir, for insulting a defenseless girl!"

"Oh, come now, chicken, that didn't hurt you! I'm only a jollier. Forget it, and I'll give you a big box of candy."

"I'll never forget it, sir, and if you try that again——"

The dire threat was not pronounced, for just then the car reached the ground floor, and the girl flung the door open.

Nearby at the telephone switchboard was another girl, who looked up curiously as the Bun man came out of the elevator. She had overheard the angry voice that seemed to be threatening him, and she was not without knowledge of his ways herself.

But Sir Herbert waved his hand gayly at the telephone girl and also at the news stand girl. Indeed all girls were, in Binney's estimation, born to be waved at.

He had recovered his good nature, and he went along the onyx lobby with a quick stride, looking at his watch as he walked.

"Taxi ready?" he said to the obsequious doorman.

"Yes, sir,—yes, Sir Herbert. Here you are."

"And here you are," the Englishman returned, with a generous bestowal of silver.

"To the Hotel Magnifique," he said, and his cab rolled away.

During the evening hours the attendants of The Campanile shifted. The elevator girls were replaced by young men, and the telephone operator was changed. The doorman, too, was another individual, and by midnight no one was on duty who had been on at dusk.

After midnight, the attendants were fewer still, and after two o'clock Bob Moore, the capable and efficient night porter, was covering the door, telephone and elevator all by himself.

This arrangement was always sufficient, as most of the occupants of The Campanile were average citizens, who, if at theater or party, were rarely out later than one or two in the morning.

On this particular night, Moore welcomed four or five theater-goers back home, took them up to their suites and then sat for a long time uninterruptedly reading a detective story, which was his favorite brand of fiction.

At two o'clock Mr Goodwin came in, and Moore took him up to the twelfth floor.

Returning to his post and to his engrossing book, the next arrival was Mr Vail. He belonged on the tenth floor and as they ascended, Moore, full of his story, said:

"Ever read detective stories, Mr Vail?"

"Occasionally; but I haven't much time for reading. Business men like more active recreation."

"Likely so, sir. But I tell you this yarn I'm swallowing is a corker!"

"What's it called?"

"'Murder Will Out,' by Joe Jarvis. It's great! Why, Mr Vail, the victim was killed,—killed, mind you,—in a room that was all locked up——"

"How did the murderer get in?"

"That's just it! How did he? And he left his revolver,———"

"Left his revolver? Then he did get in and get out! Must have been a secret passage——"

"No, sir, there wasn't! That is, the author says so, and all the people,—the characters, you know, try to find one, and they can't! Oh, it's exciting, I'll say! I can't guess how it's coming out."

"I suppose you wouldn't peek over to the last page?"

"No, that spoils a story for me. The fun I get out of it is the trying to ferret out the solution, on my own. That's sport for me. Why, you see, Mr Vail,—but, excuse me, sir, I'm keeping you."

The elevator had stopped at the tenth floor, and Vail had left the car, but he stood waiting till the enthusiastic Moore should pause.

"Oh, well, go on,—what were you saying?"

"Only this, sir. To me, a good detective story is not the one that keeps you guessing,—nor the one that keeps you in fearful suspense as to the outcome, but the one that gives you a chance to solve the riddle yourself. The one that puts all the cards on the table, and gives you a chance at it."

"And you can usually work it out?"

"Sometimes,—not always. But the fun is in trying."

"You ought to have been a detective, Moore. You've the taste for it evidently. Well, good-night; hope you discover the clue and solve the mystery. Shall you finish your book to-night?"

"Oh, yes, sir. I'm more than half way through it."

"Well, tell me in the morning if you guessed right. Good-night, Moore."

"Good-night, Mr. Vail."

The elevator went down, and Bob Moore left the car to return to his book.

But he did not return to the story. A more engrossing one was opened to him at that moment. A glance toward the front doorway showed him a figure of a man, lying in a contorted heap on the floor, about half way between himself and the entrance.

He went wonderingly toward it, his heart beating faster as he drew near.

"Dead!" he breathed softly, to himself, "no, not dead!— oh, my God, it's Sir Herbert Binney!"

In the onyx lobby, at the very foot of one of the tall ornate capitaled columns was the prostrate Binney. Apparently he was a dying man; blood was flowing from some wound, his face was drawn in convulsive agony, from his stiffening fingers he let fall a pencil, but his lips were framing inarticulate words.

Bob Moore's wits did not desert him. Instead, his thoughts seemed to flash with uncanny quickness.

"Binney's dying," he told himself, "he's been murdered! Gee! what an excitement there will be! He's babbling,—he's going to tell who killed him! If I scoot for

Doctor Pagett, this chap'll be dead before I get back,—if I wait,—I'll be called down for not going—but I must get it out of him,—if I can—what is that, Sir, try to tell me   "

Bending over the stricken man, Moore listened intently, and caught the words,—or words which sounded like,—"Get—them—get J—J—anyway,—get—J——"

With a sudden gasping gurgle, the man was dead.

Bewildered, but striving hard to grasp the situation and do his exact duty, Moore looked about, and quickly concluded his next move was to call the doctor.

Pagett, on the second floor, was the physician of the house, and Moore raced up the stairs to his apartment.

Ringing the bell continuously brought the doctor to the door.

"What's happened?" he said, sleepily.

"Murder!" answered Moore, briefly. "Hike into some clothes and get downstairs. Sir Herbert Binney's been done for!"

Not waiting, Moore ran back down the stairs, and took his station guarding the dead man. He resolved to touch nothing, but his attention at once fell on a bit of paper, on which Binney had evidently been scrawling some message, with the pencil that had at last fallen from his nerveless fingers.

Careful not to touch the paper, Moore devoured it with his eyes.

This is what he read:

(handwritten note): women did this get [unreadable]

Chapter 4: The Busy Police

But even the astonishing disclosure of the scrawled statement did not cause Bob Moore to lose his head. Excited and startled though he was, he was also alertly conscious that he must conduct himself with care. He had a vague fear that he might be connected with the case and weirdly enough he had a secret fear that he might not!

Already in fancy he saw himself doing marvelously clever detective work that should result in getting the criminal of whom the dying efforts of the victim strove to tell him. But he must be careful not to put himself forward, not to overstep his privileges, and, above all, not to seem too eager to help in the search for the murderer, for he felt sure his offers of assistance would be deemed presumptuous.

Doctor Pagett came running down the stairs, knotting his necktie as he descended.

"Binney!" he exclaimed; "the Englishman who makes Buns. What's this paper?"

"I haven't touched it, Doctor; I haven't touched anything. You can see for yourself what the paper says."

"Women did this," said the doctor, his eyes fairly bulging; "what—what does it mean? Where were you?"

"Up at the tenth floor, taking Mr Vail up. He came in,—there was no Binney about then!—and I took him up in the elevator to his floor, and when I came down, Mr Binney was there just as you see him now,—only, he was still alive."

"Alive!"

"Yes, sir,—just dying. He mumbled a word or two——"

"What did he say?"

"He said—'Get—get——' but he couldn't say who. That's all,—then he drew a long breath and died."

"You came straight to me?"

"Yes, sir. I flew! I thought it my duty to hesitate that moment, in case he might get out the name of the murderer."

"I think you did all right, Moore. He's surely dead,— and, just as surely, he was murdered. And by women! But how is it possible? However, that's not my province. We must get the police, and also, notify his people. He lived in the Prall apartment, didn't he?"

"No; he was there a lot; they're his relatives, I believe, but he had his own apartment, a small one on the eighth floor. Miss Prall, she's on the eighth, too, shall I call her up?"

"Oh, that's pretty awful. Call the nephew, young Bates, first."

"Shall I telephone or go up there——?"

"Go up—no, telephone,—somebody might come in, and want you."

"Hello," Richard Bates responded to Moore's telephone call.

"Mr. Bates?"

"Yes."

"Will you come downstairs, sir, right away? There's been a—an accident. Mr. Binney,—that is, Sir Binney, you know,—he's—he's——"

"Well, he's what?"

"He's—oh, come down, sir, *please!*"

Moore hung up his receiver, for his nerve suddenly deserted him when it came to telling the dreadful fact of the tragedy.

In a few moments the elevator bell sounded and Moore went up to bring Bates down.

"What is it?" Bates asked. "Is my uncle—er,—lit up?"

"Oh, no, sir," and Bob Moore looked shocked, "it isn't that, at all. It's worse than that,—it's an accident."

"What sort of an accident? Taxi smash-up? Any kind of a stroke?"

But by this time they were down to the street floor, and the two men stepped out of the car.

Seeing the doctor, who was still bending over the inert figure on the floor, Bates hurried along the onyx lobby till he reached the scene, and could see, without being told, what had happened.

A moment he gazed in silence at his uncle's face, and then said, excitedly, "Who did this? How was he killed? Why should anybody——"

Silently the doctor pointed to the paper on the floor at the dead man's side.

Bates read it, and looked up wonderingly.

"Don't touch it," warned the physician as the young man stretched out his hand. "It's a clew,—the police must take charge of it."

"The police! Oh, yes,—of course,—it's a murder, isn't it?"

"You bet it's a murder!" exclaimed Moore. "And done by women! Oh, gee! what a case it will be!"

"Hush up!" Bates cried, angrily. "Don't talk like that in the presence of the dead! We must send for an undertaker."

"Not yet," demurred Doctor Pagett. "In a case like this, the police must be notified first of all."

"Not first of all," said Bates, slowly, as his mind began to work; "we must tell my aunt, Miss Prall."

"Yes, of course, but the police must be sent for."

"Sure," put in Bob Moore, who was gaining confidence in his own importance, "I must get this matter hushed up before people begin to get around. Lucky it happened in the night! It's none too good an advertisement for the house!"

"I think I'll go up and tell my aunt myself," said Bates, thoughtfully. "You stay here by—by the body, Doctor. And, I say,—what—how was he killed?"

"Stabbed," said the doctor, shortly.

"What with?"

"I don't know,—except that it was with a sharp blade of some sort. There's no weapon in sight."

"No weapon! How queer!"

"Queer or not, I can't find any. It's a pretty strange affair, to my mind. Yes, I'll stay here, you go and tell your aunt's people, and,—Moore, you come right back after you take Mr Bates up."

In silence the return trip was made in the elevator, for Bates was thinking how he should break the news to the two excitable women upstairs, and Bob Moore's thoughts were in such a riot, that he was trying hard to straighten them out.

In front of Miss Prall's bedroom door, her nephew hesitated for some time before knocking. Not only was his courage weak but his brain was receiving so many sudden jolts that he could scarcely control his voice. Why, now, he was his uncle's heir. Unless he had already changed that will! Had he?

At last, with a gentle knock, repeated more loudly, and finally with a fusillade of raps, he succeeded in rousing Miss Prall, who demanded, with asperity, "Who's there?"

"Me; Rick. Open the door, please."

"What's the matter? You sick?" his aunt exclaimed, as she unlocked her door.

"No; now, listen, Aunt Letitia, and don't faint—for anything. Uncle Binney is—has been—why, somebody killed him!"

"Killed him! Is he dead?"

"Yes, ma'am"; both were unaware of the absurdity of the words, "he's downstairs,—in the lobby,—and he's been stabbed."

Richard's teeth were chattering from the tension of his nerves, and the horror of the situation, but Miss Prall's nerves were strong ones, and she said, "I'll dress and go right down. And I'll tell Eliza,—you needn't. Go in the living-room and wait for me there."

Rather relieved at not being sent back downstairs and decidedly willing to let his aunt break the news to Miss Gurney, Bates went to his own room and added some finishing touches to the hasty toilet he had made. Then he awaited his aunt, as directed, and in an incredibly short time she appeared, all dressed and impatient to go downstairs.

"We won't wait for Eliza," she said; "come along. Oh, no, wait a minute!" She returned to her bedroom, and shortly reappeared.

Her vigorous push of the elevator button brought Moore quickly, and he took them down.

Miss Prall strode rapidly along the lobby and spoke brusquely to the doctor.

"What are you doing? Why do you touch him before the police arrive?"

"Good Lord, how you startled me!" exclaimed Doctor Pagett, who in his absorption had not heard her approach. "I have a perfect right to examine the body, ma'am," he went on indignantly. "Do you suppose I don't know my business?"

"I've always heard no one must touch a murdered man until——"

"Then how are we to know it is a murder?" he countered, looking at her keenly. "Will you read that paper, Miss Prall? Don't touch it!"

"Women did this," she read, aloud. "Well, I'm not surprised. If ever a man was mixed up with women,—of all sorts, it was Sir Herbert! But what women did it? Where are they?"

She looked about, as if expecting to see the criminals cowering in the shadows or behind the great columns of the lobby.

"They have disappeared,—not an uncommon procedure," returned the doctor, dryly. "And they have taken with them the weapon with which the crime was committed, thus removing a most important clue! Have you any suspicion—in any direction?"

Doctor Pagett shot this query at her with such sharp suddenness that Miss Prall almost jumped.

"I!" she exclaimed loudly. "How could I know anything about this man or his women? He's nothing to me!"

"He is your nephew's uncle."

"Well, that makes him no kin of mine, does it? Don't you dare mix me up in this thing!"

"Nobody's mixing you up in it, ma'am," and, indifferently, the physician returned his attention to the dead man, and became engrossed in studying the writing on the paper.

And then, as three men from Police Headquarters appeared at the front end of the long lobby, Eliza Gurney stepped from the elevator at the other end. Apparently she was holding herself well in hand, for, though her face was white and drawn with fear, her firm set lips and clenched hands betokened a resolve not to give way to nerves in any fashion.

"Let me see him," she said, in steady tones.

"Who are you, madam?" said Officer Kelsey, resenting her determined push forward.

"I'm Miss Gurney, the companion of Miss Prall," and the air with which she made the announcement would have fitted a grand duchess.

Impressed, the policeman made way for her, and then continued his questioning.

"Who's in command here?" he said. "Who's nearest of kin?"

At the first question, Miss Prall stepped forward, but at the second, she fell back in favor of Richard Bates.

"I am," Bates said, quietly. "He is my uncle, Sir Herbert Binney."

Further statistics were ascertained and then the police began actual investigation. The detective was the smallest and least conspicuous man of the three, and his unassuming air and somewhat stupid-looking face would have carried a conviction of his utter incompetency, save for his alert, darting black eyes, that seemed to look in several directions at once, so rapidly did they roll about.

Corson was his name, and he asked questions so quickly and so continuously that he scarce waited for answers.

"Where had he been?" he flung out. "Who saw him come in? Who was on door duty? What's *your* name? Moore? Well, did you admit this man?"

"No," said Bob Moore, "I was up in the elevator taking one of the tenants to his floor. There's only me on, late at night."

But Corson seemed unheeding. Already he had turned to Miss Prall.

"Does this man live with you? Did he, I mean. Where did he set out for when he left home? What time did he go?"

"Now you look here!" said Miss Letitia, angrily. "I can't answer forty-seven questions at once! Nor other people can't, either. You talk more slowly, sir, and more rationally."

But Corson heeded her not at all. He turned to Bates.

"Your uncle, eh? You his heir?"

"Yes, he is!" Miss Prall answered for him, and Corson's roving glance took her in and returned to Bates. "Where were you when he was killed?"

"In bed," replied Richard, shortly.

"Oh; all right. Now, I'll take charge of this paper, for there's little doubt but it's mighty important." He folded it carefully into his pocket-book. "Was this gentleman— er, addicted to ladies' society?"

"That he was," Moore spoke up, involuntarily.

"I didn't ask you," said Corson. "I asked Mr. Bates."

"Why, yes," said Richard, "he did like the society of ladies,—but most men do."

"We're not discussing the matter, Mr. Bates," and for once Corson looked steadily at him, "we're just looking into it. And—" he paused, impressively, "and these immediate, right-away-quick questions are pretty good first aid, as a rule."

"Go ahead, then," and Richard folded his arms, in a resigned manner.

Doctor Pagett motioned the two ladies to take seats on the red velvet sofa and seated himself also.

"There's no doubt," Corson went on, "that this writing is the true explanation. Dying men don't leave anything but truth as a last message. It seems pretty steep to believe that women managed this affair, but that's the very reason he made such a desperate effort to let it be known."

"And he tried to tell me who it was," broke in Moore, irrepressibly.

"He did?" and Corson's eyes flashed toward the speaker. "What did he say? Did he mention any names? How did you come to be listening? Were you here when——"

Miss Prall interrupted. "If you'd listen a minute, and not talk all the time, you might learn something, Mister Detective!"

"Thank you, ma'am. Answer me, Moore. Just what did this man say after he was hurt,—that you heard?"

"He said 'Get—get—' and that was all, except that he tried hard to say a name,—or it seemed like that,—and he said something like something beginning with a J."

"Well, you're guarded in your statements. But I understand. I suppose he was struggling for breath, really——"

"He could just speak and that's all. He kept saying 'J—J—' and then he gave a gasp and died."

"How do you know he died?"

"Why, he sort of relaxed—limp like,—and stopped trying to speak."

"And he seemed to be after some name beginning with J,—say James or John."

"That's the way it sounded."

"All right. Now, how long had you been absent from this place when you returned and found him?"

"Just long enough to take Mr Vail up to his floor,—the tenth."

"Vail? Who's he?"

"One of our tenants. He lives on the tenth floor. He came in and I took him up——"

"And came right down again?"

"Yes; and when I got down, I saw the—the heap in the lobby."

"You knew at once who it was?"

"Not who it was, but I saw it was a man, evidently knocked down, or fallen in a fit,—as I thought. So I ran to see, and—I've told you the rest."

"What time was all this?"

"It was twenty minutes after two."

"When you found him?"

"When I found him."

"How do you know so certainly?"

"I'm—I'm fond of detective work, and I thought there'd be some in this matter, and so, I did everything I could think of to help along."

"Oho, fond of detective work, are you? What have you done in that line?"

"Nothing! I didn't mean practically. But, well, theoretically. You see, I've read a great many detective stories——"

"Yes; you were reading one this evening? Where is it? Let me see it."

Slightly embarrassed at Corson's manner, Bob got the book and passed it over.

"'Murder Will Out.' H'm——Say, Mr. Bates, do you know where your uncle spent the evening?"

"I do not." Richard was not at all pleased with Corson's way, and he had turned sullen.

"No idea? Have you, Miss Prall?"

"I've an idea, but I suppose you want only definite statements. Such I cannot give."

"Well, well, what *do* you know about it? Remember, evasion or refusal to answer is by no means a point in your favor."

"What! Are you implying there's anything in my disfavor? Am I being questioned as a possible suspect?"

"Lord, no, madam! Don't jump at conclusions."

"She didn't!" put in Eliza Gurney. "Seems to me you're an addlepated young fellow for a detective."

"Yes? Does any one present know where Mr Binney—is that the name?—spent this evening? Or any way to learn of his whereabouts?"

"He went out about before I came on," volunteered Moore. "The day doorman will know, or the elevator girl who brought him down."

"All right. That's keep. Now, I want to get at the actual facts of his discovery here. It would seem, Moore, that you're the only one who can give any information in that respect."

"I've already told you all I know."

"And this Mr Vail you took upstairs,—he wouldn't know anything?"

"I can't answer for that, but when Mr Vail came in, and I took him up in the elevator, there wasn't any sign of Sir Herbert Binney about, dead or alive!"

"No; that's so. Well, then, when you came down, and found the wounded man, you went at once for the doctor?"

"Almost at once. I paused a moment, because he was trying so hard to speak, and I reasoned that if he succeeded it would be of utmost importance that some one should hear his words."

"H'm—yes, that's so. Well, and then, he gave over trying and died, you say; and then?"

"Then I ran up at once to Doctor Pagett's apartment, it is only one flight up, and he came down as soon as he could."

"Go on from there, Doctor."

"I came right down, as soon as I could hurry on some clothes. I found Sir Binney dead, and can asseverate that he had been dead but a few moments."

"He was stabbed?"

"Yes, and the weapon used was removed and must have been taken away by the murderer, as it cannot be found."

"H'm there are other explanations. But never mind that. The wound was such as to cause almost instantaneous death?"

"Apparently it *did* do so. Death was, of course, hastened by the immediate removal of the knife. Had that remained in the wound, the victim would doubtless have lived long enough to make a clear dying statement."

"What was the weapon? Can you divine?"

"A sharp knife, dagger, or some such implement."

"A paper-cutter, say?"

"Not likely. Unless it was an unusually sharp one. The cut is so cleanly made that it presupposes a very sharp blade."

"And your diagnosis of the killing corresponds in all points with this night porter's story?"

"So far as I can judge, there is no discrepancy in his narrative."

Dr Pagett was of the pompous school, and dearly loved to be in an important role. But he was evidently a learned and skilled physician and his words were spoken with a positive air that carried conviction.

"There is little more to be learned from viewing the scene," the detective said, at last, after he had put a few more direct questions to Bob Moore and had advised some with his companion policemen.

"Nope; might as well let in the undertakers," agreed Kelsey.

"Oh, do," urged Moore. "It's really imperative that we get all traces of the tragedy away before daylight. And it's almost four o'clock now!"

"Good gracious, so it is!" exclaimed Miss Prall. "Well, I suppose I shall be consulted as to the funeral, at least! I seem to be of little importance here!"

"Don't talk like that, Aunt," urged Bates. "These inquiries are necessary. The funeral services and all that, will of course be under our control."

"I should hope so," the lady sniffed; "I shall stay here until the undertaker arrives. I want some say in these matters."

"I think, Letitia," suggested Miss Gurney, "you'd better go to your room and tidy up a bit. You dressed very hastily."

"What matter! Such things are unimportant in a crisis of this sort! Oh, I can't realize it! The awful circumstances almost make one forget the sadness of death! Poor Sir Herbert! He enjoyed life so much!"

Miss Prall buried her face in her handkerchief, and so was unable to see the quizzical glances given her by Detective Corson.

CHAPTER 5: WIIO WERE THE WOMEN?

The usual and necessary routine was followed out. The Medical Examiner came and did his part; the undertakers came and did theirs; and at last Bob Moore's nervous restlessness was calmed, somewhat, by a hope of getting all signs of the tragedy obliterated before the morning's stir began in the house.

"I'll wash up these blood stains, myself," Moore volunteered,—speaking to Corson, after the body had been taken away to a mortuary establishment and the Prall family had gone up to their rooms.

"Oh, I don't know," demurred Corson. "It's evidence, you know——"

"For whom? Can't you get all the deductions you want, and let me clean up? We can't have the tenants coming down to a hall like this! If there's any evidence in these blood spots, make a note of it. You know yourself they can't be left here all day!"

This was reasonable talk, and Corson agreed. "All right," he said. "I'll make pencil marks around where the spots are,—pencil won't wash off, you know,—and as I can't see any trace of footprints, I suppose there isn't anything further to be learned from the condition of the floor."

"Thought you Tecs got a lot from looking at the scene of the crime," Moore jeered. "You haven't deduced a thing but that the man was stabbed,—and Dr. Pagett told you that."

Corson took the taunt seriously.

"That finding of tiny clues, such as shreds of clothing, part of a broken cuff-link, a dropped handkerchief, all those things, are just story-book stuff,—they cut no ice in real cases."

"I'll bet Sherlock Holmes could find a lot of data just by going over the floor with a lens."

"He could in a story book,—and do you know why? Because the clews and things, in a story, are all put there for him by the property man. Like a salted mine. But in real life, there's nothing doing of that sort. Take a good squint at the floor, though, before you remove those stains. You don't see anything, do you?"

Elated at being thus appealed to by a real, live detective, Moore got down on hands and knees and scrutinized the floor all about where the body of Sir Herbert had lain.

There was nothing indicative to be seen. The floor of the lobby was always kept in proper condition and beyond the slight trace of dust that naturally accumulated between the diurnal washings, the floor gave up no information.

So the gruesome red stains were washed away, and once again the onyx lobby took on its normal atmosphere.

"How you going to work on the case?" asked Moore, eagerly interested.

"I'm going to get the truth out of you!" declared Corson, so suddenly and brusquely that Moore turned white.

"What!" he cried.

"Yes, just that. You know a lot about the matter that you haven't told,—so you can just out with it!"

"Me? I don't know anything."

"Now, now, the thing is too thin. How could Binney get in here, and then his murderer come in and have the whole shooting-match pulled off in the short time it would take you to run Vail up to the tenth floor and drop your car down again?"

"But—but, you see, I—I stood quite a while talking to Mr Vail after we stopped at his floor."

"What'd you do that for?"

"Why, we were talking about the book I was reading—
—"

"You were both talking—or you were talking to him?"

"I guess that's it. I was so crazy about the book I'd talk to anybody who'd listen, and Mr Vail was real good-natured, and I guess I let myself go——"

"And babbled on, till he was bored to death and sent you away."

"Just about that," and Moore grinned, sheepishly. "I'm terribly fond of detective stories."

"Yes, so you've said. Well, your book is called, I believe, 'Murder Will Out,' so, as that's pretty true, you might as well own up first as last."

"Own up to what?"

"That you killed Sir Binney! Where's the knife? What did you do it for? Don't you know you'll be arrested, tried, convicted and sentenced? Yes—sentenced!"

Corson's habit of flinging out rapid-fire questions took on new terror from the fierce frown with which he accompanied his speech, and Bob Moore's knees trembled beneath him.

"W—what are you talking about? I—I didn't k—kill him!"

"Yes, you did! You got all wrought up over those fool story books of yours and you went bug, and killed him in a frenzy of imagination!"

"Oh, oh! I didn't—I,——"

"Then explain your movements! You came down from your talk with Vail, full of murder thoughts. You saw Binney come in, and, moved by the opportunity and obsessed with the murder game, you let drive and killed him, in a sort of mania!"

"Oh, no! no!" and Moore fell limply into a seat and began to sob wildly.

"Stop that!" Corson ordered. "I've got to find out about this. I believe you did it,—I believe I've struck the truth, for the simple reason that there's no other suspect. This man Binney had no enemies. Why, he's a peaceable Englishman, in trade,—and a big trade. I know all about him. He wanted to place his Bun business over here. He'd confabbed with several Bakery men in this city, and was about to make a deal. He was on good terms with his people here,—sort of relatives, they are,—and he was a gay old boy in his social tastes. Now, who's going to stick up a man like that? There was no robbery,—his watch and kale were all right there. So there's no way to look, but toward you! *You!*" A pointed forefinger emphasized Corson's words and Moore broke into fresh sobs.

"I tell you I didn't! Why, it's too absurd—too——"

"Not absurd at all. I know something of psychology, and I know how those murder yarns, read late at nights,—when you're here alone, get into your blood, and—well, it's a wonder you didn't stick Vail! But I suppose his indulgent listening to your ravings helped along your murder instinct, and you——"

"Oh, hush! If you keep on you'll make me think I did do it!"

"Of course,—you can't think anything else. Now, here's another thing. You say you went up for Dr Pagett at twenty past two."

"Or a few minutes later."

"Well, Pagett said,—I asked him privately,—that it was at least quarter to three! What were you doing all that time?"

"It wasn't—I didn't—oh, Mr Corson, I told you the truth. I waited to catch the last words of——"

"Yes, of your own victim! And then, frightened, you hung around twenty minutes or so before calling the doctor."

"I did not! But," and Moore pulled himself together, "I'm not going to say another word! You've doped out this cock-and-bull story because you don't know which way to look for the real murderer. And you think you can work a third degree on me—and railroad me to the chair, do you? Well, you can't do it!"

Moore's eyes were glittering, his cheeks were flushed and his voice rose to a shrill shriek as he glared wildly at his tormentor.

"Shut up on that!" Corson flung at him. "Calm yourself down, now. If you're innocent, it's all right. But I'll keep my eye on you, my boy. Now, tell me any theory you have or can invent that will fit the facts of the case."

Corson asked this in the honest hope that Moore could give him a hint. The detective was a good plodding sleuth when it came to tracking down a clew, but he was not fertile of imagination and had little or no initiative. He really believed it might have been Moore's work, but he thought so, principally, because he could think of no other way to look.

"The facts are not so very strange," began Moore, looking at the detective uncertainly. He didn't want to give any unnecessary help, for he had a half-formed theory that he wanted to think out for himself, and he had no intention of sharing it with an avowed enemy. But he saw, too, that a few words of suggestion of any sort might lead Corson's suspicions away from himself and might make for leniency.

"Wait a minute," he said, on a sudden thought. "The writing the dying man managed to scribble said that women did the murder."

"That's my best bet!" cried Corson; "I've been waiting for you to mention that! You wrote that paper! That's what occupied you all that time. Of course women didn't do a deed like that. You conceived the fiendishly clever idea of writing such a message to mislead the police!"

"You—you——" but words failed Bob Moore. He reverted to his plan of silence and sat, moodily staring in front of him, as the dawn broke and the time drew near for the day shift of workers to come on.

"Don't you think so?" and Corson now spoke almost ingratiatingly. "I mean don't you think it pretty impossible for women to put over such a crime?"

"No, I don't," Bob blurted out. "Nor you wouldn't either, if you knew Binney! Why, his life just one—h'm—one woman after another! And they were all after him!"

"What do you mean?"

"Why he was a regular feller, you know. He took the chorus girls,—or some of their sort,—out to dinners and all that, and, here in the house, he jollied the elevator girls and the telephone and news-stand Janes,—and yet he detested girls' service. Many a time he'd blow out to the manager about how he'd ought to fire all the girls and put back men or boys,—like we had before the war."

"Your story doesn't hang together. Binney seemed to adore and hate the girls, both."

"That's just it, he did. He'd storm and rail at Daisy,—she's on his elevator, and then he'd turn around and chuck her under the chin, and like as not bring her home a big box of chocolates."

"Oh, well, I've heard of men like that before."

"But not so much so. I don't believe anybody ever went for the girls rough-shod as bad as he did. He called them down for the least thing,—and then, sometimes he'd make it up to them and sometimes he wouldn't."

"And the chorus ladies? But I suppose you don't know much about them."

"Don't I? Well, I guess I do! Why, Mr Binney—Sir Binney, I mean,—he used to tell me the tallest yarns I ever heard, about his little suppers,—as he called 'em. He'd come 'long about two G. M. pretty mellow, and in an expansive mood, and he'd pour out his heart to old Bob,—meaning me. Yes, sir, I know a thing or two about Binney's lady friends, and there's a few of them that wouldn't mind knifing him a bit,—if they were sure they wouldn't be found out. And,—if you ask me, that's just what happened."

"H'm; you mean they followed him home, and slipped in after him——"

"Yep."

"But how did they know they'd find the coast clear,—that you'd so very conveniently be up in the elevator, and would stay up there such an unusually long time? You'd better shut up, Moore. Everything you say gets you deeper in the net. If your chorus girl theory is the right dope, you were in on it, too. Otherwise it couldn't have been worked!"

"All right, Mr Corson, I'll shut up. You'll see the time when you'll be mighty glad to turn to me for help. Till then, work on your own; but you needn't aim this way, it won't get you anywhere."

Meantime there was consternation among the nearest of kin to the dead man.

In the Prall apartment, Miss Letitia was conducting conversation ably aided and abetted by Eliza Gurney, while young Bates sat listening and joining in when there was opportunity.

"Worst of all is the disgrace," Miss Prall was saying. "There's no use my pretending I'm over-come with grief,— personal grief, I mean, for I never cared two straws for the man, and I'm not going to make believe I did. But the publicity and newspaper talk is terrible. Once it blows over and is forgotten we'll be able to hold up our heads again, but just now, we're in the public eye,—and it's an awful place to be!"

"But who did it, Aunt Letitia," said Bates. "We've got to get the murderer——"

"I don't mind so much about that," his aunt returned, with a sharp sniff. "All I want is to get the thing hushed up. Of course, you're the heir now, Ricky, so you must put on suitable mourning and all that, but those things can be attended to in due course."

"Where you going to have the funeral and when?" asked Eliza. "I don't think I'll go."

"You needn't, if you don't want to," Miss Prall agreed. "I don't blame you,—I don't want to attend it myself, but I suppose I ought to. It will be in the undertaker's chapel, and it will soon be over. Let's have it just as quickly as possible, Rick. To-morrow, say."

"Oh, Aunt Letitia! Do observe the rules of common decency! We can't hurry the poor man into his grave like that. And I shouldn't wonder if there'll be a lot of red tape and inquiry before we can bury him at all."

"Maybe the body'll have to be sent back to England," suggested Eliza, and Richard was just about to say he supposed it would, when the doorbell of the apartment rang.

As Miss Prall's maids did not sleep in the house, Bates opened the door and found Corson there, with a bland but determined look on his face.

"Sorry to trouble you people," he said, stepping inside without being asked, "but I've some talking to do, and the sooner the quicker."

He smiled, importantly, and, selecting a comfortable chair, seated himself deliberately and looked in silence from one to another.

"Well," said Miss Prall, stiffly, "what do you want to know?"

The angular, spare figure of the spinster, upright in a straight-backed chair, was not of a demeanor to put a man at ease, but Corson showed no uneasiness, and almost lolled in his seat as he cast a slow glance at her.

"Naturally," he began, "what I want to know is, and what I propose to find out is, who killed Sir Herbert Binney. And what I want to know here is, anything any of you can tell me that will throw any light, side light, or full glare, on the question."

"We don't know anything that is illuminating in any way," Miss Prall informed him.

"I will be the judge of the powers of illumination if you will tell me what you know," was the suave retort. "Will you make a statement or shall I ask questions?"

"Neither," and Letitia Prall rose. "You may bid us good-night, sir. This is no time to intrude upon the ladies of a family,—especially a family in deep and sudden mourning."

"You weren't mourning very deeply as I entered." Corson made no move to get up, although Bates rose as his aunt did. "I think, Miss Prall, you'd better sit down again, and you, too, Mr Bates. This may be a lengthy confab."

"I think you'd better listen to this man, Letitia," advised Eliza. "He's got a right to be heard, and I, for one, want to know how matters stand."

Whereupon Letitia sat down and Bates came and stood behind her chair.

"First, Mr Corson," Richard said, "let me understand just how far your authority goes——"

"All the way," returned Corson, promptly. "I'm the police detective on this case. I shall have a helper,—a colleague, undoubtedly, but for the moment I'm working alone. However, I've all the authority in the world. I represent law and justice, I represent the government, I represent the United States!"

"The United States is honored, I'm sure," said Miss Prall with unconcealed sarcasm.

Such things never ruffled Corson, and he went calmly on.

"This man's relation to you?" he said, interrogatively, looking at Letitia.

"He was no kin of mine," she snapped; "he was the uncle of my nephew, Mr Bates, and Mr Bates is the sole heir."

"Indeed; he is to be congratulated. Now, this man,— Sir Binney——"

"Don't call him that!" put in Eliza. "It does annoy me so! Say Sir Herbert Binney or Sir Herbert. Have you never known a knight?"

"No, ma'am, I never have. Well, Sir Herbert, then,— did he live here?"

"In this building,—not in this apartment," Richard answered, as the two haughty ladies seemed disinclined to accommodate their inquisitor.

And then, by dint of slow and persistent questioning, Detective Corson drew out the vital statistics of the deceased gentleman and of the members of the Prall household.

"Now as to the 'women,'" Corson went on. "You know Sir Herbert left a paper stating that women killed him. This is a most peculiar message for a dying man to leave."

"Why so, if it is true?" and Letitia Prall's eyes gave him a curious look.

"Yes,—that's just it,—if it is true."

"It's got to be true," burst out Bates, impulsively. "No man is going to write a thing like that with his last ounce of dying strength unless it's true!"

"I agree to that," and Corson nodded, "if he did write it."

"What?" Miss Prall started up in amazement. "Who says he didn't write it?"

"Nobody says so, I only say it might be so. Suppose the murderer himself wrote it to turn suspicion toward some one else,—some woman."

"I never thought of that!" and Miss Prall fell into a brown study, as if the new thought moved her profoundly.

"Nor I," said Bates, looking intently at the detective. "But, I say, that writing looked to me amazingly like my uncle's."

"And the porter,—Bob Moore, you know," broke in Eliza,—"he said, the pencil dropped from Sir Herbert's fingers just as he fell back dead——"

"Oh, no, he didn't say that! That's the way stories get repeated. There's no such thing as direct, undistorted evidence! Moore didn't see the pencil in Sir Herbert's fingers at all. He saw it lying on the floor beside the dead man's hand,—or, he says he did."

"Good Heavens! You don't suspect Moore!" cried Richard. "Why, he's the best chap going!"

"I don't say he isn't, and I don't say I suspect him, but I want you people to understand that he *might* have done it all,—might have committed the murder and might have written the scribbled paper to turn suspicion away from himself. As for the handwriting, that trembling, shaky scrawl can't be identified with anybody's ordinary writing."

"Oh, I can't think it," Richard objected. "Why, Bob Moore couldn't do such a thing, and, besides, what would be his motive?"

"We haven't come to motive yet. We're finding out who had opportunity."

"Any passer-by had that," Miss Prall said, positively; "while Moore was up in the elevator, what was to prevent any pedestrian going by from stepping in and killing Sir Herbert?"

"Nothing; but there are few pedestrians at two o'clock in the morning, and fewer still who have a reason for a murder."

"Oh, it must have been prearranged," said Bates, thoughtfully. "There's not the slightest doubt," he went on hurriedly, "that whoever killed him,—man, woman or child!—came in from the street to do the deed."

"Why, of course," agreed Miss Prall; "where else could they have come from? Nobody in the house would do it!"

"No; I suppose not," admitted Corson. "Well, then, ma'am, we have the assassin coming in from the street, while Moore is upstairs. And, according to the victim's own statement, the assassin was feminine and there were two, at least, of them. For I've studied that paper, and it says, clearly, 'women did this.' Want to see it?" his hand went toward his breast pocket.

"No,—oh, no," and Miss Prall shuddered.

"Well, supposing a couple of women came in, having, we'll say, watched their chance, what more likely than that it was two chickens,—beg pardon, ma'am, that means gay young ladies,—with whom Sir Herbert had been dining? Why, like as not they came in with him. They didn't hang round outside waiting for him. You see, they'd been with him, and he had in some way offended them, let us say, and they wanted to kill him——"

"Seems to me you're drawing a long bow," and Bates almost smiled at the mental picture of two gay chorus girls committing the gruesome deed.

Corson spoke seriously. "No, Mr Bates, I'm not. If we take this written paper at its face value, and I don't know why we shouldn't, it means that women killed that man. And *if* women, who more likely than the chorus girls? Unless you people up here can suggest some other women,—some, any women in the man's private life who wished to do him harm or who wished him out of the way. That's why I'm here, to learn anything and all things you may know that might aid me in a search for the right women—the women who really killed him. Chorus girls are wholly supposititious. But the real women, the women who *are* the criminals, must and shall be found!"

CHAPTER 6: THE LITTLE DINNER

The next morning at eight o'clock, Morton, the day doorman, came on duty.

Corson eagerly began at once to question him, and he told the story of Sir Herbert Binney's departure from the house, but there his information ended.

"All I know is, Mr Binney went away from here in a taxicab, 'long about half-past six, I think it was. And he went to the Hotel Magnifique,—at least, that's what he told the driver. And that's the last I saw of him. But his man, Peters, is due any minute,—maybe he'll know more."

"Peters? A valet?"

"Yes, and general factotum. He comes every morning at eight, and takes care of his boss."

And in a few moments Peters arrived. His shocked astonishment at the news was too patently real to give the slightest grounds of suspicion that he had any knowledge of it before his arrival.

"Poor old duffer!" he said, earnestly, "he was awful fond of life. Now, who would kill him, I'd like to know!"

"That's what we all want to know, Peters," said Corson. "Come, I'll go up to his rooms with you, and we can look things over."

Up they went, and the detective looked about the apartment of the dead man with interest. There were but two rooms, a bedroom and bath and a good-sized sitting-room. The furniture was the usual type of hotel appointments and there were so few individual belongings that the place gave small indication of the habits or tastes of its late occupant.

"Nothing of a sybarite," commented Corson, glancing at the few and simple toilet appurtenances.

"No," returned Peters, "but he was accustomed to finer living in his English home. He's no brag, but I gathered that from things he let drop now and then. But when he was on a business trip, he didn't seem to care how things were. He was a good dresser, but not much for little comforts or luxuries."

"What about his friendships with ladies?"

"Aha, that was his strong point! As a ladies' man he was there with the goods! He liked 'em all,—from chorus girls to duchesses,—and he knew English ladies of high life, I can tell you."

"But over here he preferred the chorus girls?"

"I don't say he preferred them. He went out a lot to fine homes and hobnobbed with some big people. But he was in his gayest mood when he was getting off for a frolic with the girls."

"As he was last night?"

"Yes; he didn't say much about it, but he did tell me that he was to take a couple of peaches to dinner, and afterwards see them in a Review or something they dance in."

"Can't you be more definite? Don't you know what revue? Or the girls' names?"

"No; I've no idea. Sir Herbert didn't mention any names, and of course I didn't ask him anything."

"Then, I'll have to go to the Magnifique to get on with this. First, I'll take a look around here."

But a careful investigation of the late Sir Herbert's papers and personal effects cast no light on the mystery of his death. There were several photographs of young women, quite likely theatrical people, but none had a signature. However, Corson took these in charge as well as some few notes and letters that seemed significant of friendships with women.

"As young Bates is, I believe, the heir to Sir Herbert's estate, I suppose he'll take charge of these rooms, but, meanwhile, I'll lock up as I want to go downstairs again now. You're out of a job, my man!"

"Yes,—why, so I am! It's the first I've realized that!"

"Maybe Mr Bates will keep you on."

"Not he! Those young chaps don't want valets. He doesn't, anyhow. No, I'll be looking for a new berth. Oh, it'll be easy enough found, but I liked Sir Herbert mighty well. He was a queer dick, but a kind and easy-going man to live with."

"And he never chatted with you about his young lady friends?"

"Never. He was a reserved sort, as far as his own affairs were concerned. You could go just so far and no farther with Sir Herbert Binney."

"Well, he left a paper stating that his death was brought about by women."

"He did? Why, how could that be?"

"That's what I've got to find out. He tried to write a message, and died in the very act. But he wrote clearly and distinctly the words, 'Women did this,' and we've got to believe it."

"Oh, yes; if it was the other way, now, if women did it, he might try to put it up to a man, to shield the girls. But if he wrote that, it's so, of course. Must have been some of those skylarking kids, and yet, it ain't likely, is it now? Some vamp, I should say."

"That's it! Not a young chorus chicken, but an older woman, or women. Adventuresses, you know."

"Yes, that's what I mean. I suppose your first move is to trail his steps of last evening."

"Yes, and I must get about it before the trail gets cold. I've so many ways to look. You know, Peters, he wasn't liked by the girls of this house."

"Well do I know that,—and small wonder. The girls in this house are as nice a bunch of young ladies as ever lived. And the tenants are decent men,—they don't chuck an elevator girl under the chin or try to kiss her every time they ride up or down in her car alone with her!"

"And Sir Herbert did?"

"That he did! I heard it time and again. All the girls were right down mad about it. They're not that sort of girls."

"But I suppose they're not the sort of girls to stab him in their righteous wrath?"

"Oh, good Lord, no! Though there's one of 'em, now,—
—"

"Which one?"

"No, I'll mention no names. Why, I've no right to hint at such a thing."

"But if you know anything——"

"I don't. Go ahead with your investigations. If there's anything to start your suspicions, let me know which way you're looking."

Corson went downstairs again, and rounded up all the girls employed in the house who might be apt to come in contact with the tenants.

Daisy Lee, an elevator girl, and Julie Baxter, a telephone girl, were the only ones who seemed to have rancorous or vindictive feelings toward the dead man.

Daisy, a frail, pale girl with a soft pretty face and lovely eyes, said frankly she was glad he was dead, for he bothered the life out of her with his attentions.

"He'd wait till I took other people up or down," she said, angrily, "so's he could ride with me alone, and then he'd kiss me."

"Why didn't you report his actions to the management?" Corson said, sharply.

"Well," Daisy blushed and hesitated.

"Speak up, Day!" said Julie. "I'll tell you, sir. She didn't tell 'cause he brought her candy and flowers if she wouldn't."

"That's so," Daisy admitted, pouting. "I like flowers and candies as well as anybody, and they're scarce nowadays."

"Where were you last night?" Corson inquired, suddenly.

"Home and in bed," declared Daisy, and when Julie gave her a quick, surprised look she said, defiantly, "Well, I was!"

"And where were you?" The detective turned to Julie.

"Home and in bed," she said also, but her tone was not convincing.

Corson was about to ask further questions of them, but just then Mr Vail came down in the elevator, and the detective turned to him.

"What!" Vail exclaimed, as the news was told him. "Binney! Why, who did it?"

"Women," said Corson, succinctly, and Vail looked mystified.

"Women! What women? And how do you know?"

He was enlightened as to the written message, and he looked utterly amazed.

"I never heard of such a thing! How could he write all that after he was stabbed with a stroke that killed him?"

"Well, he did! He was just dying when Bob Moore came down from taking you up."

"Oh, then? Yes, Moore and I chatted a few moments about detective stories, and do you mean to say that at that very moment poor old Binney was being murdered a few floors beneath us?"

"Just that, sir."

"What an awful thing! Have you any idea of the identity of the women? How *could* women do it?"

"That's what everybody says! To me it's just as easy to think women did it as men,—and a heap more logical! Why, a man wouldn't have dared to come into a brightly lighted place like this and stab somebody and get away again! But an angry woman—that's just what she would do!"

"That's true: I mean it's true no man would take a chance like that,—no sane man. But a woman, in a towering rage or insanely jealous or something—well, anyway, it's the most astonishing case I ever heard of!"

"It's all of that! You knew Sir Herbert Binney pretty well, didn't you, Mr Vail?"

"In a business way; not socially. We had several conferences as to his Bun bakery. I've a Bread business of my own, and we talked about a combine, but we finally gave up the plan and Sir Herbert took his offers to the Crippen concern,—or, said he was going to do so."

"You and he friendly?"

"Oh, yes; the affair was entirely amicable. The whole thing resolved itself into the fact that his Buns were really more cake than bread,—at least, from the American point of view,—and so better adapted to Crippen's use than to ours."

"And you came in last night just before Sir Herbert came?"

"So you tell me now. Naturally, I didn't know he followed me in."

"Where'd you spend the evening?"

"With a friend, Dr Weldon, in Fifty-first Street."

"Mind if I call him up and ask him?"

Vail stared at the detective.

"Meaning you're questioning my veracity, or connecting me with the crime?"

Corson reddened, but stuck to his suggestion. "No, sir, but,—well, you're the nearest I've found to a material witness, and——"

"Well, do you know, it strikes me you don't know what a material witness is! However, I've not the least objection to your calling up my friend,—go to it! Here's his number."

A little sheepishly, Corson took the number and called up Dr Weldon. The hearty response of a genial voice assured the inquirer that Mr Vail had spent the evening before with the doctor, that he had arrived late, having been to a theater, and that the two had played chess until nearly two o'clock, when Mr Vail, surprised at the lateness of the hour, had started for home. That was the extent of Dr Weldon's information.

"And quite satisfactory," Corson said, with a relieved air. "I had to know, sir, that you weren't with Sir Herbert. Now, I must find out who was with him,—of either sex."

"You're all right, Corson," Vail said; "I think you see your duty clearly, and if I can help you in any way, call on me. And, look here, don't you let any suspicion fasten itself on Bob Moore. That chap's all right. He's everlastingly reading murder yarns, but he's interested in the detective side of them, not the crime side. I wouldn't say this, but I heard something about his being questioned and I want to stand up for him. In a general way, I mean. And as to this case, it's very strange, I know, but don't let its strangeness lead you into impossible theories. You know, already, that at the time of Sir Herbert Binney's murder, Bob Moore was up at the tenth floor,—I can testify to that,——"

"Now, I don't know, Mr Vail," and Corson looked deeply perplexed. "What you say's true enough, but look here, we've only Moore's word that he found that man dying when he came down. Suppose Sir Herbert came in and Moore stabbed him——"

"And Sir Herbert wrote a paper saying it was women?"

"Well, no,—but maybe Bob wrote that paper himself——"

"You're getting pretty well tangled up, Corson. Why don't you put a handwriting expert on that paper, and see if it's in the dead man's fist or not?"

"Good idea, Mr Vail! I never thought of it!"

"Try it, and, excuse me, Corson, but I say this in all honesty, I think you'd better get some help. I believe this is a big case and a mysterious one, and it wouldn't do you any harm to have a colleague to advise with. Do as you like, or as you're told, but that's how it looks to me. Now I must be off, but I'll come home early, for I'm interested to know how things go."

"Hold on a minute, Mr Vail; you know Moore pretty well. Do you think it's possible that he knows who did it, knows who the women are, even perhaps saw the thing done, and then helped them to get away and disposed of the weapon?"

"Anything is possible, Corson, but I think what you suggest is exceedingly improbable. I know Moore only from my chats with him now and then in the elevator, and that's all I can say. To me, anything crooked in that young man seems decidedly unlikely."

Vail went off leaving a sadly perplexed detective behind him, who felt that he didn't know which way to turn, and was inclined to follow the advice he had received regarding a colleague.

Corson was anxious for further talk with the members of the Prall household, but they had not made appearance yet and he hesitated to call them.

He decided to run down to the Magnifique at once, when he received unexpected help from the telephone operator, Julie Baxter.

"Sir Herbert has a lot of telephone calls from ladies," she said, with a meaning glance.

"Is that so? Did he have any yesterday?"

"Yes, he did. About five o'clock, a skirt called him up and they had a merry confab."

"Who was she?"

"Dunno; but he called her 'Babe.'"

"Not very definite! Most girls get called that! What did she say?"

"How should I know that?" and Julie's big eyes stared haughtily at him.

"By the not unheard of method of using your ears. What did she say?"

Really eager to tell, Julie admitted that she listened in, and that an appointment was made for dinner at the Magnifique. Further details she could not supply.

Whereupon Corson carried out his plan of going to the big hotel at once.

He hunted down the head waiter of the grill room of the night before, and, having found him asleep in his room, waked him up and proceeded to interrogate him.

"You bet Sir Herbert Binney was here," the man declared, when he got himself fully awake; "he had two of the prettiest little squabs I ever saw, along, and they had a jolly dinner."

"And then?"

"Then they all went off to the theater, and after the show he brought them back, also two more,—four of 'em in all,—and they had supper."

"All amicable?"

"Oh, yes,—that is, at first. Later on, the girls got jealous of each other, and—well, the old chap's a softy, you know, and they pretty much cleaned him out."

"Just what do you mean?"

"Well, he made them presents, or promised them presents,—he's terribly rich,—and each of those girls was afraid somebody else would get more than she did. So, they squabbled quite a lot."

"Sir Herbert was good natured?"

"Yep; he just laughed and let 'em fight it out among themselves."

"Now, look here, did any of those four girls get angry enough to wish Sir Herbert any harm?"

"Did they? Why, I heard Babe Russell say she was going to kill him, and Viola Mersereau, she said, if she was sure it would never be discovered, she'd shoot him herself."

"Are you sure of these things? Because—somebody did kill Sir Herbert Binney about two o'clock this morning."

"What! Who did it?"

"We don't know, but we've reason to suspect women."

"That's the bunch, then! Lord, I didn't think they'd go so far as that! But that Viola is a ring-leader,—she's a vamp, if there ever was one! And little Russell! Well, she's soft and babyish looking but she's got the temper of a wildcat! And they were out for the goods, those young she's! They're all straight, you know, but they're just little greedies. And that man was their natural prey. Why, they could get anything out of him! Not pearl necklaces and diamonds,—I don't mean that,—but fans and vanity-cases and silk stockings and lockets and such trifles. Not trifles in the aggregate, though. That man must have spent a good big roll on 'em last night."

"How do you mean, spent it?"

"Why, he'd give this one or that one a yellowback to buy a new hat, say,—and then the others would tease for new hats. And maybe, if he didn't have the kale, he'd give 'em checks, or he'd tell 'em they could have the hat or the scarf or whatever charged to him. But he was strict. He told each one the limit she should pay, and if she paid more, they couldn't be friends any more. It was a queer mix-up, but all friendly and decent. He was just like a big frolicsome boy, and the girlies were like soft little kittens, playful,—but, kittens can scratch."

"And they did?"

"Yes, there was more real ill nature shown last night than ever before. Sir Herbert wasn't as generous as usual; I daresay he's tired of the game,—anyway, they couldn't bamboozle him to more than little trinkets, and I think Viola was out for furs. And furs mean money. But he only smiled when she hinted and she spoke more plainly, and then when he didn't agree she got mad."

"You seem to know all about it."

"Couldn't help knowing. They took no pains to be quiet, and I was around most of the time, and finally I became interested to see how it would come out."

"And how did it?"

"They all went off together,—I mean the girls did. He bundled 'em into a taxicab, gave the driver a bill and said good-night. That's the way he always does. He never escorts 'em home. Then he came back in here, settled his account, lit a cigar and strolled off by himself."

"At what time was this?"

"Abut one, or a little before. Not very late. Sir Herbert's no villain. I read him like a book. He just liked to see those girls enjoy a good supper, same's he liked to see 'em dance on the stage. Anyway, there's the history of the evening, so far as I know anything about it."

Corson went away, went to the theater where the girls belonged,—found out where they lived and went there.

The four lived in the same boarding house, and one and all refused to appear at any such unearthly hour as ten A. M.

But the strong arm of the law was used as an argument, and, after a time, four kimonoed and petulant-faced maidens put in an appearance.

Corson meant to be very intimidating, but he found himself wax in their hands. One and all they denied knowing anything of Sir Herbert Binney after he had entertained them at supper and sent them home in a cab.

They expressed mild surprise at his tragic fate, but no real regret. They seemed to Corson like four heartless, brainless dolls who had no thought, no interest outside their silly selves.

But in the dark eyes of Viola Mersereau and in the blonde, rosy face of Babe Russell he saw unmistakable signs of fear,—and, working on this, he blustered and accused and threatened until he had them all in hysteria.

"You've not got a chance!" he declared. "You're caught red-handed! You two said in so many words that you wished the old chap was dead, and after you got home, you sneaked out,—whether there were others to know it, or not, I can't say,—but you two sneaked out, went to The Campanile, waited your chance, dashed in and stabbed the man and dashed away again. And you'd been safe, but for his living long enough to tell on you! 'Women did this!' Of course they did! And *you're* the women! Who else could it be? What other women,—what other sort of women would commit such a deed? Come now, are you going to own up?"

Chapter 7: Enlightening Interviews

The avalanche of denial, the flood of vituperation and the general hullabaloo that was set up by the four girls at Corson's accusation reduced the detective to a pulp of bewilderment. The girls saw this and pursued their advantage. They stormed and raged, and then, becoming less frightened they guyed and jollied the poor man until he determined that he must have help of some sort.

Moreover, he felt sure now that these youngsters never committed murder. Even the Mersereau girl, the vamp, as she had been called, was a young thing of nineteen, and her vampire effect was only put on when occasion demanded.

"S'posen I did say I'd like to kill him!" she exclaimed, "that don't mean anything! S'posen I said I died o' laughin', would you think I was dead? Those things are figgers of speech,—that's what they are!"

She paraded up and down the room with a tragedy-queen air, and rolled her practiced eyeballs at Corson.

And Babe Russell was equally scornful, though her soft, gentle effects were the opposite of Viola's ways.

"Silly!" she said, shaking her pinkened finger at the detective. "To think us nice, pretty little girls would kill a big grown-up man! First off, we *couldn't* do it,—we wouldn't have the noive! And we'd be too 'fraid of getting caught. And we, wouldn't do it anyway,—it isn't in the picture!"

They seemed so straightforward and so sensible that Corson began to think it was absurd to suspect them, and yet the two he watched most closely were surely afraid of something. They talked gayly, and babbled on smilingly, but they glanced at each other with anxious looks when they thought the detective wasn't looking.

Whatever troubled them concerned them anxiously, for beneath their gayety they were distinctly nervous.

Corson convinced himself that they had no intention of running away and could always be found if wanted, so he left, with immediate intention of following the advice of Mr Vail and attaching an assistant.

"Not in a thousand years!" was the opinion of the assistant, one Gibbs, after he heard Corson's tale of the chorus girls. "Those little chippies might be quite willing to kill a man, theoretically, but as for the deed itself, they couldn't put it over. Still, they must be remembered. You know, the statement that women did it, is surely the truth. Dying messages are invariably true. But it may mean that women caused it to be done,—that it was the work of women, even though the actual stab thrust may have been the deed of a man."

"I don't think so," mused Corson. "You haven't seen the paper. It said, not only, 'Women did this,' but it said afterward, 'Get——' and then there were two letters that looked like b-o——"

"No; I hadn't heard that! Why, it might have been Ba—and might have meant Babe Russell, after all!"

"No; it's bo,—but it isn't a capital B. I studied it closely, and I have it put away. I'll show it to you."

"But the capital doesn't matter. A man writing, in those circumstances, with his last effort of fading strength, might easily use a small letter instead of a capital. Know anybody beginning with Bo?"

"No—why, oh, my goodness! Bob Moore!"

"Well, there's a chance. You've had your eyes on Moore, haven't you?"

"Only because he was right there. But Mr Vail,— George Vail, of the Vail Bread Company,—stands up for Moore. To be sure, it was only in a general way,—we only talked a few moments,—but he seemed to think Moore is on the detective order,—not of a criminal sort."

"Why must Moore necessarily be either?"

"Only because he's a detective story shark. Reads murder yarns all the time, and goes to detective story movies."

"That proves just nothing at all. But the 'Get Bo—' is important. Anybody else around, beginning with Bo,—or Ba? You see, he naturally wouldn't form the letters perfectly."

"Ba? There's Julie Baxter, the telephone girl."

"He'd hardly speak of her as Baxter."

"But,—oh, I say, Gibbs, Moore testifies that, as the man died, he tried to say something and it sounded like 'Get J—J——' some name beginning with J!"

"Hello! We must inquire as to the fair Julie. Any one else?"

"No; no women, that I know of. Young Bates, the heir, begins his name with Ba, but he's not a woman."

"Have you looked up his record for last evening? What was he doing?"

"No, I haven't. A man can't do everything at once!"

"This thing seems to have a dozen different handles. First of all, I think we want to see the family.

"But he hadn't any family."

"Well, relatives, connections, anybody most interested. Especially the heir."

So the two went to the apartment of Letitia Prall, and there found the family connections of Sir Herbert Binney in a high state of excitement.

It was nearly noon, and Richard Bates was impatiently waiting the arrival of the detective, whom he had been expecting all the morning.

"Look here," he said to the two men when they came in, "I want you to take hold of this case with me,—if you can't do it, I'll get somebody who can. I don't want you to be off skylarking on a wild goose chase, while I sit here waiting for you——"

"One moment, Mr Bates," said Corson, sharply; "we're not detectives in your employ; we're police officers, and we're conducting this case in accordance with orders."

"Well, well, let's get at it, and see where we stand. What do you know?"

"Only the message on the paper left by your uncle, and such testimony as we could gather from the employees downstairs. Now, we want to interview you."

"And I want to be interviewed. Go ahead."

"Interview all of us," put in Eliza Gurney, who with Miss Prall had sat silent during the men's colloquy, but was quite ready to talk.

"One at a time," and Gibbs took up the conversation. "Mr Bates, where were you last evening?"

"That," said Richard, "I decline to state, on the grounds that it has no bearing on the question of my uncle's death. If you ask me where I was at the time of the tragedy, or shortly before, I will tell you. But last evening or yesterday afternoon or morning are not pertinent."

"You refuse to state where you spent last evening?"

"I do."

"Not a good thing for you to do," Gibbs shook his head, "but let it pass for the moment. Where were you at two o'clock this morning?"

"In bed and asleep."

"You can prove this?"

"By me!" spoke up Letitia Prall. "I heard him come in about twelve and go to his room."

"H'm. Proof to a degree. How do you know he didn't leave the apartment later?"

"Because I didn't hear him do so."

"Where is his room, and where is your own?"

After being shown the respective bedrooms, Gibbs remarked that in his opinion Bates could easily have left his room without Miss Prall's knowledge, if she were asleep at the time.

"Unless you are unusually acute of hearing, are you?"

Now this was a sensitive point with the spinster. Her hearing was not what it had once been, but she never acknowledged it. She greatly resented the busy finger of time as it touched her here and there, and often pretended she heard when she did not. Both her nephew and her companion good-naturedly humored her in this little foible, and at Gibbs' question they looked up, uncertainly.

"Of course I am!" was Miss Prall's indignant reply to the detective's question. "I hear perfectly."

"Are you sure?" said Gibbs, mildly; "for I have noticed several times when you have seemed not to hear a side remark."

"Inattention, then," snapped Letitia. "I am a thoughtful person, and I often take little notice of others' chatter."

"But you are sure you could have heard your nephew if he had gone out of his place last night after——"

"But I didn't go out!" declared Bates. "You're absurd to imply that I did, unless you have some reason on which to base your accusation!"

"We have to locate you before we can go further, Mr Bates," insisted Gibbs, who had assumed leadership, while Corson sat, with folded arms, taking in anything he found to notice.

And Corson, though lacking in initiative, was a close observer, and he saw a lot that would have escaped his notice had he been obliged to carry on the inquiry.

"Let's try it," Corson said, suddenly. "Go into your room, please, Miss Prall, and shut the door, and see if you can hear me go out."

"Of course I can!" and with a determined air, Miss Prall went into her room and closed the door quite audibly.

Lifting his finger with a gesture of admonition, Corson made every one sit perfectly still and without speaking for about two minutes.

Then, rising himself, he opened Miss Prall's door and bade her come out.

"Now," he said, "I admit I made as little noise as possible, but did you hear me go out of the front door?"

"Of course I did!" declared the spinster, haughtily. "I heard you tiptoe to the door, open it stealthily and close it the same way."

She looked calmly about, and then seeing the consternation on the faces of Richard and Eliza and the amused satisfaction on the countenances of the detectives, she saw she had made a false step, and became irate.

"What is it?" she began, but Richard interrupted her.

"Don't say a word, Auntie," he begged; "you see gentlemen, Miss Prall is a little sensitive about her slight deafness, and sometimes she imagines sounds that are not real."

"I'm not deaf!" Letitia cried, but Eliza interposed:

"Do hush, Letitia. You only make matters worse! Will you be quiet?"

The tone more than the words caused Miss Prall to drop the subject, and Gibbs proceeded.

"Now, you see, Mr. Bates, we can't accept your aunt's testimony that you didn't leave your room last night."

"I didn't ask you to," retorted Richard; "nor do I need it. I tell you I was in bed by or before midnight, and did not leave my bed until I was summoned by Bob Moore after the tragedy had occurred. Now, unless you have some definite and sufficient reason to suspect me of falsehood, I have no need to bring any proof of my assertion."

"That's so, Gibbs," said Corson, meditatively. "There's no reason, I know of, to inquire into Mr Bates' doings."

"There's reason to inquire into the doings of everybody who had the slightest connection with this matter," said Gibbs severely. "But unless there's a doubt, we needn't yet ask for proof of their words."

He glared at Miss Prall, with the evident implication that he might feel a doubt of her word.

However, when she and Miss Gurney stated that they had retired at about eleven and had not left their rooms until called up by Richard to hear the tragic news, no comment was made by Gibbs and Corson merely looked at them abstractedly with the air of a preoccupied owl.

"Then," resumed Corson, "now that we've placed your whereabouts and occupations, will you state, any or all of you, what opinion you hold as to the identity of the women who are responsible for the death of Sir Herbert Binney?"

"Those chorus girls," said Miss Letitia, promptly. "I always told him he'd get into a moil with them, and they'd fleece him. They are a smart lot, and Sir Herbert, though a shrewd business man, was putty in the hands of a clever or designing woman!"

"But these girls are mere children—"

"In years, perhaps," Miss Prall broke in, "but not in iniquity. A gentleman of Sir Herbert's mild and generous nature could be bamboozled by these wise and wicked little vampires until they'd stripped him of his last cent!"

"You seem to know a lot about them, Madam."

"Because Sir Herbert has told me. He often described the cleverness with which they wheedled and coerced him into undue generosity, and though he laughed about it, it was with an undercurrent of chagrin and vexation. And so, the time came, I feel certain, when Sir Herbert, like the worm in the proverb, turned, and what he did or said, I don't know, but I haven't the slightest doubt that it led, in some way, to such hard feeling and such a deep and desperate quarrel, that the affair resulted in tragedy."

Gibbs looked at the speaker.

The Grenadier, as some people called her, sat upright, and her fine head nodded with stern denunciation of the young women she accused.

Her tight-set lips and glittering eyes showed hatred and scorn, yet her fingers nervously interlaced and her voice shook a little as if from over-strained nerves.

Even more nervous was Miss Gurney. Unable to sit still, she moved restlessly from one chair to another,— even now and then left the room, hurrying back, as if afraid of missing something.

"Do sit still, Eliza," said Miss Prall, at last; "you're enough to drive any one distracted with your running about like a hen with its head off!"

"I feel like one! Here's poor Sir Herbert dead, and nobody paying any attention to it,—except to find out who killed him! I think our duty is first to the dead, and after that——"

"Keep still, Eliza," ordered Bates, who was never very patient with his aunt's irritating and irritable companion. "Sir Herbert's body and his affairs will be duly taken care of. It's necessary now to discover his murderer, of course, and the sooner investigation is made the more hope of finding the criminal."

"Or criminals," put in Gibbs. "Since seeing that paper, I feel convinced that the dying man tried to write 'get both,' meaning to insure punishing to the women who killed him."

"Then you think women really did the deed?" asked Bates, a strange fear in his blue eyes.

"Yes, I do;" Gibbs stated, "but Corson thinks women were merely at the root of the trouble. However, that isn't the point just now. That will all be learned later. First, we must get an idea of which way to look. And, too, I may be wrong. The illegible word on that paper may mean, as Corson thinks, the beginning of some name. The fact that the B is not a capital doesn't count for much when we realize the circumstances of the writing."

"I should say not!" and Miss Prall looked straight at him. "Think of that poor dying man trying to write, while his life blood ebbed away! And can you fail to heed his dying message? Can you fail to get those wicked, vicious little wretches who heartlessly lured him on and on in their wild orgies, until it all resulted in his fearful end! I, for one, shall never be satisfied until those foolish, flippant little things are punished——"

"Oh, Letitia," wailed Miss Gurney, "bad as they are, you wouldn't want to see them all stuffed into an electric chair, would you, now?"

The mental picture of the chorus girls crowded into a single electric chair was almost too much for Richard's sense of humor, and he smiled, but Miss Gurney went on:

"But, anyway, if a pack of girls did do it, don't think it was the chorus girls. They're too frivolous and light hearted. I think you'd better look nearer home. The girls in this house were all down on Sir Herbert. None of them liked him, and he was always berating them, both to us, and to their very faces. That telephone girl, now,——"

"Eliza, *will* you keep still?" fumed Miss Prall. "Why do you suggest anybody? These detectives are here to find out the murderers and they not only need no help from you, but they are held back and bothered by your interference. Please remain quiet!"

"I'll talk all I like, Letitia Prall; I guess I know what's best for your interests as well as my own."

"You haven't any interests separate from mine, and I can look after myself! Now, you do as I tell you, and say nothing more on this subject at all. If Sir Herbert was the victim of his foolish penchant for those light young women, I'm not sure it doesn't serve him right——"

"Oh, Auntie!" exclaimed Bates, truly pained at this. "Don't talk so!"

"What right have you got to dictate to me? You keep still, too, Rick,—in fact, the least we any of us say, the better."

"Oh, no, Miss Prall," said Gibbs, suavely, "if there's anything you know, it will really be better for all concerned that you should tell it. As to your opinions or ideas or theories, I hold you quite excusable if you keep those to yourselves."

"And you'd prefer I should do so, I suppose! Well, I will. And as to facts, I know of none that could help you, so I will say nothing."

"Miss Gurney," and Gibbs turned toward her with a determined glance, "you spoke of the young women employed in the house; had you any one in mind?"

"Eliza——" began Miss Prall, but Gibbs stopped her.

"Beg pardon, ma'am, but I must request that you let Miss Gurney speak for herself. You have no right to forbid her, and I insist upon my right to ask."

"Nobody in particular," Miss Gurney asserted, as she looked timidly at Letitia. "But Sir Herbert's chambermaid,——"

"Yes, go on."

"Well, she refused to take care of his room, he was so cross to her. But I don't suppose she'd kill him just for that."

"I'll look up the matter. Glad you mentioned it. Andy they gave him another maid?"

"Yes, the same one we have."

"I must have a talk with her. Much may be learned from a room servant. That's what I want, facts,—not theories. We've got the big primal fact,—'women did it.' We've got a possible fact,—an uncertain statement,—'get both'—or, maybe, get some particular person. Now any side lights we can get that may throw illumination on that uncertain bit of writing is what is needed to show us which way to look. Isn't that right, Mr. Bates?"

"Why, yes, I suppose so. Personally, I can't seem to see women doing such a deed——"

"That, sir, is the result of your own manly outlook and your lack of experience with a desperate woman. You know, 'Hell hath no fury like a woman scorned,' and we can readily imagine a woman scorned by this Sir Herbert."

"He could do the scorning, all right——"

"And they could do the rest! Oh, yes, sir, it isn't a pleasant thing to believe, but it is a fact that women can be just as revengeful, just as vindictive, just as cruel as men,—and can commit just as great crimes, though as we all know, such women are the exception. But they are in existence and that fact must be recognized and remembered."

"But the circumstances—" demurred Bates, "the time——"

"My dear sir, it seems to me the circumstances and time were most favorable for the work of women. Granting some women wanted to kill that man, or had determined to kill him,—or even, killed him on a sudden irresistible impulse, what more conducive to an opportunity than this house late at night? The great lobby, guarded, as it is at that hour, by only one man and he often up in the ascending elevator car. You see, the women could easily have been in hiding in that onyx lobby. The great pillars give most convenient and unobservable places of concealment, and they could have been tucked away there for a long time, waiting."

"Oh, ridiculous! Supposing my uncle hadn't come in?"

"Then they could have slipped out again. They may have been hidden there night after night, waiting for just the chance that came last night."

"But, suppose Moore had been downstairs when Sir Herbert entered—"

"Just the same," Gibbs explained, wearily. "Then they would have gone away and tried again the next night. A woman's perseverance and patience is beyond all words!"

"It's all beyond all words," and Richard folded his arms despondently. "I can't get a line on it."

"Well, I can," asserted Gibbs; "they came, no doubt, prepared. Else, where'd they get the knife? Now, naturally one criminal would be assumed,—that's why *women* was written so clearly. Several who know, have agreed the handwriting is positively that of Sir Herbert Binney,—so, there's nothing left to do but *cherchez les femmes.*"

CHAPTER 8: JULIE BAXTER

Richard Bates and the two detectives stood waiting for the already summoned elevator to take them downstairs.

"You see," Gibbs was saying, "in nearly every investigation there's somebody who won't tell where he was at the time of the crime."

"I will tell that," exploded Bates, "only I won't tell where I was through the evening, and, you know yourself, that has nothing to do with the case."

"I know, and, nine times out of ten, it doesn't matter what the people were doing who refuse to tell. But it might make a difference, and it's always a bother to be worrying about it."

"Why worry?"

"Because it may pay. According to Corson's hunch, two of those chorus chicks don't want to tell where they were at the time of the crime——"

"Oh, well, they wouldn't——"

"I know; but it's an uncertainty. Now, take your aunt. She falsified about hearing your front door close just now. I've a full belief that was merely because of a piffling vanity about her deafness,—a thing nobody wants to admit,—but, I wish she hadn't, for it proves that she is not above prevarication."

"I don't think she would fib in any serious matter," vouchsafed Richard.

"You don't think so because you don't want to think so. That can't cut any ice with me, you know."

The elevator stopped and the three went down.

In a business-like way, Gibbs rounded up all the girl employees available and put them through a rigid investigation.

They were a voluble lot, and it was easier to get information than to prevent it.

Daisy Lee was among the most vindictive. Although a frail, pale little thing, she was full of indignation at the late Sir Herbert's ways, and expressed herself without reserve.

"He was an old nuisance!" she averred; "he was free with his presents and he was a gentleman,—I'll say that for him,—but he thought he could pat any girl on her shoulder or even snatch a kiss, without making her mad. He made me so mad I wanted to kill him,—and I told him so, lots of times. I didn't, and there's no way I could have done it, so I am not afraid to say that I would have stabbed him myself if I'd had a good chance!"

"You don't mean that, Miss Lee," said Gibbs, coolly, "and you're only saying it to make a sensation."

"Why, what a story!" and Daisy turned on him. "Well, that is, I don't suppose I really would have done the actual killing, but I'd have the will to."

"Quite a different matter," said the detective, "and your will would have fizzled out at the critical moment."

"Of course it would," put in Julie Baxter, the telephone girl. "Daisy's an awful bluffer. None of us girls would kill anybody. But one and all we are glad to be rid of Sir Herbert, though I can't help being sorry he's killed."

"You mean you'd have been glad to be rid of him in some more peaceable fashion?"

"That's exactly what I mean. He was insufferable——"

"In what way?"

"Not only, as Daisy says, because he had free manners, but he was silly, beside. Always saying, 'Well, little one, how do you like my new necktie?' or some foolishness like that."

Richard Bates looked uncomfortable. "Need I stay?" he inquired. "You must realize I dislike to hear this talk about my uncle."

"Stay, please," returned Corson, briefly; "and, young ladies, don't give us any more of your opinions of Sir

Herbert, but tell, if you know, of any circumstance bearing on his death."

Apparently none knew of any such, and the girls looked at each other in silence.

"And now, tell me where you were at two A. M., each of you, and then you may be excused."

Every one declared that she had been home and in bed at that hour, except Julie Baxter. She, with a fine show of independence, refused to disclose her whereabouts at that time.

"There it is again," said Corson in despair. "Now, Miss Baxter, I don't think that your reticence necessarily incriminates you at all, but it leaves room for doubt. Take my word for it, it would be wiser and far better for you to tell frankly where you were, even if it calls for criticism from your mates."

"But I won't tell," and Julie looked very stubborn.

"You'd rather be arrested and held on suspicion?"

"You can't arrest me without a speck of evidence! Nor you can't scare me by such threats."

"It isn't an idle threat, and you can be held for further inquiry, if I say so."

"You won't say so, and anyway I won't say where I was last night. But I will say I was up to no harm, and had no hand in the death of Sir Herbert Binney."

"I don't, as yet, think you did; but let me remark that if you *were* implicated in the matter you would act and speak just as you do now. You would, of course, asseverate your innocence——"

"Of course I should. So, now, Mr Smarty-Cat, what are you going to do about it?"

Julie's eyes snapped with anger that seemed almost vicious, and she tossed her head independently, while the other girls showed little or no sympathy. She was not a favorite with her fellow-workers; they called her stuck-up, and she not only refused to take them into her confidence as to her amusements and entertainments, but she often whetted their curiosity by mysterious hints of grand doings of which she never told them definitely.

She lived in herself during her hours on duty, and even in the rest room she was never chummy or chatty like the rest.

Wherefore, there were surprised glances and nodding heads in her direction, and Daisy Lee sniffed openly.

"Huh," she said, "Julie Baxter, you're too smart. You were more friendly with Sir Binney than any of us. He gave you twice the candy he did any one else, and I know you've been out to dinner with him!"

"I have not!" declared Julie, but a flush on her cheeks and a quiver of her eyelids left room for doubt as to her truthfulness.

"Also," and Corson flung this at her, "also, on the paper was written 'get B-a-' and *also*, we've been told that the dying man tried to articulate a name beginning with J!"

"Now, Miss Baxter, do you still deny all implication in the affair?" Gibbs leaned forward and stared into her eyes.

"I do!" she cried, but her voice was hysterical and her manner agitated. Vainly she strove to keep her self-control, but, unable to do so and broke into a fit of uncontrollable weeping.

"Oh, I say, Corson," said tender-hearted Bates, "you oughtn't to bully her! That's nothing short of third degree!"

"Well, I'll put it through, if I can get the truth that way. Now, Miss Baxter, if you'll tell us, in your own self-defense where you were that night, you may go. If not, I think we'll have to ask you to go away with us to——"

"Don't take me away!" moaned Julie, "and don't ask me about last night! I didn't kill him—truly, I didn't!"

"But you know something about it,—you must be detained as a material witness——"

"Wait till I talk to somebody—ask somebody's advice——"

"She means Bob Moore," Daisy informed them; "they're engaged, and Julie'll say just what Bob tells her to."

"Oho! You're engaged to Moore, eh?" and Gibbs gazed at her with fresh interest.

And then, stepping from the door of the elevator, came Dorcas Everett, and Richard Bates lost all desire to hear further evidence from the questioned girls.

With a brief but determined apology, he left the alcove, where they had been talking, and hurried to Dorcas' side.

"Have you heard?" he said, as he fell into step and walked with her toward the door.

"Yes; I can't talk here,—I can't breathe! Can we go for a walk?"

"Of course, why not?"

"I thought you were busy with those—people."

"Perhaps they think so, too, but I don't care! Come on; hasten your steps just a little and don't look back."

Apparently carelessly, but really with a feeling of stealth, the pair made their way to the street, Bates feeling guiltily conscious of the detectives' disapproval, and Dorcas afraid of her action being reported to her mother.

"I've been waiting so to see you," she exclaimed, as soon as they were at a safe distance from The Campanile. "Do tell me all about it! My mother has gone to call on your aunt,—and I thought I'd come down and see if I could run across you. Mother'll be there some time, I've no doubt, and I took a chance."

"Bless you! But, tell me, how did your mother hear? What do you know? I mean, what's the general report?"

"Nothing definite, but all sorts of rumors,—which mother tried to keep from me. But she and Kate were talking, and I found out that the chambermaid told them that woman had killed Sir Herbert. Mother told me he had died suddenly, but she didn't know I overheard about the murder."

"Yes; it's true. He was murdered and he left a dying statement that women did it. It's a horrible affair, and I wish you needn't know the details. Can't you go away or something till it is all past history?"

"Oh, I don't want to. I'm no child to be put to bed like that! But Mother has been urging me to go away,—and yesterday she said she's going to move anyway. If she should send me to Auntie Fayre's—but she won't——"

"If she should, what?" cried Richard, eagerly; "Do you mean that in that case, we might meet now and then?"

"Yes, that's what I meant,—but, we couldn't if this matter is public property, and I suppose it is, or will be?"

"Yes, of course; but it can't last long. You see, dear, there's bound to be an awful disclosure of some sort. Women don't kill a man without some big reason,—at least big to them."

"But who did it? What women?"

"We don't know. The probabilities are that it was some girls he had flirted with. Oh, Dork, don't ask questions; it's a disgraceful affair, I fear. I don't know,—if a man had done it, I should think it merely the result of Uncle's wild temper. He was awful when in a rage. But the feminine element makes only unpleasant theories possible. And yet, Uncle was a gentleman and a decent one. I believe it was the work of some women who had a fancied grievance and who were jealous or revengeful for some foolish reason. But, of course, there's no telling what evidence will turn up. And I must be prepared for embarrassing disclosures."

"You're the heir, aren't you, Rick?"

"So far as I know. Uncle made me that, but he may have changed his mind. His lawyers have his will, and I've made no inquiries as yet. You see, Dork, there's so much to see to. Why, I've got to take care of Aunt Letty and Eliza,—I mean, shield them from publicity and reporters and all that. I've no business to sneak off here with you, but I couldn't help it!"

"But tell me this; what women are suspected? What ones are possible suspects?"

"Some chorus girls and the house girls, so far."

"House girls? You mean the elevator girls——"

"Yes, and telephone operators and perhaps chambermaids,—oh, Dorrie, Uncle Bin was the sort of a man who is jolly with any woman. I'm willing to bet there was never a really wrong idea in his head, but he was so carelessly gay and chummy with them all, that a vicious or wicked woman could play the devil with him!"

"Poor Sir Herbert,—I rather liked him."

"He liked you,—he said so. And he was in favor of our marriage, which is more than we can say for any of our nearer relatives."

"Yes, indeed! Mother gets more and more wrathy about Miss Letty every day of her life,—and I expect this matter will just about finish her!"

"I suppose so. Now, we must get back, for my reasons and your own good. When can I see you again?"

"Oh, I don't know. It all depends on the outcome of the present meeting of the two. If your aunt seems to want sympathy or help I daresay Mother would feel kindly toward her in this trouble. But if Miss Letty is uppish and reserved,—as I fear she will be,—then Mother will go for her! I'm only imagining all this; I've no idea what will really happen."

Poor little Dorcas, it was well for her present peace of mind that she hadn't!

The two walked slowly back to The Campanile, almost forgetting the tragedy that had come so close to them, in the content of being together.

Corson met them at the door.

"Been looking for you," he said to Bates. "And, Miss Everett, your mother is inquiring where you are. She left word for you to go to her the moment you appeared."

"Yes," Dorcas returned, and then, shyly, "Please don't say I was with Mr Bates, will you?"

Corson looked at her, with interest. Pretty Dorcas, her shy, brown eyes falling at the idea of asking for secrecy, but her judgment, already trained in diplomacy, telling her it was necessary.

"I won't," and Corson smiled at her, "if, you'll answer a question or two. Where were you last night at two o'clock?"

"In bed and asleep," said the girl simply.

"Thank goodness you don't refuse to tell! And at what time did you retire?"

"About eleven."

"And where had you spent the evening?"

"Oh, I say, Corson," and Bates interrupted, "that's in the class with your grilling of me. You know Miss Everett isn't implicated, you know you're asking her that because you've got the habit. Run along, Dorcas, you don't have to be quizzed any more."

Dorcas turned quickly, and just managed to catch an up-bound elevator as its door was about to close.

"Now, you let her alone, Corson," said Bates, sharply. "I don't mind telling you she's the girl I intend to marry, but we're not really engaged. That is, it isn't announced. And I ask you, as man to man, to say nothing of it, to say nothing to her, and to keep her out of it all you can. Lord knows, you've no reason to think of her in connection with the horrible affair!"

"No; except as she's interested in you, and you're the heir."

"Forget it. Who told you I was the heir?"

"Everybody knows it,—it's in all the papers."

"I haven't looked at a paper! Lord, I don't think I can!"

"Better not; they're not pretty reading."

"What do you mean? Any aspersions against my uncle's character?"

"No, not that. But when the word women occurs in connection with the murder of a rich and influential man, there's bound to be surmise,—at least."

"Oh, I suppose so. Well, do you want me down here? I'd like to go up to see my aunt."

"Wait a minute. Have you ever thought, Mr Bates, that the feud between your aunt and Mrs Everett is a mighty queer affair?"

"I've often thought that, but,—pardon me,—don't get outside your own proper boundaries!"

"Oh, I'm not. Now, a queer thing, like that feud, has to be taken into consideration."

"Not in connection with the murder of my Uncle Binney."

"Maybe not in direct connection, but as a side light. You know the feud has a decided bearing on your affair with Miss Everett."

"I object to your use of the word 'affair.' My friendship with Miss Everett is in spite of, even in defiance of, the feud between her mother and my aunt. I make no secret of it to you, but as I advise you, the matter is confidential. I'm treating you as a fellow-man, Corson, and I don't want you to abuse my confidence in your fellowship, or your—manliness."

Corson fidgeted a little and returned, "I've got to do my duty, Mr Bates, and part of my duty seems to me to be to tell you that I'm not allowed to observe confidences if they affect my orders."

"They don't! How can your investigations of this murder case be affected by my friendship for Miss Everett?"

"They can,—in a way. You see, I know a lot about this feud business. I know how inimical, how full of vicious hatred those two women are, and have been for years. And I know how your recent special interest in Miss Everett has roused the renewed anger of not only your aunt, but her mother——"

"Phew! You do know it all, don't you?"

"I do. Therefore, I felt I must inform you of the extent of my knowledge, so you and I can understand each other. Now, drop the subject for the moment, for I've other matters to speak of. Where do you suppose the weapon is?"

"I've not the slightest idea! How could I have?"

"Do you know what the weapon was?"

"Only what the doctor said, a very sharp knife of some sort."

"Yes; now did you know that the doctor has also said that the stroke delivered by that same sharp knife was so well planted, so skillfully driven home, that it implies the work of some one with a knowledge of anatomy?"

"A doctor?"

"Not necessarily,—unless a woman doctor. But, what other idea suggests itself?"

"Oh, I don't know. Don't ask me riddles."

"A nurse, then. Can't you see the reasonableness of suspecting a trained nurse, after Dr Pagett's opinions?"

"All right; where's your trained nurse in Sir Herbert's bright galaxy of beauty?"

"That's a point to be looked up. But, I may tell you that Julie Baxter studied nursing before she took up telephone work."

"H'm. Might be coincidence."

"Of course it *might*. But we have to investigate coincidences. You don't know of any nurse or ex-nurse in your uncle's circle of friends?"

"Friends seems to me an inappropriate word."

"Look here, Mr Bates, you let my choice of words alone, and answer my questions."

"All right, I will. I don't know of any nurse at all and I shouldn't tell you if I did!"

"Not a very wise remark on your part, Mr Bates," and Corson looked at him meaningly.

"I don't care whether it's wise or not. You make me disgusted with detective work! Why do you go around sneaking up on any woman you can hear of? Why don't you go about it from the other side? Find a motive for the murder and then find the criminal who had the motive! Don't suspect this one because she studied nursing and that one because the old gentleman kissed her! It isn't a unique case, my uncle's fancy for chorus girls,—but it by no means indicates the result of murder! Get the weapon, then find its owner. Get a clue,—a real, material clue, and then trace the criminal. Get some evidence,—actual, spoken or circumstantial,—and deduce your facts from it. For heaven's sake, do some real detective work, and not just dance around questioning any kiddy-girl you happen to see!"

"Your words are not without reason," and Corson gave Bates a peculiar smile. "Indeed, I had some idea of doing just what you suggest. But one of the first things to do in the hunt for evidence is to find out where your uncle was last night between twelve and two. You see, the people at the Magnifique say he sent the girls home by themselves and then soon after went off himself in the neighborhood of midnight. Next he's heard of at two A. M. dying on the floor of the onyx lobby! Where was he in the meantime?"

"That's truly a most important question to be answered," said Richard, very seriously. "On that depends far more than on the frightened admissions or denials of a lot of excited young women."

"I quite agree with you," said the detective.

Chapter 9: The Library Set

But it proved no easy matter to trace the whereabouts of Sir Herbert Binney between the hours of twelve and two on the night he met his tragic death.

The detectives were aware that he said a pleasant good-night to the chorus girls he had entertained at supper, and had left the Magnifique, alone, about midnight, but then all trace was lost. Naturally enough, for peaceable citizens are not noticed if they follow a beaten or usual path.

Nor could it be discovered whether he came into the onyx lobby alone, or accompanied by the person or persons responsible for his death. The absence of the weapon precluded all thought of suicide, therefore, he had been murdered and the murderer was still at large.

There was no witness to his dying moments but the night porter, Bob Moore. His testimony was not doubted, for, so far, no reason was apparent for his having any ill will toward the victim of the tragedy.

The two police detectives on the case worked well together. Corson was the more clever minded of the two, and Bates more energetic and active. But they felt decidedly baffled at the stone wall they found themselves up against.

Sir Herbert had left the Hotel Magnifique, walking. Where had he gone or whom had he met? A highwayman or thug was improbable, for such a person would not follow a victim into his own home before attacking him. This added plausibility to the written statement incriminating women.

Angry or vindictive women might accompany him to the lobby of his own hotel, pleading or threatening in their own interests and then, in their final despair at gaining their point, stab him and run away.

Which, the detectives concluded, was just what had happened, and the thing now, was to find the women.

In default of any other way to look, they were still investigating the women employed in The Campanile.

But they had narrowed their search down to a few of those. Principally of interest was Julie Baxter, the telephone girl,—but more for the reason of her relations with Moore, than because of her own admissions.

A persistent quizzing of Moore had proved to the detectives' satisfaction that he did not know where Julie was the night of the murder, and that he was himself anxiously worried at her refusal to tell.

For the girl would not tell even her *fiance* where she had been. She persisted in her story that she had been up to no harm but she was determined to keep her secret. This, in connection with her strong will and blunt manner, convinced the detectives that, though she need not have been criminally implicated, she, at least, knew definite and indicative facts about the murder.

Moore said he was in a quandary. Full of detective interest, he longed to work on the case, and felt sure he could be of use to the police, but the attitude of Julie deterred him.

"You see, she's my girl," he said frankly to Corson. "And she does act queer! I don't understand her, but I can't dig into this thing and maybe run up against something she doesn't want me to!"

"You have faith in her own innocence, then?"

"Oh, yes,—that is, she wouldn't kill a man! And yet,— who can say that? In a fit of anger a woman would do anything,—more especially, if she wasn't alone."

"What do you mean by that?"

"I mean a woman, working alone, would hardly dare to kill a man,—but, accompanied, maybe egged on by another woman, she'd be daredevil enough to——"

"Who would? Julie Baxter?" Corson flung the question at him.

"Yes," Moore declared, "Julie or any woman of her fierce, intense nature. I know Julie well, and I love her, and I'm going to see her through,—but it's quite in the picture that she knows something about this thing."

"You're pretty frank for a man engaged to——"

"That's just it! I'm going to save her from herself! Julie is stubborn,—she's positively pig-headed, if she takes a notion. Now, if she's keeping something back,— and she is,—it's to shield some friend, or,—or to shield herself; but not from conviction of crime,—rather from some circumstances that might falsely incriminate her— or some one else."

"But if she knows who did this thing——"

"Oh, she doesn't. At most, she only suspects. But I'll find out. She's my girl, and I'm going to discover the truth about her,—and then about the murder."

"Oho, you're going to be a detective!"

"Not so's you'd notice it. But I'm going to do a little sleuthing on the side and if I find out anything that will help justice along, I promise to tell you,—let the chips fall where they may."

"I haven't any too much faith in Moore's protestations," Corson confided to Gibbs. "He's crazy to be a detective, but he's afraid he'll catch his own girl in his net. That's the truth in a nutshell. I do think, though, he'd be good help to us, for he knows all about this house and its occupants, and I can't help thinking the murderers belong here."

"I don't think so," returned Gibbs. "I'm sure they are rank outsiders. They were with him during those missing two hours and they followed him home, hoping to get what they were after,—black-mail, most likely, and then at the last minute opportunity presented itself and they killed him."

"Must have been prepared for it, as they had a weapon, used it deftly, and carried it off."

"They did that, and there's an important clew. None of those little chorus babes could have stabbed with that deft touch, which the doctor vows shows skilled medical or surgical knowledge."

"Maybe, and maybe it was a chance blow. Well, I'm going off on a new tack. I'm going up to see the dead man's people and get, if I can, some new angle on the case."

Corson went up to the Prall apartment and found the members of that household in a high state of excitement.

Miss Letitia Prall paused in what was evidently an angry harangue and somewhat grudgingly accorded a greeting to the caller.

"Must you have an interview just now, Mr Corson?" she asked, acidly. "I'm sure you know all we can tell you."

"I'm not sure of that, Miss Prall. There are, I think, some points yet to be cleared up."

"The whole case is yet to be cleared up. I can't see that you detectives have solved any part of the puzzle."

"I doubt it can be solved in parts. I think we must ferret about here and there and at last we will strike the truth all at once."

"Well, can't you go and strike it somewhere else?" spoke up the pert voice of Eliza Gurney. "We have much to attend to, with funeral arrangements and business matters."

"As to business matters, you are sole heir, I understand, Mr Bates?"

"Yes, I am so informed by the lawyer who has my uncle's will in his keeping," answered Richard, with an air of cold politeness.

"And you will take up the Bun business?"

"He will not," Miss Prall replied for him. "He will devote himself to his great work of inventing—Mr Bates is a genius and now he will have the means and the opportunity to carry on his life work."

"Just so. And you will be getting married?"

"Of course he will," Miss Prall still gave the responses; "not at present, of course, but as soon as he finds the right young lady——"

"He won't have to look far afield for that!"

"Leave me out of the conversation," Richard growled. "These private affairs of mine in no way affect your detective work."

"But, you must pardon me if I seem intrusive, I am assuming that we are at one in this matter of investigation?" Corson spoke sharply.

"Of course," agreed Bates.

"Then I must ask if you are engaged to Miss Everett."

"He is not!" Miss Prall almost shrieked the words. "He is not and never will be. The death of his uncle, deplorable as are the circumstances, leaves Mr Bates free to pursue his occupation with all his time and attention. He will not think of other matters for a year at least, and then the lady in the case will *not* be Miss Everett!"

The Grenadier sat stiffly upright, and her black beady eyes, darted from her nephew's face to that of the detective as if challenging contradiction from either of them.

Bates replied only by a shrug of his shoulders, but Corson said, "I assume then, Miss Prall, that outside the natural shock of the tragedy you feel a certain relief that your nephew is now the heir to great wealth and can pursue his career? But I understand his uncle wished him to associate himself with the Bun business."

"Quite so," Letitia snapped. "The late Sir Herbert was deeply interested in my nephew, but he did not understand or appreciate his achievements and possibilities in his own chosen line. Wherefore, I am rejoiced that now my nephew can proceed unhindered."

"But, I believe the late Sir Herbert favored the match between Mr Bates and Miss Everett?"

"Drop that!" Richard blazed forth. "Leave that lady's name out of this conversation!"

"Yes, indeed!" Letitia cried; "I forbid the mention of the name of Everett in my presence!"

"Yet it may be necessary," Corson went on, calmly. "You know, Miss Prall, the ends of justice may call for the mention of a name——"

"What in the world can the mention of that name have to do with justice?" Eliza broke in. "You don't connect the Everetts with the murder, do you?"

"I don't connect any one with the murder, as yet," Corson replied, "but it is my great desire to find some connection, and so I have to make inquiries."

"If that's your motive, I still must request that you omit the name of Everett from your conversation," said Bates. "Look here, Corson, are you getting anywhere, or aren't you?"

"I am," was the quiet reply; "now, Miss Prall, you'll be obliged to answer a few questions, whether you like it or not."

Corson's tone, though courteous, was severe, and the Grenadier, while not frightened, gave him a look of curiosity and intense interest.

"Go on," she said, briefly.

"This feud between yourself and Mrs Everett is a matter of long standing, I believe. You can't, therefore, object to my reference to it. What was its cause?"

"Oh, it's so old now, that its cause is sunk in oblivion." Letitia smiled sourly. "But it has been added to by other causes as time went on, and thus new fuel has kept the fire burning."

"Keep the home fires burning," said Richard, with a mocking smile at his aunt, who heeded it not.

"And so," she went on, "the feud, as it has come to be called, is as strong and well-nourished as ever."

"Yet you two ladies elect to live under the same roof."

"To nurse the feud along," Bates asserted, and the Grenadier nodded assent.

"However," she added, "Mrs Everett is about to move away."

"What!" cried Richard.

"Yes," repeated his aunt, evidently pleased with the fact, "she is going soon."

"Thus," offered Corson, "you will be relieved of two undesirable people at once."

"Meaning Mrs Everett and her daughter?" queried Eliza.

"Not at all. Meaning Mrs Everett and Sir Herbert Binney."

"Oh!" gasped Miss Prall. "Don't put it that way!"

"Why not? Since it's the truth. You now can have the pleasure of seeing your nephew pursue——"

"Don't talk about me as if I weren't here!" exclaimed Richard. "Or as if I were a minor or an incompetent! I'm devoted to my aunt; I love, honor and obey her, but I'm a man with a mind of my own. And when it runs counter to the desires or plans of my aunt—well, we must fight it out between ourselves. However, Mr Corson, I can't see that the affairs of my aunt and myself, or the affairs of my aunt and her fellow-feudist, Mrs Everett, have any connection with or bearing on the murder of Sir Herbert Binney. If they seem to you to have such a bearing, I think it is right that you should tell us all about it."

"I take it, then, that we are working in unison,—at least, in concord?"

"You may certainly assume that as far as I am concerned," said Bates, but the two women present seemed by their silence to reserve judgment.

"First, Miss Prall, I'd like to hear from you what plans Sir Herbert had, so far as you know, regarding the sale of his great bakery business."

"I know a great deal about that, Mr Corson, as Sir Herbert not only discussed the matter with me, but did me the honor to ask my advice, considering that my judgment was of value."

"No doubt. And you advised him?"

"I advised him to sell out to Crippen,—of *Crippen's Cakes*. You know of the firm?"

"Yes, indeed; who doesn't? It's the largest of its sort in the country."

"Unless one excepts the Vail Bakery. But that's bread."

"And aren't buns bread?"

"That was part of the controversy. However, Sir Herbert and Mr Vail had their bout before the matter was taken up by the Crippen people. Mr Vail didn't see his way clear to combine his bread with Sir Herbert's buns. But Mr Crippen thought the buns would go well with his cake business, and they were on the point of coming to an agreement in the matter. Indeed, Sir Herbert told me he expected to see Mr Crippen last evening——"

"He didn't. I've interviewed Mr Crippen and he told me so."

"Might they not have met after the Magnifique supper?"

"What!" Corson looked at Miss Prall in surprise. "You mean——"

"Oh, nothing,—nothing connected with the—the tragedy, of course. But perhaps the interview did occur, and for some reason Mr Crippen doesn't want it known—can't you see, Mr Corson, that it's a queer thing that nobody comes forward to tell where Sir Herbert was those last two hours of his life? Well, mightn't he have been with Mr Crippen,—remember, he told me he expected to see him,—and whatever their conference resulted in, might not Mr Crippen have wished it kept quiet——"

"And so, denied it? Why, it might be so, Miss Prall,—but in such a serious case Mr Crippen would hesitate before he would be anything but sincere in his story. It's a risky matter to falsify when a murder case is being investigated!"

"I know it," and Miss Prall smoothed the folds of her gown placidly. "But, you see, I know Mr Crippen."

"Oh, come now, Auntie," broke in Richard, "just because Crip was an old beau of yours, don't say things against him."

"I'm not saying anything against him, Ricky, I only say I know him. If that's a damaging admission, it's his fault, not mine."

The Grenadier set her lips in a straight line, and looked sternly at Corson. "You can draw any deductions you wish, Mr Corson," she went on, acidly, but positively; "I tell you that I know Mr Crippen very well, and I wouldn't believe a word he says, unless I had the corroboration of another."

"Be careful, Letitia," warned Miss Gurney.

"You shut up, Eliza! I'll say what I choose."

"Do, Miss Prall," urged Corson. "You're decidedly interesting. May I be forgiven if I look about a little. What unusual curios and treasures you possess."

"I do; but this is no time to examine or comment on those. If you have questioned me all you wish,—though, for my part, I don't think you've questioned me at all,—suppose we consider this interview at an end."

"Why, Aunt Letitia, have you no wish to find out who killed Uncle Herbert?" asked Richard.

"I can't say that I have. He's dead; no punishment of his murderer can bring him back. He was no relative of mine, nor was he such a friend that I'm thirsting to avenge his life. For my part, I only want to have the matter hushed up. The unavoidable publicity and notoriety are most distressing!"

"I haven't questioned you much, I admit, Miss Prall," observed the detective, "but I have found out a great deal since I have been here."

"Yes?" she returned, coolly, with a haughty nod.

"Yes; are you interested to know what I have learned?"

"I am not. It is all beneath my notice. I assume you will use your information in any way you see fit—but the way, nor the result, interests me not at all."

"Don't talk like that, Letitia," and Eliza looked deeply concerned. "Mr Corson will think you a hard-hearted woman."

"He has my permission to do so."

"Oh, stop, Auntie!" Bates cried, earnestly. "You get yourself misunderstood by such talk. You're not hard-hearted,—except regarding your foolish feud. In all other ways you're normally kind and generous minded."

"Thank you, Rick, but I don't care for compliments."

Corson was fingering some library appointments on the large table near which he sat.

"These brass sets are convenient things," he remarked, referring to an elaborate array of fittings spread out on the large green blotting pad. "These long clipping shears are most useful, and the pen-holder, letter opener and ink eraser, all to match, are of admirable workmanship."

"Yes," said Miss Prall, carelessly, "I had the set made to order. It is, I think, unique."

"Why are you interested in them?" Miss Gurney said, abruptly.

"Oh," Corson returned, easily, "I love desk fittings. They always have a peculiar fascination for me. I have several sets myself, but none so fine or costly as these."

"Why don't you stick to your subject, Corson?" said Bates, a little impatiently. "Are you and Gibbs going to make a success of this case or not? And I wish you'd let me know all you've done. You have a frank air about your disclosures, but I can't help thinking you're sounding us."

"Sounding you?" and Corson looked mystified.

"Yes; as if you suspected us of knowing more than we've told. I assure you *I* don't."

"No, I never dreamed that you did. You've been most outspoken, Mr Bates, and, while I can't plume myself much as yet on my findings or those of Mr Gibbs, you must remember that the matter is not many days old, and it is not what is called an 'open and shut' case."

"No; and yet, it ought to be. For a man who does not belong to this country to come over here and be killed, seems to imply not such a very large number of possible suspects."

"As to that," and Corson sighed, "I don't know of even one possible suspect. I wish I did,—it might lead to others. But we have the assurance that the deed was done by women; that simplifies the search."

"Yes and no, to that," spoke up Miss Prall. "Sir Herbert, of course, wrote that in good faith, but may he not have meant by the influence of women, or at the orders or desire of women,—and not, necessarily, that women committed the actual deed?"

"Granting all that," returned Corson, "it is the women we want. If they hired gunmen,—as they may be called,— we must find out the identity of the women all the same. And if they actually committed the deed——"

The ringing of the telephone interrupted his speech and proved to be a message for the detective to come downstairs at once.

Corson went and on reaching the ground floor he was met by Gibbs, who took him to a small reception room and closed the door.

"Here you are," Gibbs said, and handed the other a paper-wrapped parcel which when opened proved to contain a long sharp paper-cutter. The blade, apparently hastily wiped, still showed traces of what was unmistakably blood.

"Where'd it come from?" Corson said, staring at the thing.

"A boy connected with the service department found it stuck between the palings of a fence near the delivery entrance. It may have been placed there by the murderer of Sir Herbert Binney."

"Where is this entrance? Why wasn't this found sooner?"

"The place is around the corner,—a sort of obscure entrance on the side street, used only by the tradesmen, for delivery. A cleaner found this just a short time ago."

"Well," said Corson, very gravely, "this is the paper-cutter belonging to a set of writing implements on Miss Prall's library table; and I have just come from there, and

I noticed that, though the sheath of this was up there, the paper-cutter was missing!"

CHAPTER 10: SEEK THE WOMEN

Late that night,—in fact it was about midnight, when the onyx lobby was practically deserted save for an occasional late home-comer,—the two detectives arrived for a confab with Bob Moore.

This greatly pleased the night porter for he hoped to be looked upon as a sort of assistant detective, and felt sure he could be of valuable help.

"You know, Moore," Gibbs began, "there are people who are looking askance at you, with a sort of half-formed suspicion that you know more about this thing than you have told. But I don't think that,—at least, I think you are willing to tell all you know, if you haven't already done so. How about it?"

"Why, it's this way, Mr Gibbs. I am ready to tell all I know, and I think I have done so, but you can't expect me to tell what I suspect or surmise or imagine. Can you, now? It might lose my place for me. Also, I might injure an innocent person."

"I think," spoke up Corson, "you ought to tell us anything you suspect; it need go no further and if your suspicions are mistaken ones, they can't harm the innocent."

"Well, then, I've got my eye on two of the chambermaids. They are great chums, and one is on the seventh and eighth floors, the other on the ninth and tenth. But floors don't matter; they chum around with each other. Well, these two are the most canny old hens you ever knew. They're no chickens, and they have an eye out for the main chance all the time. I mean they toady to the people who are rich or generous and they scamp their work in places where they're not 'remembered.' Also they're specially attentive to the work of gentlemen who live alone. Why, Sir Herbert's rooms were kept as neat as a bandbox. And Mr Goodwin and Mr Vail,—they're both up on the tenth,—their rooms are immaculate. And yet, there's the Prall place neglected, 'cause Miss Prall don't believe much in fees, and as for the Everetts, why, *she* says she can't get anything tended to!"

"Doesn't she 'remember' the housemaid, either?"

"Some; but in her case, it's more her sharp tongue and her fussy ways. Miss Prall, now, she's on the outs with Mrs Everett,—I know that,—but she's decent-spoken to the maids. Only, she's stingy. Well, what I'm getting at is, those two chambermaids are regular devils, if you ask me, and though Sir Herbert Binney was generous enough when he liked the work people, he didn't like his chambermaid, and he was as ugly as Cain to her. Used to call her down for the least thing and laid her out cold if she sauced him back."

"Then you think the 'women' might have referred to these two maids?"

"That's just it. I only think it may have done so. I've no evidence except that they are more the type of women it seems possible to suspect. These little girls,—it don't seem's if they could manage the deed. But Jane and Maggie could have worked it if they'd wanted to. They're big, husky women and they've dogged, sullen tempers. And, of course, what made me think most about it, was your finding that paper-knife of Miss Prall's. Now, if Miss Prall had killed Binney,—which is ridiculous on the face of it!—she'd been too cute to leave the knife around, but those ignorant chambermaids——"

"I don't agree," Corson interrupted. "The woman,—which one is the Prall's chambermaid?"

"Maggie."

"Well, Maggie then,—she couldn't have taken the knife from Miss Prall's table without its being missed, and Miss Letitia is not the one to lose her property without a word! No, sir, that paper-knife points straight to Letitia Prall. Moreover, she had motive; she wanted the old gentleman out of the way for two reasons. First, so Pet Nephew could inherit the old man's money, and, second, because the uncle was in favor of the marriage of young Bates with Miss Everett, the daughter of Miss Prall's deadly enemy!"

"Where'd you get all that dope, Corson?" Gibbs said in astonishment.

"Partly by quizzing round and partly by putting two and two together. Anyway, it's all true, the motives, I mean. Now, confidentially, just among us three here, could she have done it? I mean, was it physically possible?"

"Anything is possible for Miss Prall," said Moore, quite seriously. "She is a Tartar, that lady is. And whatever she sets out to do, she does,—irrespective of whether it can be done or not!"

"I mean this. Could she have come downstairs from the eighth floor without being seen——"

"Of course she must have been seen," broke in Moore. "Whether she came down in the elevator or walked down the stairs she must have been seen. She could have come down the servants' stairs, but that would have been even more conspicuous."

"At two in the morning?"

"No; there'd probably be no servants around then."

"So she could have done that, and waited, say, outside,——"

"Oh, nonsense! Waited out in the street at that hour?" Gibbs demurred; "that's too much to swallow!"

"But she may have known just about the hour Sir Binney expected to return. Anyway, suppose she did do that, and then, having succeeded, she slipped back to the servants' entrance and hid the knife where it was found and then scuttled back upstairs the way she came."

"But the paper said, 'women,'" mused Moore.

"That companion person was with her," declared Corson, triumphantly. "Those two are great in teamwork. Miss Gurney doubtless acted as scout and kept a lookout and Miss Prall did the deed."

"Oh, Mr Corson, I can't think it!" exclaimed Moore.

"Because you know Miss Prall only as a tenant of this house. You know nothing of what she may be capable of when her spirit is fired. And as far as I'm concerned, it's far easier to believe that she did it, than that it was the work of some foolish little girls scarcely out of their teens! Miss Prall is not only a strong-minded woman, and a strong-muscled woman, but she has a strong personality with practically illimitable powers of loving and hating. For her the sun rises and sets in young Bates, and in the other direction she is all wrapped up in her hatred of Mrs Everett.

"What's Mrs Everett got to do with the murder?" growled Moore.

"Nothing, that I know of, but she works in this way. Her daughter is in love with Richard Bates, and neither of the women will stand for the marriage of the two young people. Why, I think Mrs Everett and Miss Prall would see their young charges dead rather than married to one another. Now, Sir Herbert Binney favored the match. Therefore Miss Prall wanted him out of the way. Again, he favored young Bates going into the Bun business instead of sticking to his inventions. Therefore, again, Miss Prall wanted Binney out of the way. So, what would a woman of her caliber and her determination do, but put him out of the way?"

"Plausible enough," and Gibbs thought deeply.

"And so, I'm asking Moore," Corson went on, "how he thinks Miss Prall could have compassed her awful plan and he's solved any uncertainty by suggesting the servants' staircase at an hour so late that it was almost certain to be unused."

"I don't say I believe she did do it," Moore began, "but I have to say she could have done it that way. She must have known just about the time he'd come home——"

"That's not difficult to assume," Corson defended his theory, "he probably told her that. And she could have waited around some time,—it was a mild night."

"But how could she be sure she'd have the chance in the lobby?" asked Gibbs, his incredulity fast dwindling.

"Oh, she wasn't sure. She took a chance. I mean, she may have waylaid him outside, don't you see, and kept him there talking until she saw Moore go up in the elevator with somebody. This place is so brightly lighted that any one outside could see that. Or they could have been inside, standing in the shadow of the big pillars for a long time,—unnoticed."

"Have you any clews?" asked Bob Moore of the detectives.

"Dropped handkerchiefs and such like?" asked Gibbs, mockingly. "No; and if there were footprints, they're washed away now. But those things are only for story-books,—such as you're eternally reading, Moore."

"I do read a lot of 'em, and it's astonishing, but most always a criminal leaves some trace."

"In the stories,—yes. In real life, they're not so obliging. But let's look at the spot. We might get an idea,—if nothing more tangible."

The three went along the lobby till they reached the place where Sir Herbert had breathed his last. Marks had been drawn to indicate the blood spots that were so quickly washed off, and these still showed clearly. The body had been found crumpled on the floor, in the angle made by the great square base of an onyx pillar and the wall.

They saw, of course, no traces of any personality, but as they looked each began to reconstruct the scene mentally.

"I think they were concealed here for some time," Corson said. "If they stood here talking, the pillar would partly shield them from view of others entering. Nor could they be easily seen by Moore, in the back of the lobby."

"Maybe," Moore agreed hesitantly, "but if Miss Prall and Sir Herbert had come in together I bet I'd seen 'em."

"Not if you were up in the elevator," said Corson.

"No; of course not. That might have been the case."

"And then, when you took Mr Vail up, was no doubt the moment she chose to stab him and immediately pulled out the knife and ran away."

"We know," said Moore, positively, "that whoever did it, did it while I took Mr Vail up, and that the murderer then pulled out the knife and ran away. But that's not saying it was Miss Prall. And I've got to have some sort of evidence before I'll believe it was. Her desire to be rid of Sir Herbert isn't enough, to my mind, to indicate that she killed him. Can you tie it onto her any more definitely?"

"Her ownership of the knife, and her making no effort to find it, though missing, are evidence enough for me," said Corson doggedly. "And, how'd those little chorus chickens get it, if they're the ones?"

"I don't think they're the ones," Moore declared; "but I do think it was those two chambermaids. They could get the knife from the Prall apartment easy enough, and maybe Miss Prall did question Maggie about the missing knife and maybe Maggie gave a plausible explanation for its disappearance."

"Maybe and maybe and maybe not!" observed Gibbs, cryptically. "This sort of talk gets us no-where——"

"Yes it does," Corson interrupted. "It's shown us how Miss Prall could have done it. And when you remember that Sir Herbert declared with his dying heartbeats that women did it, and when we have no other women with half as much motive,—those little girls' jealousies are puerile by comparison,—I think we are bound to conclude we're on the right track."

"If so, let's forge ahead," and Gibbs nodded energetically. "What's the next move?"

"Don't move too fast," advised his colleague. "And, too, we want to interview those chambermaids. Though I think Miss Prall is at the back of the thing, she may have been aided by those women. They might have been paid——"

"Now, look here," put in Moore. "I know Miss Prall better than you two do. And I know if she undertook a thing of this desperate nature, she never called in any outside help. She'd be afraid to trust those women. And that companion of hers is all the help she'd want. No, sir, if the women Sir Binney recognized were Miss Prall and Miss Gurney, that's all there was of them. Likewise, if it was those two chambermaids, that's all there was of *them*. But they never combined forces; no, sir, they didn't!"

"I believe that." Gibbs nodded his head. "Now, let's take a look at this paper again."

The paper left by the dying man had been carefully placed between two small panes of glass, in order to keep it intact and undefaced.

As Gibbs studied the passe-partout, he said, thoughtfully, "We must make up our minds what he meant in this second line. It's unintelligible, but what *could* he have meant? 'Get bo——'"

"I think it means get both," said Corson, positively; "but it mayn't be that at all. As it was the very last effort of his spent muscles, it is far from likely that he wrote just what he meant to write. He might have intended that second letter for a or o or g or, in fact, almost any letter! He lost control of his fingers and the pencil fell away from them."

"All right; I grant you all that," Gibbs agreed. "But we've got to start somewhere. Now we know women killed him; he states that. Next, if this word is both, we know there were two women and two only."

"Marvelous, Holmes, marvelous!" guyed Corson. "And Miss Prall and Miss Gurney count up just two! Correct, so far."

"Don't be funny. The chambermaids in question number two also. And there were most likely only two, for women don't go round murdering in squads. But the point is, he says, get both,—if the word is both. That would seem to imply that one is more probable as a suspect than the other, but he adjures us to get the other one also."

"There's something to that, Mr Gibbs," and Bob Moore looked at the detective admiringly. "Now, if it was a case of Miss Prall and Miss Gurney, they're so much together, that such a message would be practically unnecessary. So it may point to the chambermaids. You see, Maggie is on his floor, but he may have meant that Jane, too, was implicated."

"Oh, rubbish!" cried Corson. "A dying man isn't going to use his last gasp to tell the police to get a certain chambermaid! That word isn't 'both' at all. It's something far more significant. I think it's a name. I think it's a name that begins with Ba or Bo. Now, I'm as well aware as you two men are, that my own name begins with Bo and my girl's last name with Ba. But I'm not afraid, for I didn't do it. I was upstairs at the time, and anyway I'd no grudge against the old fellow. Nor did Julie do it. And he never would have called her Baxter, if she had! So, I say that I think it represents some name, and all possible names ought to be investigated."

"The trouble is it might represent so many names," Gibbs said. "I think myself that he might have meant to make a capital letter and only achieved a small one, but never mind that. Ba could be Babe Russell,—but I can't seem to think he'd take that method of accusation. If it had been a man who killed him he would be more likely to feel revengeful."

"Good heavens, Gibbs!" and Corson's eyes opened wide; "I guess if you'd just been fatally stabbed by your lady friends, and had enough spunk to tell that women killed you, you wouldn't hesitate at bringing a name into the limelight! I've had a hunch it was that Baby Doll all along,—but it looked like an impossibility."

"So you see," offered Bob Moore, "you can't deduce much from that second line. And we may be 'way off. It might have been meant for, 'Get busy' or 'Get Bob Moore to find the criminal,' or lots of things."

"This is no time for fooling, Moore," said Corson, gravely, "but you're right that it's wasting time to puzzle over that phase of the message. We're lucky in having the clear direction as to the sex of the criminal,——"

"Unless it's all faked," suggested Gibbs. "How about the murderer being a clever man, who had this paper all ready, and brought it with him and laid it beside his victim?"

"Not a chance," said Moore. "I've checked up that handwriting and it's his. Mr Bates says so, and I've compared it to his writing,—lots of it. That's Sir Binney's fist, all right."

Feeling they had learned all they could from Moore, and also feeling decidedly tired and sleepy, the two detectives went home and to bed.

Not at once to sleep, however, for each had lots of thinking to do and each felt that there were more ways to look than had yet appeared.

But, also, each thought the Prall suspicion justified, and each planned to keep a wary eye in that direction.

Next morning, after waiting till such an hour as he thought late enough, Gibbs went to see Miss Prall.

He found a visitor already there, and he was presented to Mrs Everett.

To his surprise, Miss Prall made the introduction as casually as if it had been a meeting of social acquaintances, and Gibbs felt a little awkward at being expected to join in a general conversation.

But he was alertly interested in meeting Mrs Everett, and especially in circumstances where he might hear or see some manifestations of the feud he had heard of.

"My friend, Mrs Everett, is about to move away, so you're lucky to chance upon her here," Miss Letitia said, in honey-sweet tones.

"As to your luck, I express no opinion," said the other lady, "but as to moving away, I've not the slightest intention of such a thing."

Mrs Everett was inclined to be fair, afraid of being fat and unwilling to admit being forty. She was pretty in a soft, faded way, and her voice, though low and pleasant, had a sharp tang to it, which, one felt sure, could increase at will.

"You said you would!" Miss Prall declared, "but I long ago learned to put no faith in your assertions."

"You're saying I lie?" asked Mrs Everett, and her voice was still placid.

"If the shoe fits, put it on," Letitia laughed. "Only, you can't blame me for saying that of you, when you know it's the truth."

"Dear friend," murmured Mrs Everett, "how can you think I'd go off and leave you while you're in such trouble? I feel I must stand by."

"That's quite like you! Don't lose a chance to gloat over any sorrow or grief I may have!"

"Do you call it sorrow and grief? I didn't know you thought so much of the departed nobleman—he was a nobleman, wasn't he? Tut, tut, Letitia! and at your time of life! Well, I suppose it's habit that makes you set your cap for any man you chance to meet."

"You always were the greatest for judging others by yourself, Adeline. You were the celebrated cap-setter of your day. Ever since you worried poor, dear Mr Everett into his untimely grave, you've pursued the honorable business of cap-setting, alas! to no avail."

"Don't you dare call my husband dear! I'll let you know, Letitia Prall, he was not in the habit of calling you dear!"

"Tee hee," tittered Eliza Gurney. "Don't be jealous of Letty, Mrs Everett. She's had more beaux than you ever saw, with all your yellow curls and red—a little too red cheeks!"

"Hush, Eliza," admonished Miss Prall, "our caller will think we're quarrelsome neighbors. As a matter of fact, Mr Gibbs, we're——"

"Dearest enemies?" he suggested, smiling, for he saw he was expected to recognize the situation.

"Yes," assented Letitia with a nod at Mrs Everett that seemed to convey all sorts of inimical intent, undiluted by friendliness.

Gibbs realized that these two women took such pleasure in their bickerings and faultfindings that they really enjoyed their antagonism.

And Miss Eliza Gurney was equally interested in the exchange of sarcastic repartee.

They kept on with their sparring until Gibbs began to feel not only uncomfortable but impatient.

"I called, Miss Prall," he began, but Mrs Everett interrupted:

"Oh, I know what for," she cried, clasping her fat hands, and giving an unpleasant little giggle, "to talk about the murder! Yes, yes, and please don't mind me. I want to hear the details; have you found out who did it? Who was it? Was it those sweet little dancing girlies? I can't think it!"

"Keep quiet, Adeline," said Miss Prall; "how you do run on! I should think you'd have the tact to take your leave,—but you never had even ordinary good manners. I can scarcely invite you to depart, but I do feel privileged to say you may go if you feel you must."

"Oh, I don't feel I must at all! On the contrary, I want to stay and hear the news. For I'm sure this gentleman has some news. I can see it sticking out all over him! Go ahead, sir, tell your story. I feel I'm entitled to be in the audience."

She settled herself in her chair and looked as if nothing less than a really severe earthquake would move her. Her big round eyes danced from Letitia's face to the detective's. Her smile broadened as she enjoyed the discomfiture of her enforced hostess. And she positively reveled in the awkward and embarrassed silence that fell on all in the room.

Then Eliza Gurney said, "Adeline Everett, if you take my advice, you'll go away before you're put out!"

"I've never taken your advice yet, Eliza, and I don't propose to begin now. Also, you'd better not put me out, for if you do, I shall think that what Mr Gibbs is about to reveal is something you don't want known,—something incriminating to some of your own people!"

Apparently she had heard something, Gibbs thought quickly, and he was more than ever anxious to get her away. But, not knowing how to manage such an unusual type of womankind, he said instead that he thought he should retire and make his call some other time.

CHAPTER 11: THE OLD FEUD

And Detective Gibbs did retire and did make his call some other time, but he made it not on Miss Prall, but on Mrs Everett.

He had fancied from her attitude that he could learn much from her if he could manage to gain her attention and enlist her sympathies.

With this end in view he went to see her later the same day, and found her not unwilling to talk with him.

"I thought I should die," she exclaimed, clasping her plump little hands and rocking back and forth in a becushioned wicker chair, "to see Letitia Prall wriggle around! Why, Mr Gibbs, it's clear to be seen she knows more than she has told or means to tell! Aren't you going to make her talk?"

"Why do you think she knows something?" countered the detective.

"Oh, I know her so well. When she purses up her thin lips and then widens them out to a straight line again, several times in succession, that's a sure sign she's terribly upset. Didn't you notice her do that? It's a peculiar habit, and I know what it means! Letitia Prall was nearly frantic for fear you'd find out something she doesn't want you to know!"

"Now, mother," interposed Dorcas, who was present, "I don't think you ought to say such things about Miss Prall,—this is a serious matter, and talking to a detective is very different from your every-day spats and squabbles with Miss Letty."

"Hold your tongue, Dorcas; and you'd better leave the room. This is no subject for a young girl to be mixed up in. Go to Kate and let her fit your new guimpe."

"I'm just ready to try it on," and Kate, the maid, appeared in the doorway, her mouth full of pins, and her hands full of voluminous breadths of tulle.

"But I'd like to hear what this man has to say," she went on, dropping her work on a table as she took a chair for herself. "I know a thing or two about this murder," she declared, as she looked curiously at Gibbs, "and it would be to your advantage, sir, to listen to my tale."

"Oh, nonsense," put in Mrs Everett, "you don't know anything, Kate. She's a visionary creature, Mr Gibbs, and greatly given to romancing."

"Nothing of the sort," spoke up Kate, briskly, and Gibbs wondered at the strange apparent relation between mistress and servant.

But as he listened further, he gathered that Kate had been so long the stay and dependence of the Everett household, that her position was more that of a housekeeper and general manager than an underling.

It seemed that Mrs Everett depended on the woman for service, yet was chummy with her as with a companion. Kate sewed for Dorcas and kept her clothing in order, looked after Mrs Everett's social engagements and was useful in so many ways that it was not difficult to see why she was made much of by her employer.

Then, too, it was clear that she was entirely conversant with the feud, its progress and present condition. She was deeply interested in the murder mystery and, though Gibbs rather doubted it, she might have something of importance to tell him.

So, as Dorcas obeyed her mother and left the room, the detective listened to the chatter of the two women, and from the volume of inconsequent talk he gleaned much of interest.

Especially he learned the character of Miss Prall, or, rather, the traits of her character that interested the Everett household.

Their tales may have been exaggerated, probably were, but he decided they contained internal evidence of Letitia's insincerity and untruthfulness.

He found out to his own conviction that he could not rely implicitly on the word of Miss Prall, and, this granted, her whole story might fall to the ground.

The feud was talked over and detailed to him until he was positively sick of it, but he persevered in the talk, trying to lead it toward the murder.

But the women were wary of this subject. Whether it was too grewsome for their taste or whether there was some other reason, Gibbs tried hard to find out.

"But you told me you had something to communicate," he insisted, to the canny-looking Kate.

Her sharp eyes scrutinized him.

"Oh, I don't know anything definite," she said, with a somewhat defiant glance at Mrs Everett. "And if I did, I'm not allowed to tell it."

"If you know anything at all,—definite or suggestive, you're to tell it, whether you're allowed or not!" Gibbs cried, willing to try intimidation. "Don't you know, woman, that you can be jailed if you withhold information from the police?"

Mrs Everett giggled. "You can't frighten Kate," she said; "she has no fear of anything."

"Why should I have?" and Kate looked belligerent. "I know all about the police. I'll tell anything I see fit to, and nothing more."

Calmly, she took up the mass of white tulle, and began to sew on it.

"That attitude won't do, Kate," said Gibbs, seriously. "Bluff and bravado won't get you anywhere."

"I don't want to get anywhere; I haven't set out for anywhere," and with a flippant swish of the tulle stuff, Kate rose and started to leave the room.

"Wait a minute," ordered Gibbs. "You've gone too far to back out now. You said, or implied, you had something to tell,—now, you tell it!"

"Goodness, Kate, tell it,—if you've anything to tell!" Mrs Everett spoke with a sharp glance at the woman.

"Well, I will, then. But it's no tale of happenings or that. It's only that I know Miss Prall was wishing Mr Binney out of the way. She was wishing it so hard that I myself heard her say, 'If I was sure I wouldn't get caught, I'd kill him myself!'"

"She said that?"

"Yes, sir, she did. Mrs Everett heard her, too."

"I did," admitted Mrs Everett as Gibbs looked at her inquiringly. "But don't take it too seriously. Letitia Prall and I are enemies, have been for years,—but I'm not the one to brand her with the mark of Cain! That I'm not."

"Well, I will," declared Kate. "She's quite capable of it, she has expressed her willingness, and she had strong motive. What more do you want?"

"What was her motive?" asked Gibbs in a casual tone, hoping to draw further light on these remarkable statements.

"Why,——" Kate hesitated, but Mrs Everett smiled and nodded permission, and Kate went on; "why, you see Miss Dorcas and young Mr Bates are friendly-like, and old Binney——"

"Sir Herbert," prompted Mrs Everett, pointedly.

"Well, Sir Herbert, then, he was in favor of the two marrying."

"And neither Mrs Everett nor Miss Prall approve the match?" Gibbs put in quickly.

"Of course they don't! Well, Miss Prall, she's one who would try and try to persuade Sir Herbert to change his mind——"

"And his will," suggested Gibbs.

"And his will," agreed Kate, "and then, when she couldn't persuade him,—he had the devil's own stubbornness,——"

"And so has she," observed Mrs Everett.

"That's right! Well, when she couldn't do anything with him, she up and killed him."

"Women, he wrote."

"Of course; Eliza Gurney helped. Probably Eliza did the actual deed. She'd cut off anybody's head that Letitia Prall told her to! But those are the women you're looking for, and if you want to jail me for telling you, go ahead!"

"No," Gibbs told her, "you won't be jailed for telling that,—if it's true. But, if it isn't,—you want to be careful about slander, you know."

Kate looked a little startled, but Mrs Everett laughed.

"Don't be afraid, Kate; Mr. Gibbs can't punish you for an opinion. You haven't stated any facts."

"Except that she heard Miss Prall's threat to kill Sir Herbert," Gibbs reminded her.

"It wasn't a threat at all. I heard her say it, and it was merely an outburst of anger. I doubt if she meant it——"

"Do you doubt her capable of committing such a crime?" the detective asked, so suddenly that he took his listener by surprise.

But she was not to be caught. "My theory is," she smiled, "that as Goethe says, 'We are all capable of crime, even the best of us.' I truly think that most human beings could commit crime, given sufficient motive and opportunity."

"All very fine in theory," said Gibbs, smiling, "but are you willing to assert that Miss Prall or—or yourself, would be capable of the murder of Sir Herbert Binney, if you had a perfect opportunity and if you considered your motive strong enough?"

"Oh, *I* wouldn't have done it!" and Mrs Everett looked shocked, indeed, "but,—well, maybe I do think Letitia Prall would have done it."

"Aided and abetted by Miss Gurney," the detective egged her on.

"Yes; Eliza would have been not only a help but a commander,—a tyrant, even."

"And Miss Gurney wished the old gentleman out of the way?"

"Oh, yes; as much, perhaps, as Letitia. You see, if he died just now, his fortune would be young Bates' and the boy could go on with his chosen career, without being pestered to make buns! Moreover, Sir Herbert favored Rickey's marriage——"

"To your daughter?"

"To anybody,—any nice young woman. My daughter is out of the question and not to be spoken of in this connection."

Mrs Everett drew herself up in with an effect of injured dignity and looked scornfully at Gibbs.

"But you seem to eliminate the young people themselves as factors in the romance part of it all."

"They are not factors. My daughter has sufficient confidence in my judgment to agree to my advice. She knows my attitude toward Miss Prall and she would not encourage or accept the attentions of her nephew."

"You're sure of this?"

"Of course I'm sure of it! Dorcas is a sweet, obedient child, and she would not deceive her loving and beloved mother. Also, she knows the despicable and unworthy nature of Miss Prall, and she assumes, as I do, that Richard is of the same stamp."

"Then you don't know the young man? You only assume his character? Is that quite fair?"

"Fair enough for anybody belonging to the Prall family! They cannot expect fairness! They wouldn't even appreciate it! Letitia Prall is a mean, low type of womanhood,—a deceitful, unjust, disloyal, contemptible snake in the grass!"

"That's so," chimed in Kate; "she's proved all that over and over,—and more too! She has no notion of common decency toward her neighbors; she is a two-faced, backbiting, sneaky, tattletale!"

"But this doesn't prove young Bates——"

"Yes, it does!" the detective's argument was cut off; "she brought him up, and she taught him all her own evil principles, and her own way of thinking and talking——"

"But you scarcely know the man,——"

"That's doesn't matter! He's the nephew of Letitia Prall,—and that's enough for me! My daughter shall never speak to him,—never meet him,—and lest such a chance should occur accidentally, I am planning to move away."

"You don't think your daughter is—is interested in Mr Bates?"

"I know she is not! Dorcas is a wayward-tempered child, but she is loyal to her mother and her mother's wishes. She wouldn't dream of seeing Richard Bates against my will."

Now, as it happened at that very moment, the loyal child was apparently quite oblivious of the wishes of her beloved mother, for she was sitting by the side of the objurgated Richard on a bench in Central Park.

When told to leave the room by her mother, she had also left the Everett apartment, and later, the house.

By some discreet telephoning she had summoned the despised young man and the two had sauntered out of The Campanile, separately, and joined company soon after.

"It's a risk," Dorcas was saying, "and if mother, catches on, she'll give me Hail Columbia, but I just had to see you! Do you know what they're saying about your uncle's murder, now?"

"No; and I don't want to hear from you. Please, dear, let's leave all that horror out of our conversation. We get so few moments together and I need every one of them to tell you how I love you."

"Then," the red lips pouted, "when am I to tell you how much I love you?"

"Oh, Dork! you do say the sweetest things! Tell me, darling, tell me, first, then I'll tell you——"

"We may as well both talk at once," Dorcas laughed. "We can say the same things,—it'll really be a duet!"

"All right, say with me,—I love you. Ready, one, two, three, go!"

"I love you!" they said in concert.

"No fun," decided Dorcas; "I want you to tell me separately."

So Richard did, to such an extent and with so much detail and reiteration that the moments flew by, and it was time to go home before the other side of the shield was painted.

"But, Ricky, dear," Dorcas said finally, "I must talk a little about this awful thing. I've heard a lot of hints and whispers,—for mother and Kate shut up as soon as I come into the room,—and I want to know this: Is your aunt, Miss Prall, suspected of killing Sir Herbert?"

"Good Lord, no! What an awful idea! Where did you dig that up?"

"I've heard a lot, I tell you. And some people do think so!"

"But it's absurd! Impossible! Also, I won't have such talk going around! You must tell me, Dork, where you heard it! Tell me all you know."

"I don't *know* anything, Rick, but I think you ought to do something definite in the way of detective work. Those men don't get anywhere?"

"Why, what do you mean? What do you know about that, Little Peachbloom?"

"I don't know anything. And you don't, either. But unless you find out something there'll be trouble. Now, Rick, stop treating me as a baby and talk about it. Who do you think killed him?"

"Honestly, Dorrie, I think, just as he wrote, some women did it. I don't know who they were, and I'm not sure I care to know,—for they were, no doubt, some— some people with whom we have no concern."

"That may be," said the girl, very soberly, "and it may not be. You must realize, Rick, that those silly little chorus girls might have had reason to hate the man, but they could scarcely compass that killing."

Bates looked at her in astonishment.

"What *do* you mean?" he said, slowly; "that is, what are you hinting?"

"Only that I think the murderers are of a higher type of women than giddy youngsters,——"

"Murderers can't be of a very high type——"

"I don't mean high type of character, but of brains. To my mind, that deed implies women of cleverness and mental power."

"Such as,——?"

"Oh, I don't know. But girls in our house are all older and wiser than a lot of giddy chorus girls. Why not suspect them?"

"Why suspect anybody? I mean, what do we care? In one sense, I'd like to see the death of Uncle Herbert avenged, but on the other hand I'd hate to see women's names dragged through the police court——"

"But if they were guilty?"

"That's just the point! Ten chances to one they wouldn't be. I mean those dunder-headed detectives are quite capable of getting the wrong ones and then railroading them through."

"Perhaps so. But I think you ought to do more than you have done. Why, Rick,—if,—if you don't, first thing you know they'll suspect you!"

"What! Don't be foolish, dear. I'm not a woman."

"I know, but some people think that's a blind,——"

"It can't be a blind. There's Uncle Bin's writing,—and I know him well enough to be sure that with his dying breath he didn't write anything but the truth. No, sir, women are responsible for that murder, and directly, too. Uncle Bin never flung that accusation at women if they were merely implicated. Now, don't you see, dear, that investigation must result in tragedy for *some* women,— and, as I say,—probably not the guilty ones."

"But it must be fastened on the guilty ones. They must be found——"

Dorcas' red lower lip quivered, and the big tears gathered in her eyes. She strove to keep her calmness but she was rapidly losing control over her emotions.

"Why, Dorrie, darling, what is it? Tell me,—I'll do whatever you want,—whatever you say! Do you know something you haven't told me? Something you don't want to tell me? What *is* the matter, dearest?"

"That's it; I do know something,—or I fear something, I don't want to tell you,—at least not yet,—but——Rick, let's do something, you and me,—toward solving the mystery."

"Oh, no, dear. Please don't mix your own sweet self into this horrid moil. I'll do what you tell me to, but don't dip into the trouble yourself,—I beg of you, don't!"

"Richard," and Dorcas stood up, her face taking on a determined look, "come on home with me, and go with me to talk to a woman,—one of the maids of the house. Don't interfere,—don't even interrupt, just stand by me, and be ready if I call on you for help."

Bewildered, and not entirely willing, Bates consented and the two went back to The Campanile.

Unhindered by any message from Dorcas' mother or Richard's aunt, they went up in the elevator and on one of the highest floors, Dorcas sought out the head chambermaid's office.

"I want to know about Maggie and Jane," she said, straightforwardly. "Maggie is our chambermaid, and Jane is a friend of hers. I have a reason, that I don't wish to state at present, but I ask you frankly if those two girls are honest and reliable?"

The woman addressed hesitated.

"They are, miss, so far as I know. But I think it's my duty to tell you, that I've heard other whispers of complaint. We're very particular about the help in this house, and I can't keep any girl on, who's even so much as suspected. Have you any definite complaint to make, Miss Everett?"

"There, you see," broke in Bates. "You mustn't harm those girls' reputation by a vague suspicion, Dorcas. If you know anything against them, that's one thing. But a hint goes so far, and it may be against an innocent girl."

"I know it," Dorcas looked very earnest, "so I ask you, Mrs Malone, not to mention this. But tell me, where were those two girls the night of the murder of Sir Herbert Binney?"

"Oh, that!" and Mrs Malone looked greatly relieved. "They were in their own beds asleep,—both of them. That I can swear to. I thought you meant they'd been dishonest,—stealing something."

"No, I didn't," said Dorcas, frankly. "I really wanted to know just what I asked. Will you forget it,—since you've answered me as you have?"

"Yes, indeed, miss," the woman agreed, her decision influenced perhaps by the bill that was quietly slipped into her not unready hand.

"Well, I must say," and Bates looked at his companion as they went slowly along the hall to the elevator, "you did stir up a tempest without even a teapot! What's the big idea?"

"Don't speak like that, Rick," Dorcas implored. "Try to see things as I do. Or must I tell you right out that if there's no chorus girl, no chambermaid, no elevator girl to fasten suspicion on, it is going to be fastened on some one else. Can't you guess who?"

"That I can't," and Bates looked blankly at her. "Do you mean some of Uncle Bin's English people came over here and did for him?"

"I do not. I mean that there are people who will think,—who are already thinking there's reason to direct their inquiries toward—toward your aunt."

Bates stared; "Aunt Letitia?" he said, half understandingly; "she didn't do it."

"I don't think she did!" Dorcas was irritated at his bewilderment. "But I tell you the detectives think so!"

"Oh, Dork, what awful rot! Dear child, you must keep out of this affair. It makes you crazy."

"I'm not crazy! But you're blind. I tell you, Rick, the detectives *do* suspect Miss Prall,—I heard them tell mother so,—and you *must* wake up and look into things."

"I should say so!" Bates seemed to get awake all at once. "You heard this, Dorcas? I'm glad you told me. Go home, dear, and I'll look up Gibbs or Corson at once!"

CHAPTER 12: ONE WOMAN AND ANOTHER

Bates' search for Gibbs or Corson resulted in finding the former in the rooms of the late Sir Herbert Binney. Peters was also there, packing up the personal effects of the dead man preparatory to vacating the apartment.

As sole heir, Bates was in authority regarding these effects, but he had paid little attention to them beyond giving orders to have them packed and stored for the present.

"Thought I'd dig around a bit," Gibbs vouchsafed, "but there's no indicative evidence that I can find. No papers of an incriminating sort, no sign of any special woman friend—or feminine enemy, for that matter."

"Never mind generalities or suppositions. Look here, Mr Gibbs, what about my aunt's connection with this matter?"

Gibbs looked up quickly. "Just what do you mean by that?"

"Only that I've heard that you are considering the possibility of her being implicated. Are you?"

"I'm considering any possibility I can find to consider. Yes, since you ask me, I am looking into the question of your aunt's connection with the case. I know you want me to be frank."

"I do. Have you any real evidence to work on?"

"Only talk. Only somewhat vague reports that I have yet to investigate."

"Reports, no doubt, from Mrs Everett, my aunt's longtime foe."

"Yes, that's the source of the hints I had given me. But Mrs Everett does not accuse your aunt——"

"She'd better not!"

"Oh, she doesn't. But the matter must be looked into, for there is a motive, and your aunt——Really, I can't discuss this thing with you, Mr Bates!"

"But you must. I'm in charge,—I'm going to find out who killed my uncle. I admit I hadn't a great desire to know his murderer, when I supposed it was some girls or women with whom he was mixed up in a frivolous way. But if my aunt's name is so much as breathed, of course, I must discover the real murderer to save her reputation. She no more did it than I did,—but I daresay the people who suspect her would also implicate me!"

"Don't speak like that. I've only a hint to go upon, and though I must follow it up, it's an easy matter, no doubt, for all your aunt's household to state an alibi and that settles it."

"Real alibis are not always easy to prove. It's your faked alibi that's glibly detailed and sworn to. There's no one in my aunt's household but herself, myself, and Miss Gurney, her companion. We three were in our beds and asleep at the time of the murder, but we can't prove it by eye witnesses! Naturally, there's no one to swear to it, except ourselves. Now, where does that lead you?"

"To further investigation. You know your aunt's paper-cutter was found——"

"That proves nothing. You must connect that knife undeniably with the crime before you can use it against her."

"I grant that. But first, let's look into the motive. Your aunt did want Sir Herbert out of the way. She did say she wished he was dead. She did say she would kill him herself if she were sure she'd never be found out."

"I know she said those things, for I heard her,—not once, but repeatedly. But my aunt is a quick-tempered and thoughtless-speaking woman. She has time and again wished various people dead. She has often expressed her willingness to kill certain people. But it meant no more,—as she said it,—than for another to wish bad luck to them, or say they hate them. She is most unguarded in her expressions and exaggerates always. These things must be understood by you before you accuse her. She has frequently wished herself dead, but she didn't mean it any more than she meant it regarding Sir Herbert."

"All that will be considered and remembered, but we must question her."

"You'd better question me. I can tell you anything she can, and in a more satisfactory manner."

"Tell us all you like,—all you will, but we must also question Miss Prall and Miss Gurney."

"All right, but there are other directions in which to look. Don't be too sure that women committed the deed."

"No use your trying to throw over that dying statement. No use looking for a man in the case, with that note before our eyes. You know yourself if a man or men had killed Sir Herbert nothing could have influenced him to write a denunciation of women. Why would he? What possible circumstance could explain it? Have you any theory that would fit the facts?"

"No, unless a man killed him at the instigation of or in behalf of some women and Sir Herbert wanted the deed traced to its true source."

"Even that doesn't seem to make plausible a positive assertion that 'women did this.' No, there's no getting away from that avowal. And, you must see that the use of the plural,—women,—signifies collusion. Two or more must be implicated. Not necessarily two or more present at the moment of the crime, but two or more to be found and punished."

"Yes, I see all that,—and I want to find the criminals as much as you do. Especially now, since Miss Prall's name has been dragged in. But I do want you to understand how little her hints at 'killing' anybody really mean. You know what an extravagant talker she is."

"I do know that, and I assure you I'll make all allowances. But I can't leave any stone unturned."

The man Peters had been in and out of the room and, as he reappeared, Richard said, "You know Miss Prall, Peters. You know how carelessly she speaks of serious things?"

"Yes, sir, I do. But you needn't tell me them little chickens ever had any hand in the murderin'! Why, they just couldn't have had."

"Anything is possible, Peters," said Bates, sternly. "And I don't want you to make those definite statements. They mean nothing, save that such is your opinion."

"But my opinions is pretty sound ones, Mr Bates, an' founded on a lot of personal knowledge of Sir Herbert,— rest his soul. And I tell you, gentlemen, that that deed could never ha' been done by young girls,—neither the little ladies that Sir Herbert was fond of kitin' round with nor yet the girls employed in this house. No, sir, that fearful crime was planned and carried out by older heads than theirs. Men or women might 'a' done it,—but never little half-baked flappers like them you're suspectin'."

"There's sense in that," mused Gibbs, and Bates flared out: "I suppose that leads you more certainly to suspicion of my aunt. But you're wrong, Gibbs, all wrong! Now, look here, suppose, just for a moment, there had been no written message,—which way would you look then?"

"Toward some business complications," said Gibbs, promptly. "You see, Sir Herbert Binney was putting over an awful big deal in that matter of his Bun business. He had dickered with several big bakery companies and he was a shrewd man at a bargain."

"And he was in bad with some of the men he was bargaining with," vouchsafed Peters, who was a privileged participant in the conversation, because Gibbs hoped by this means to learn something from the valet.

"Who, for instance?" demanded Bates.

"Graham, of the Popular Patisserie concern; Vail, here in the house, and Crippen of Crippen's Cakes."

"Nothing doing," returned Gibbs, shortly. "I've dug into all those issues. He was off with the Patisserie people weeks ago. He finished discussion with the Vail company some days since, and the only one pending was the Crippcn bunch."

"Yes, and my aunt says he expected to see Crippen the night he was killed."

"Well, he didn't," returned Gibbs. "I've looked up Crippen's alibi and it's gilt-edged. Vail was in the elevator with Bob Moore at the time of the murder,—that lets him out and the Patisseries are back numbers. I mean they got through with Binney's Buns as a working proposition, long ago."

"They might have come back to it," suggested Bates.

"Sure they might,—so might Crippen or Vail. But they didn't,—or if they did, we've no tiniest speck of evidence of it. If you can get any, go ahead. You don't know of anything against the Bakery men, do you, Peters?"

"No, sir. But Mr Crippen and Mr Vail have both been here——"

"Here! In Sir Herbert's rooms?" cried Bates. "What for?"

"Mr Vail, he just dropped in, as he was passing by, and he looked round the room, like in idle curiosity. He said, 'Poor old chap, he was a good sport,' and went away. That wasn't so strange, for he often used to drop in for a chat with my master. But Mr Crippen, now, he never came here, that I know of, while Sir Herbert was alive. But the day after he died, Mr Crippen comes with a sort of determined air, and he wants to look round,—and more, he wants to look over Sir Herbert's papers. Of course, I didn't let him do that, but it seemed sorta queer,—didn't it, now?"

"Maybe and maybe not," said Gibbs. "I suspect there might have been a letter from himself that he wanted to get possession of, or something like that. I say, as I have said from the first, if it were not for the written paper, I might have suspected these business men, but I'm sure that's the very reason Sir Herbert did write the paper, so we would not go off on a wrong tack. It proves to me the determination of his strong mind to lead us in the right direction and not let us pursue the most obvious but mistaken course of looking into the Bun matters."

"I agree with you on the face of things," said young Bates, with a sigh, "and if you hadn't mentioned Miss Prall, I'd let you go your own gait, but now you have mentioned her, I shall get into the game myself and spare no effort or expense to dig up the truth! And, first of all, I'm going back to Bob Moore. I don't think he knows anything more than he's told, but I do think I can learn more from him now I've got my mad up!"

"Come on, I'll go with you," and Gibbs accompanied the young man to the elevator.

Moore was not in the house, and Bates, determined to learn something, went to Julie Baxter, who was at her switchboard.

He took her, Gibbs following, to a small reception room, where they could be by themselves.

"Now, Julie," Bates said, "you've got to come across with the true story of your doings the night of the murder. You are not suspected, but you will be if you don't 'fess up. It's a fool thing to do, to refuse to tell, when continued silence may get you in very bad. So, out with it."

"You did the same thing yourself, Mr Bates," and Julie glared at him. "You refused to tell——"

"But I'm not a woman; they can't suspect me. Also, I'll tell, if I have to. My story won't incriminate me. Go ahead, now,—let's hear."

"I'll tell where I was, if you'll promise not to tell anybody else." Julie looked obstinate, though evidently a good deal frightened.

"I'll promise, if the secret can be kept without hindering our investigation. Agree to that, Gibbs?"

The detective agreed, and Julie went on. "Specially, I don't want Bob Moore to know. We're engaged and he's awful particular about where I go, when he isn't along. And I've never gone any place or done anything he wouldn't want me to, except that very night. I went with a crowd on a trip to Chinatown. It wasn't any harm, but we were out late, and if he knew it, he'd give me the dickens. You won't tell, will you? And, too, if the manager knew it, he'd think I was a different sort of a girl from what I am. So, please don't tell."

"No; we won't tell," promised Bates. "Unless, of course, we find you haven't told the truth, or the whole truth,—in that case, you'll be shown up! I never suspected any connection of yours with the whole matter, but if you've told the truth just now, it will go no further. I know you're not given to frisking about, and I think myself it's just as well Moore shouldn't know of this one occasion. By the way, did you study to be a nurse?"

"I began the course of training, but the work was too hard for me and I gave it up the first year and took up telephoning."

"Did you," asked Gibbs, suddenly, "did you know any one else in the hospital, or wherever you were, who studied nursing, and who is in any way connected with the people interested in this murder?"

Julie hesitated and her face flushed a little.

"I don't think I ought to mention it,——" she began, and Gibbs cried:

"Of course you ought to mention it! If you're innocent it can do you no harm, and if the one you tell us of is innocent it can do her no harm."

"But it may stir up suspicion quite wrongly," objected the girl.

"Then the suspicion will fall to the ground. Don't be afraid; you are only helping justice along. If it's a real help you must give it, and if not, it won't be followed up."

But Richard Bates looked grave.

"Oh, I don't know, Gibbs," he said; "somebody must have started this trend toward my aunt, and it's made me pretty miserable already. Now, need we take up a new trail with only a sort of surmise on this girl's part. For, surely, she is by no means ready to make a positive accusation."

"Out with it, Julie," commanded the detective with no apparent notice of Bates' demurrer.

"Well, it's only this," and Julie looked relieved at the thought of unburdening herself; "when I was in training, the girls used to talk of Kate Holland, who was there many years before, but who seemed to be a sort of a star pupil. I don't remember much that they said, only she was renowned for her surgical skill, and when I heard Bob tell how the murderer of Sir Binney was a knowing one, I couldn't help thinking about her. You know she's Mrs Everett's maid."

"Oh, Lord!" Bates groaned, "don't drag the Everetts into this thing! It's bad enough to have my people spoken of without attacking the Everetts too!"

"Nobody has attacked them yet," said Gibbs, dryly; "don't go too fast."

"But you will! You'll suspect Kate because of what Julie has said, and then you'll go on to Mrs Everett and——"

"H'm,—you seem to inherit your aunt's trait of hasty speaking. Better stop where you are, Bates. Don't put ideas into my head!"

"I don't have to! You're all primed to take up this new outlook. I knew Julie's tales would upset things! Just because Mrs Everett's maid has had training, doesn't argue her a murderess!"

"Nobody said it did!" exclaimed Gibbs, angered at the young man's words, partly because they were so in line with his own thoughts.

"In fact," and Bates looked very sober, "in fact, Gibbs, I'd rather you'd suspect my aunt than the Everett crowd!"

"But nobody has voiced any suspicion of the Everett crowd——"

"You don't have to voice it, for me to know what you have in your mind——"

"And that Kate Holland is a terrible woman——" began Julie.

Richard silenced her with a look.

"Julie," he said, sternly, "don't you dare mention one word of Kate Holland in connection with this matter! If you do, I'll tell both Moore and the house management of your Chinatown trip."

"That's right," agreed Gibbs. "You're not to mix into this thing in any way, Julie. You run along now, and remember, it's just as Mr Bates said; if you breathe a word of anything you've heard or said in here with us, we'll show you up good and plenty, and we may do a little exaggerating, too! Is it a bargain?"

"Yes, sir, it is!" and Julie Baxter went out of the room, glad to be assured of the safety of her own secret.

"Now, Bates, you may as well face the music," Gibbs began. "You must know that in the back of everybody's head has been an unspoken thought of higher up people than chorus girls or elevator attendants. Those youngsters don't commit murder,—such a thing is unknown. But older women with deeper motives must be considered. You say you want to find the murderess in order to relieve your aunt from any hint of suspicion. Do you want to do so if the trail leads toward the Everett household?"

Richard Bates seemed suddenly to have grown years older. His good-looking young face turned to an ashen hue, and his eyes were wild and staring.

His voice shook as he replied, "I say, Gibbs, I don't know what I want! I'm knocked galley-west. I don't believe for the thousandth part of a second that either Miss Prall or Mrs Everett have one speck of knowledge of the deed, but you know the very mention of their names would be like fire to tow in the newspaper reports."

"Of course it would. Yet what can we do? However much I keep my investigations quiet, there's a gang of reporters nosing about everywhere. They've likely got hold of Julie already——"

"She won't tell anything."

"She won't mean to,—but they'll frighten or trap her into it. There's nothing so dangerous as a woman with a secret of her own to guard. She'll babble of everything else."

"What do you advise?" Bates was clearly at the end of his rope. He was beseeching of manner and despairing of tone.

"Straightforwardness, first of all. I'm going at once, either to Miss Prall or to Mrs Everett, and make them come across with something definite. If they don't know anything,—I'll find that out, at least."

"Go first to my aunt, then. I'll go with you,—come along. Get all you can out of her, I'm not in the least afraid!"

The two men went up to the Prall apartment and Bates opened the door with his own key.

"Here's Mr Detective, Aunt Letty," he said, trying to speak lightly; "he wants a little chatter with you."

Miss Prall looked up from her book.

"Be seated, Mr Gibbs," she said, with quiet dignity. "How do you do?"

"How do you do?" the detective returned, not quite at ease, in the presence of her forbidding manner. "I'm sorry to intrude——"

"Then don't," interrupted Letitia, her large, strong face frowning at him. "Why make us both sorry?"

"Because it must be done." Gibbs gathered firmness from her own attitude. "This matter of the murder of Sir Herbert Binney is of sufficient importance not to wait on convenience or pleasure."

"Quite right. And what have you done? Nothing, as usual? When one remembers that the crime occurred nearly a week ago, and no steps have yet been taken to apprehend the criminal——"

"Pardon me, Miss Prall, many steps have been taken, and they have led in a definite direction."

"Good gracious, where!" The spinster was startled out of her calm and a look of concern spread over her face.

"First, tell me if you have any suspicions?"

"I have not, but if I had I'd never tell you, so long as they were merely suspicions. If I could prove them, I'd tell quick enough!"

"But I may help you to prove them—or disprove them."

"That's just it; if you disprove them, I'm covered with shame and confusion at having hinted them."

"All right, I'll do the hinting. Or, rather, I'll speak right out. What did you do with the paper-cutter from your library table,—I see there is an empty sheath still there?"

"That?" and Miss Prall glanced casually at the sheath in question.

"The paper-knife was broken and I gave it to Sir Herbert Binney, who had promised to get it mended for me at some specialty place he knew of. Why?"

"Because that was, probably, the weapon that killed him."

If Gibbs had expected any sudden telltale blush or confusion on Miss Prall's part, he must have been disappointed, for she only said:

"Indeed! How could that happen?"

"I don't know, but the knife has been found, in peculiar circumstances, and I'd like to know just when you gave it to him to get it mended."

"Oh, I don't know; several days before his death. Perhaps four or five days, or a week. Go on."

"The knife,—if that was the one,—was driven into the body in such a way as to make it likely that the hand that thrust it was the hand of some one experienced in surgical lore——"

"Hah!" the exclamation given by Miss Prall was full of meaning. It seemed to imply a sort of triumphant surprise, a welcome knowledge, a looked-for and longed-for state of things.

"This gives strength to your suspicions?" insinuated Gibbs.

"It does," and the Grenadier sat up even straighter and her face was even more indicative of elation as she added, "it does, indeed!"

"And perhaps you will tell us to whom your suspicion points?" urged the detective.

"That I will do," she declared, but Bates broke in with a "Hush, Aunt Letitia! I command you not to speak!"

CHAPTER 13: MOTIVES

"I've got to speak, Ricky," Miss Prall said, but her tone was not angry now. She seemed to have changed her mood and was half frightened, half sad. "I've got to speak, to save myself. Don't you see that if that paper-cutter points towards me,—as Mr Gibbs implies, I must tell what I know——"

"What you know," assented Bates, "but not what you suspect."

"Yes, ma'am, what you suspect," directed the detective. "The time has come, Miss Prall, when suspicions must be voiced, whether true or not, in order that we may prove or disprove them."

"Then get up your own suspicions," cried Bates. "Find your own suspects and prove their guilt or innocence."

"We're doing that," Gibbs said, quietly, "but we necessarily depend also on the statements of witnesses."

"But Miss Prall isn't a witness."

"Not an eye-witness, perhaps, but a material witness, if she knows anything that we want to know."

"She doesn't know anything you want to know," exclaimed Eliza Gurney, coming into the room. "But Kate Holland does! If you're anxious for information get that girl and quiz her!"

"Hush up, Eliza," stormed Letitia. "What did you learn in at the Everett's, Mr Gibbs?"

"I learned that you said you'd kill Sir Herbert Binney yourself, if you were sure you wouldn't be found out."

"What!" Miss Prall turned perfectly white, but whether with rage or fear, Gibbs didn't know. "She said that! The little devil! Just let me get at her, once!"

"Didn't you make that remark?"

"I did not; but she did, and then, I said I would, too. Neither of us meant it, really, but that's what was said. The woman is so clever it makes her doubly dangerous!"

"But it's a queer thing for two ladies to be talking about killing anybody."

"Nonsense! It's done all the time. It doesn't mean they'd really do it—though sometimes I have thought——"

"Aunt Letty!" put in Bates, beseechingly.

"I will speak, Richard! Sometimes I have thought that Adeline Everett would be capable of—of anything! Those sleek, fat, complacent people are the very worst sort! I bluster out frankly, but that oily, deceitful woman,—and that Kate of hers,—well, if you want to know my suspicions,—there they are."

"Then, Miss Prall," Gibbs looked straight at her, "here's the situation. Both you and Mrs Everett expressed a willingness to kill Sir Herbert Binney,—no matter if it was not meant. Both of you may be said to have had a motive; both of you could have found opportunity. And, finally, each of you claims to suspect the other. Now, granting for argument's sake that one of you is guilty, would not the plausible procedure be to pretend to suspect the other?"

"Of course it would," Eliza Gurney declared. "And since Mrs Everett is the guilty party,—I see it all now! She casts suspicion toward Miss Prall! Of course, Mrs Everett didn't do it herself, but that Kate Holland did! She is a fiend incarnate, without heart or soul! She is—— "

"There, there, Eliza, you'd better be still," Miss Prall warned her. "If you go on like that, Mr Gibbs will think you're protesting too much!"

As a matter of fact, that's just what Gibbs was thinking, and he looked sharply at Letitia, marveling at her cleverness. If she had been instrumental in the death of Sir Herbert, surely this was just the way she would conduct herself. She was deep as well as clever, and Gibbs began to see light.

He was convinced now that the criminals were of a more subtle type than young girls in their teens could possibly be, and the affair, to his thinking, was narrowed down to the households of these two women who were each other's enemies.

He reasoned that the only way to learn anything from such dissemblers as they all were, was to catch them off their guard, and he greatly desired to get the rival factions together, in order that anger or spite might cause one or other to disclose her secret.

"Perhaps," Gibbs said, "it might be well for us to go to Mrs Everett, or send for her to come here, and so get the testified statement as to these assertions of willingness to kill. I don't think they're customary among the women of your class."

"You doubt my word!" flared up Letitia Prall. "Let me tell you, Mr Gibbs, that I refuse to have it corroborated by that woman! I tell you the truth,—she is incapable of that!"

"That's why I want to give you a chance to refute her, to deny her to her face——"

"Never! I don't want to see her! She shall not enter my door! Her very presence is contaminating! Adeline Everett! She is a slanderer——"

"Wait a moment, Miss Prall. What she has said of you, you have also said of her!"

"But I speak truth; she tells falsehoods. Nobody ever believes a word she says!"

"Of course not!" chimed in Eliza. "Adeline Everett is a whited sepulcher,—a living lie!"

Even more belligerent than the words was the tone and the facial expression of the speaker. Miss Gurney was not a beautiful woman at best, and her rage transformed her into a veritable termagant. Her sparse gray hair fell in wisps about her ears and her head shook in emphasis of her objurgations, while her pale blue eyes blinked with fury as she strove to find words harsh enough.

"Eliza!" and Miss Prall's warning tone was quiet but very stern. "Stop that! You only make matters worse by going on so! If you can't keep still, leave the room."

Eliza sniffed, but ceased her talk for the moment, at least.

"Now, Miss Prall," Gibbs resumed, "it is necessary, in my opinion, to have an interview at which both yourself and Mrs Everett are present. I have a right to ask this, and I offer you the choice of going there, or sending for her to come here."

"I won't do either," snapped Letitia. "I refuse to go to her home, and I certainly shall not let her enter mine."

"But, don't you see that is most damaging to your own side of the story."

"What do I care? Don't think you can frighten me, young man! Letitia Prall is quite able to take care of herself."

"That may be, but you are not able to defy, successfully, the course of the law. If I insist on this interview, I think, Miss Prall, you will be obliged to consent."

"And if I refuse?"

"Then, I am sorry to tell you, your refusal must be set aside, and you will, I am sure, see the advisability of accepting the situation."

"Oh, come, Auntie," said Bates, "you're making a lot of unnecessary trouble. Neither you nor Mrs Everett had any hand in this murder,—the mere idea is ridiculous! and if you have the interview Mr Gibbs wants, it will soon be over and then you will both be freed from suspicion and can go on with your silly 'feud.' That is a foolish thing, but trivial. This other matter is serious. You *must* get it over with at once,—for all our sakes."

"I won't." And Miss Prall set her lips obstinately.

Gibbs rose abruptly and left the room.

"He's gone for Mrs Everett," said Richard, looking severely at his aunt. "Now, you must be careful, Aunt Letty. If you don't look out, they'll accuse you of the murder, and though you'll disprove it, it will mean a whole lot of trouble for us all."

Letitia Prall adored her nephew, and, too, she saw there was no use of trying to avoid the meeting with Mrs Everett. It was bound to be brought about, sooner or later, by the determined Gibbs, and it might as well be gone through with.

She sat still, thinking what attitude it was best to assume, and she decided on continued silence.

"Eliza," she warned, "don't talk too much. You'll get us in an awful predicament if you're so free with your tongue. First thing you know, you'll tell——"

"Hush, they're coming!" and in a moment Gibbs rang the bell.

Richard admitted him, and with him came both Adeline Everett and the maid, Kate.

"I didn't invite your servant," was Miss Prall's only word of greeting, accompanied by a scathing glance at Kate.

"You didn't invite me," Mrs Everett returned, pertly, "and I shouldn't have come if you had, except that I was commanded to appear by a representative of the law. I don't see, though, why I should be mixed up in your murder case."

"It isn't my murder case any more than it is yours, Adeline Everett," her enemy faced her. "I understand you're suspected of being——"

"Oh, don't, Aunt Letitia," begged Richard, who was always distressed if obliged to be present when the two "got going," as Eliza called it. "Now, please, auntie,—please, Mrs Everett, can't you two forget your private enmity for a few minutes and just settle this big matter? Disarm the suspicions of Mr Gibbs by telling the truth, by stating where you all were at the time of the murder, and so, get yourselves out of all touch with it. Truly, you will be sorry if you don't. You don't realize what it will mean if you have to be mixed up in all sorts of witness stands and things."

"Go ahead, Mr Gibbs," and Miss Prall glared at the detective. "We owe this unpleasant scene to you,—make it as short as possible."

"I will," and Gibbs' sharp eyes darted from one face to another, for this was his harvest time, and though he expected to learn little from the wily women's speech, he hoped for much from their uncontrollable outbursts of anger or their involuntary admissions.

It was a strange gathering. Letitia Prall sat on a straight-backed chair, erect and still; but looking like a leashed tiger, ready to spring.

Beside her, trying hard to keep quiet, was Eliza Gurney, small, pale, and with a distracted face and angry eyes that darted venomous glances at the visitors.

Mrs Everett had chosen for her role an amused superiority, knowing it would irritate Letitia Prall more than any other manner. She smiled and quickly suppressed it, she stared and then dropped her eyes and she would impulsively begin to say something and then discreetly pause.

All this Gibbs took in and Richard, seeing the detective's interest, became alarmed. He felt sure there was something sinister concealed in the minds of some or all of the women present and his heart sank at the possible outcome of things.

It was inconceivable that his aunt was in any way concerned in the murder, yet it was even worse to imagine the mother of Dorcas mixed up in it. Of course, it couldn't be that either of them was really implicated, but he had to recognize the fact that Gibbs was sufficiently convinced of such implication to call this confab.

And it was a confab. The detective did not ask direct questions, but rather brought out voluntary remarks by adroitly suggesting them.

"Now, that paper-knife——" he began, musingly.

"Is what they call a clue," said Mrs Everett. "I know nothing of such things,—I can't bear detective stories, but if a paper-knife was used to kill somebody, I should think the owner of the weapon must be more or less suspected."

"Of course you think that, because you're suspected yourself," said Letitia, coldly; "naturally you think you can cast suspicion toward me, but you can't, Adeline Everett! I gave that paper-cutter to Sir Herbert to get it mended——"

"Oho! Is *that* the story you've trumped up! Clever, my dear, but too thin. Can't you see, Mr Gibbs, that that is a made-up yarn? She knows Sir Herbert can't deny it, and no one else can. So she thinks she's safe!"

"Well, she isn't," and Kate Holland gave Miss Prall a triumphant glare. "That knife will hang her yet! She not only tried to make up a plausible story about the thing, but she tried to fasten the guilt on me by saying I have surgical skill! Ha, ha,—because I took a nurse's training,—I'm to be suspected of murder! A fine how-do-you-do! Let me tell you, Miss Prall, you overreached yourself! I've been to see Dr Pagett about it, and he says that while the fatal stroke may have been delivered by somebody who knew just where to strike, yet, on the other hand, it might have been the merest ignoramus, who chanced to strike the vital point! So, your ladyship, your scheme to inculpate *me* falls through!"

Gibbs listened eagerly, gathering the news of Dr Pagett's decision, and learning, too, that this maid of Mrs Everett's was of a far higher mentality than the average servant.

"I scorn to reply," Miss Prall said, looking over the head of the triumphant Kate. "I do not converse with servants."

"Perhaps it would be well to dismiss both my servant and yours," drawled Mrs Everett, maliciously. "Let Kate and Eliza both leave the room."

"I'm no servant!" cried Miss Gurney, bristling; "I'm Miss Prall's companion, quite her equal——"

"And think yourself her superior," interrupted Mrs Everett, with her most annoying chuckle. "Well, Eliza, I look upon you as just as much a servant as my Kate,— more so, indeed, for you can't hold a candle to Kate for intelligence, education or——"

"Or viciousness," Letitia broke in. "Now, Mr Gibbs, I decline to talk to or with either of my unwelcome visitors. If you have to conduct this official inquisition, go on with it, but I refuse to speak except to answer your questions. Eliza, you are not to talk, either."

"Good!" said Gibbs, "just what I want." And he spoke sincerely, for he began to see that he would learn little from the display of rancor and temper that moved them all.

He put definite and straightforward questions, and elicited the information that they were all in their beds and asleep at the hour of the murder. This could not be corroborated from the very nature of things, but he let it pass.

There was fierce disagreement as to which had first declared a willingness to kill Sir Herbert Binney, and which had said she, too, was inclined to the deed, but it was admitted that such hasty and unconsidered declarations had been made.

In fact, the gist of the long and difficult grilling was an apparent determination on the part of each one of the two factions to accuse the other, and a most plausible and complacent assumption of innocence by both.

This seemed a non-committal situation, but Gibbs did not deem it such. He was definitely persuaded as to the guilty party, and his satisfied nods and approving smiles showed Richard Bates plainly which way the detective's opinions leaned.

And the young man was thoroughly frightened. Though, for his part, it would be a difficult matter to make a preference between the belief in the guilt of his aunt or the guilt of the mother of the girl he loved.

And the trend of Gibbs' investigation led surely to one or the other. The use of the paper-cutter that Miss Prall admitted having given into Sir Herbert's keeping gave wide-spread opportunity. Any one desiring to kill the man had a means provided, that is, reasoning that Sir Herbert had the knife with him for the purpose of getting it mended.

Again, that story might be pure fabrication, in which case the suspicion swung back to Miss Prall and Eliza.

It was Gibbs' theory that the unintelligible letters of the dead man's message implied two women and the attempted direction was to get both. This, he argued, meant either Miss Prall and Eliza Grundy or Mrs Everett and her faithful aide, Kate Holland.

It seemed to him that the case narrowed itself down to these women, either pair of which had both motive and opportunity.

The affair between Bates and Dorcas was, of course, known to both guardians, though they tried to disbelieve it, and probably didn't know to what lengths it had already gone. But Mrs Everett knew that Sir Herbert approved the match and doubtless feared that her modern and up-to-date daughter might take the reins in her own hands. Therefore her desire to have Sir Herbert removed was explainable. She felt sure that without his Uncle's insistence on Richard's entering the Bun business, the young man would return to his inventions and so forget Dorcas in his work. At least, that's the nearest Gibbs could come to her motive, though he felt sure there was more to be learned regarding that. Mrs Everett was deep and very plausible of manner. She had, he knew, underlying motives and hidden capabilities that would lead her, with the assistance of the Amazonian Kate, anywhere.

On the other hand, Miss Prall wanted the old man out of the say, so that her nephew would lack his advice and assistance concerning the affair with Dorcas, and the aunt felt that, with Sir Herbert out of it, she could easily persuade Richard to return to the great work in which he was so deeply interested and forget the girl. Moreover, she knew that Mrs Everett, no more desiring the marriage of the young people than she did herself, was planning to move away, and then all would be well.

The motives were not altogether clear, but, Gibbs reasoned, there must be many points that were hidden and would remain so, with these clever women to guard them.

He tactfully tried to draw them out, but with even greater tact they evaded and eluded his questions and contradicted each other and occasionally,—and purposely,—themselves, until the detective began to think the determined masculine mind is no match for the equally determined Eternal Feminine.

Indeed, involuntarily and almost unconsciously, they joined forces against him, and presently found themselves aiding each other, which, when they realized it, made them more angry,—if possible,—than before.

At last Mrs Everett looked at her watch.

"I've an appointment that I'm anxious to keep," she said, drawlingly; "as you don't seem to be getting anywhere, Mr Detective, can you not let me go, and finish up this absorbing discussion with Miss Prall?"

"You're quite mistaken in assuming that I'm not getting anywhere, Mrs Everett," returned the nettled detective, "but you may go if you wish. In fact, I allow it, because I have learned about all there is to learn,—not so insignificant an amount as you imply."

Mrs Everett looked at him sharply and was momentarily disconcerted enough to gasp out:

"Oh, have you a clue?"

"Several," Gibbs returned, carelessly. "Nothing that I care to make known, but I've found out enough to set me on the right track."

Covertly he watched the faces to see how this struck the two principals.

With little result, for Mrs Everett, regaining her poise, merely smiled in an exasperating way, and Miss Prall looked coldly disinterested.

"Wonderful characters," Gibbs commented to himself, for he had never before met women who could so perfectly hide their feelings.

And he was sure that one of them, at least, was hiding her emotion; that one of them was really aghast at the thought of exposure and was trying with all her powers to conceal her dismay.

The maid, Kate, and the companion, Eliza, merely mirrored the other's calm. Eliza, glancing at Miss Prall, took her cue and looked disdainful of the whole affair. Kate Holland curled a scornful lip and nodded her head in Miss Prall's direction.

And yet, if one pair were guilty the other two were innocent. Collusion between the two factions was unthinkable. But Gibbs had made up his mind, and he rose and opened the door.

"If you must keep your appointment, Madame, you are excused. I may say that you are under surveillance, but I have little fear of your trying to get away secretly, and unless you do, you will not be bothered in any way."

"Your surveillance does not interest me," and, with a sublime disregard of all present, Mrs Everett swept out of the room, followed by the large and somewhat ungainly Kate.

"I don't want to discuss this thing," Gibbs began, as he himself prepared to leave,—"but——"

"I don't want to discuss it either," said Bates, and his tone was full of indignation. "There is no room for discussion after this asinine performance of yours! You're not fit to be a detective! You get some ladies together and badger them into all sorts of thoughtless, unmeant admissions and call that testimony! I'm surprised at you, Gibbs. And I tell you frankly what I mean to do. I'm going out,—right now,—to get a detective who can detect! A man who knows the first principles of the business,—

which you don't even seem to dream of! I've had enough of your futile questioning, your unfounded suspicions, your absurd deductions! I'm off!"

Chapter 14: Penny Wise

When Richard set out to do a thing, he did it, and without consulting anybody he went at once for Pennington Wise, the detective, and by good luck, succeeding in obtaining the services of that astute investigator.

Bates told him the whole story, and Wise saw at once that though the young man was fearful of his aunt's implication in the matter, he was even more alarmed at the idea of his sweetheart's mother being brought into it.

"I look at it this way," Bates said; "Mrs Everett and Miss Prall are so bitterly at enmity, that either of them would be willing to further a suspicion of the other. I know neither was really guilty——"

"Wait a minute," put in Wise, "how do you know that?"

"Oh, I know they couldn't be! They're—they're ladies——"

"That doesn't deny the possibility,—what else?"

"Why,—they,—oh, they're women,—women couldn't do a thing like that!"

"But, 'women' did do it,—according to your story."

"Of course; but it must have been a lower class of women,—not ladies, like my aunt and Mrs Everett."

"Is that 'feud' of which you've told me, a distinctly ladylike performance?"

"No; it isn't. It's a——"

"I gather, from your report of it, it's a regular old-fashioned hair-pulling sort of feminine spitefulness."

"That's just what it is; and it is in bad taste and all that sort of thing. But murder! That's different!"

"Of course it's different, and must be treated differently. If your aunt's name is so much as hinted at in connection with crime, you must clear it,—if possible. Here we have a murder,—a mysterious murder. The police have been notified, that puts it into the public's hands. You can't afford to hold back anything now. Nor can you afford to conceal or gloss over anything. That would be to invite suspicion. Absolute frankness on your part and on the part of your aunt is imperative."

"You'll get it from me, but Solomon himself couldn't understand my aunt if she chose to be secretive."

"Why should she be secretive?"

"Oh, it's such a mix-up, Mr Wise. You'll see when you meet the two women. Either of them would do or say anything,—anything at all, if it would annoy or disturb the other."

"I think I understand, but I think I can discriminate between the truth and the pretense."

"You'll be pretty smart if you can," Richard sighed. "But get busy as soon as possible. Can you get over to-day?"

"Yes; and I must bring my assistant,—a young lady."

"You're to use Sir Herbert Binney's rooms. Where shall I put the girl?"

"Is there a matron or housekeeper? Yes? Then the girl will attend to all that herself. Don't bother."

"All right, I won't. Now, see here, Mr Wise, I want you to get at the truth, of course, but—if it leads——"

"Stop right there, Mr Bates. If I take this case, it's to get the truth, no matter where it leads. You've mentioned the two women most important in your life,—oh, yes, I see the importance of Mrs Everett. You are, you must be, interested in her daughter, for you showed it in your face when you spoke her name. Now, so far, I've nothing to connect those two women with the case, except that they are women, and the written paper accuses women. I believe that paper implicitly. I've had wide experience and no word of his murderer left by a dying victim is ever anything but the truth. I must see the paper as soon as I can; it may be informative. But, remember, the processes of justice are inexorable,—where the truth leads, I must follow, absolutely irrespective of personal prejudice."

"If you're sure it *is* the truth——"

"Right. I must be sure, beyond all doubt. And I will be before I make any important decisions. You are sole heir?"

"Yes, except for some minor bequests."

"Suspicion hasn't attacked you?"

Bates started at the question, but Pennington Wise seemed to think it a casual one, so Richard replied, frankly, "No, it hasn't,—and I rather expected it."

"Yes, it would not be strange. While, as I say, I believe, so far as I know now, that women killed him, yet others may feel the written message is faked."

"Oh, it's positively Sir Herbert's writing; it doesn't need an expert to see that."

"Were it not for the message, I should be inclined to look into his business relations."

"I think that's the reason he wrote the note. My uncle was a quick thinker, and I can see how, knowing he must die, he did all he could to assist justice. I've no doubt he realized that attention would be turned toward men, and he wrote the truth, as far as he had strength to do so, in order to facilitate the work of his avengers. Without doubt he was intending to write the names of his murderers when his muscles or his brain power gave out."

"That's the way I see it, but I can't be sure till I see the paper. There are many motives for murder, but they can all be classed as affairs of the heart, the mind or the purse. The first class takes in all love interests; the second, business deals, and the third, robbery. The last, I understand, we may eliminate; the second seems to be knocked out by that message, and we come back to some affair of the heart, which may not be love, but jealousy, revenge or a sudden, impulsive quarrel. To look for the women is not an easy task, but it is a help to be started in the right direction."

And so, Penny Wise established himself in the comfortable rooms lately occupied by the victim of the crime he was to investigate, and Zizi, his capable and picturesque assistant, found her quarters in the domain of the housekeeper.

Mrs Macey was a shrewd, capable woman, or she would not have been housekeeper at The Campanile. She looked in cold disdain at the glowing little face of the girl who unceremoniously invaded her room, and stared with increasing interest as the visitor talked.

"You see," Zizi said, nodding her correctly hatted little head, "I've just simply got to be taken in somewhere in the house, and it might as well be here. I'm too young to have an apartment by myself, and I'll promise you won't regret any 'small kindnesses' you may show me. In fact, Mr Pennington Wise, my sponsor in baptism, is the greatest rememberer of small kindnesses you ever saw!"

"My goodness!" remarked Mrs Macey, dazzled by the girl's beauty and animation, and bewildered by her insistent manner.

"Yep," sauced Zizi, with her irresistible smile, "it's your goodness that'll turn the trick. I'll confide to you that I'm here on business, most important secret business, and if your goodness pans out well and you put me up properly, you'll be what is known as handsomely rewarded. So, which is my room?"

The girl whirled through a doorway and spied a neat little bedroom. "This'll do," she said, and setting down her small handbag proceeded to push things around on the dresser and fling her gloves and veil into a drawer, then with what was indubitably a farewell smile, she gently pushed Mrs Macey out, and closed the door after her, pausing only to say, "You've good horse sense,—use it."

"So far, so good," commented Zizi, to her pretty reflection in the mirror. "That woman's a joy. Easily managed, but full of initiative. Just the sort I like."

She flew around, adjusting the appointments to suit her taste; she telephoned downstairs for her further luggage to be sent up, and soon she was as fully established in the room as if she had been there weeks.

"And now," she spoke finally to the pretty girl in her mirror, "I shall sally forth, as they call it, and see what's what in The Campanile."

Her progress through the house was so inconspicuous and casual that no one noticed her especially. It was Zizi's forte to go around unnoticed, when she chose. Though she could, on the other hand, make a decided stir, merely by her appearance.

A slender wisp of a girl, black of hair and eyes, demure without self-consciousness, and gentle-mannered, she glided here and there as she listed and none said her nay. She quickly learned the location of rooms and people, the ways of the house and certain of its tenants, and, without effort, made friends with elevator girls and other employees.

She arrived at last at the Binney rooms, now occupied by Wise.

He was not in then and she found a chambermaid dusting about.

"I belong here," Zizi said, quietly. "I am Mr Wise's assistant; and, as he has doubtless already told you, you are not to chatter about him or myself. We are here on important business matters and if you carry tales you will get into serious trouble. Do you see?"

"Yes, miss," said the woman, impressed by Zizi's air of wisdom and authority. "Mr Wise told me the same."

"Very well, then; go on with your work."

Zizi began forthwith to study the rooms. She found little of interest, for Sir Herbert had lived in them but a few months and had not cared to add any personal comforts or luxuries to those provided by the management. Therefore, the appointments were the conventional ones of furnished apartments, and were quickly passed over by the girl, who was looking for stray bits of evidence.

She didn't go through the papers and letters still on the writing table, for she felt sure they had been examined over and over by the police detectives and probably by Wise himself.

She was musing when the detective came in.

"Caught on to anything, Zizi?" he asked.

"Nope; that is, only one small hint of a possible question to be asked,—later. Where are you?"

"Progressing with the opening chapter. That's about all. But it's a corker of a case. I've seen the paper left by the dying man, and I'd stake my reputation that it's the real thing. I mean that it is the dying statement of a murdered man, and was written in a desperate effort to help along the discovery of his murderers. If he'd only been able to go on with it and tell the names!"

"Then there wouldn't have been any case, and we wouldn't be here. Go on, Wiseacre."

"Well, the two women at feud,—I told you of them,— are great! Miss Prall, spinster, and aggressively unmarried, loathes and despises Mrs Everett, a fascinating widow."

"Fascinating to whom."

"Dunno. Except to herself. But she's the dressy sort and is a blonde cat, while the Prall person is—well, I understand they call her the Grenadier."

"Who calls her that?"

"Dunno. It's in the air."

"How about these two women being the women meant on the paper message?"

"No. I thought of that, but I can't see yet how they could have joined forces, even though they both wanted the old chap out of the way. Nor can I connect them with the case separately,—as yet. But it seems to me that one faction or the other must be at fault, for there are no other women on the horizon."

"Chorus girls? Elevator girls?"

"I can't see it. To be sure, I've only dipped into things so far, but the crime is so skillfully planned and carried out——"

"It might have been impulsive and unpremeditated———"

"At the time it happened, yes. I mean, it may not have been planned for that moment, but it was planned beforehand and the criminal sprang to take his chance when it offered."

"Her chance."

"I use the common pronoun. When I say his or him, I merely mean the hand that struck the blow."

"Have you seen the paper,—the message?"

"I have it with me."

Wise produced the glass-protected paper and together they studied the writing.

"It's positively Binney's," Wise declared. "I've compared lots of his writing with it, and it's surely his. Again, it was surely written at the moment of his death, for Moore found him dying, and the pencil just dropping from his fingers."

"Oh, I don't doubt all that," Zizi said, impatiently, "but what does it mean? I've gone past the fact that women did it; I thoroughly believe that,—in fact, I think it means that women used the knife, but it may not, it may be merely that they were the primary causes. However, he knew, he was *sure* of the criminals who were to be punished. Now, if that *bo* means 'get both' there were only two. If it means something else there may be more than two women implicated."

"Oh, Lord, Ziz, don't gather in more than two suspects. Women don't form a club for murder."

"Women don't murder, as a rule, anyway. You know yourself, the small proportion of feminine murderers."

"That ought to make it easier."

"Not at all. These weren't professionals, who might be listed; they were women, two, most likely, who had a personal matter to settle with the Englishman, and—settled it."

"I grant you all that, except the personal matter. I can't help thinking the bun business is a factor, and though women did the murder, it may be they were interested in the sale of the buns."

"Reasons?"

"Because Sir Herbert Binney was a man who jollied round with little chorus youngsters and such, and they couldn't and wouldn't kill anybody. Don't look for the impossible, or so improbable as to amount to the same thing."

"I agree."

"Nothing has turned up to hint at Sir Herbert's connection, even acquaintance, with any older women or indeed any woman of a different stamp, of his own station in life, or in society at all. No woman who could be mentioned by name has ever had to do with Sir Herbert since he came to New York,—that we know of."

"There might be somebody though."

"Of course, there might. If there is, we'll find her. But we can't hunt a needle in a haystack. If she materializes, we'll spot her."

"Then, excluding the squabs, the only women tagged onto the case are the two Feudists."

"You've said it."

"And they didn't act in collusion?"

"Never!"

"Then it comes down to a decision between Miss Prall and her companion or Mrs Everett and her maid."

"Not necessarily her maid."

"Crickets! Not her daughter!"

"Oh, I don't know. I've just started, Ziz. Help me, don't jump around so."

"Well, bless his heart, he shouldn't be tormented. He should just be guided, counselored and befriended by his faithful helper. Now, to start straight, what's the motive in each of these two cases?"

"Merely to get rid of the man who was for furthering the marriage of the two young people. Miss Prall knew that if Sir Herbert were dead, his fortune would be young Bates' without any conditions and the boy could go on with his inventing in peace. Then, she felt, he'd get so engrossed he'd forget about the Everett girl, and as the Everett mother plans to move away all would be well."

"If the Everetts are leaving, why should Miss Prall go to the trouble of eliminating the Bun man?"

"Point well taken, Zizi; but, you see, as long as the Bun man was around he nagged at nephew to go into Buns and give up his more congenial occupation."

"Pretty slim reason for a real live murder, I think."

"So do I. But it's the best we can get in that direction. Now, coming to the Everett suspects, the widow may have more reason for wishing Sir Herbert dead than we yet know of."

"All we know of is so he can't push along the romance of the youngsters."

"Exactly. And here's the conclusion of the whole matter. I conclude that those two women are the ones to be looked up, not, of course, acting together, but one or the other of them. If we can get anything on either, let's do so."

"And the business men?"

"I want to look those up, too. There's one Crippen, who considered buying out Sir Herbert's business. Also, he was an old beau of the two enemy women. There may be a complication worth studying there."

"What is this bun business? I mean, does he merely sell the good will,—of what?"

"Oh, no; he sells his recipe. It's a secret process,—the making of Binney's Buns,—and the recipe is the thing. No one has ever been able to imitate them successfully. All attempts are dismal failures. But with the formula any one can make them. It's Sir Herbert's great source of anxiety lest the recipe, or formula, whatever they call it, should be discovered."

"Or stolen!"

"Stolen?"

"Yes, don't you see, he had the recipe and he was murdered for it."

"Oh, don't go off wild-goose chasing! It might be,—or it might be he was murdered for his watch and chain, which they didn't take after all,—but we have to have some shred of evidence to go upon."

"Sure we do. And, therefore, I ask you, where *is* this recipe?"

"Why, I don't know,—truly I don't."

Wise smiled at her as at a foolish child, but the saucy little brown face looked very sober as she said, seriously: "and you call yourself a detective! Why, Penny-piece of Wisdom, that recipe is the bone of contention. At least, if it isn't found, it is."

"And did the women murder him for that?"

"Like as not."

"Zizi, you're a smart little girl, but sometimes you don't see straight. Now, drop the recipe, or consider it by yourself some other time. Your stunt is to interest friend Bates."

"The nephew?"

"Yes. Don't flirt with him,—that isn't the *role*, but talk kindly to him, and thereby find out all you can about the Everett bunch. If you admire his sweetheart——"

"Haven't seen her yet."

"Well, you will. And then be real nice and girly-chummy with her, and so get both the lovers on your side. Then we can find out things otherwise out of our reach."

"Meaning the oldsters won't give up."

"Of course not, if they're guilty. I'll take hold of the Crippen end,—and then, if your hunch about the recipe has anything to it, it will come out,—and you sidle up to the lovers. We want to get quick action, for the murderer may get scared and run away."

"Shall I insinuate anything about the older women to——"

"Mercy, no! You see, Bates is scared to death now, for fear it was his aunt, and even more scared for fear it was Dorcas' mother! And those very real fears let Bates himself out,—if anybody ever had a thought of him."

"Oh, nobody could."

"No; well, there's your work cut out for you. Also——"

"Also I'll keep at the servants. I've got the housekeeper just where I want her, but there's a head chambermaid who'll bear watching and I'm rather interested in the night porter."

"Yes, he's a knowing one. Flirt with him——"

"Oh, no, he's not that sort. And, too, he's engaged to a Tartar named Julie, who would scratch out my not altogether unattractive eyes."

"Vanity Box! Well, your eyes do set off what would otherwise be a commonplace face."

Zizi made a face at him that was far from commonplace, and the talk went on.

They were indefatigable workers, these two, and what they planned carefully they carried out with equal care.

And even while she talked, Zizi was looking about the room for a possible hiding-place for the recipe, which, so far as she knew, existed only in her imagination,—and, she had a dim idea that she had found a direction in which to look.

Chapter 15: And Zizi

In her own room, Zizi was holding a confab with the chambermaid, for whom she had sent.

"Yes, miss," the girl said, staring into Zizi's magnetic eyes. "I had the care of them rooms all the time Sir Binney was in 'em."

"Yes, Molly, I know you did, and I want to know a few things about Sir Herbert Binney. Was he a fussy gentleman, about germs, say, and——"

"Germs? miss, how do you mean?"

"Was he afraid of imperfect drains, unaired mattresses or careless cleaning?"

"He was not! Lordy, the germs coulda carried him off and he'd never noticed it. He wudden't know whether I swept or dusted rightly, or whether I gave the place a lick and a promise. He was wrapped up in his own affairs so's you could hardly get his attention to ask him anythin'. Why, miss?"

"Don't ask me why,—ever!" Zizi spoke sharply but not unkindly, and the girl remembered. "Now, Molly, the day before Sir Herbert moved in, he had the sitting-room cleaned and repapered. If he wasn't afraid of germs, why have new paper?"

"Well, the old stuff was a sight, miss. All over, a dark green sorta lattice work pattern with smashin' big red roses."

"Sounds rather effective——"

"A nightmare, that's what it was. Well, Sir Herbert, the minnit he looked at it he said, 'Rip it off!'"

"Did you hear him say it?"

"No, miss, the bellboy told me. He was luggin' up bags and things and he said the new man was a peppery cuss."

"Was he?"

"Why, no, he didn't seem that way to me. Easy-goin', I sh'd say. Absent-minded, now an' then,—av'rage generous, an' not payin' much attention to his surroundin's. That's the way *I* size up Sir Binney."

"And who do you think killed him?"

"Oh, Lordy, don't ask me that!" The girl looked frightened, and quick-witted Zizi, instead of pursuing the subject then, turned it off with, "No, indeed, when detectives are busy on the case, small need to ask outsiders."

"Not that I'm exactly an outsider, neither," and Molly bridled as with a sense of self-importance. "Of course a chambermaid, now, can't help seein' a lot of what goes on."

"Of course not," Zizi said, carelessly. "But she isn't supposed to tattle and I shouldn't dream of quizzing you."

"No, ma'am. Not but what I could tell things——"

"But you wouldn't. You might get into serious trouble if you did."

Molly looked at her sharply.

"As how, miss?" she said.

"Well, you see, it's very hard to tell anything just exactly as it happened, and if you should vary a shade from the truth, and then tell it differently next time you might get arrested for—for perjury."

"Arrested! Do you mean that?"

"I certainly do. I've known girls to tell stories under stress of excitement and then try to repeat them and get all mixed up, and, oh, well, it's a dangerous performance."

"But if I just told *you*, now, miss?"

"What have you to tell? And why do you want to tell anybody?"

"I thought—I thought if I told I might get something for it."

"I like your frankness, Molly, and I don't mind offering you a fair price for your goods, *if* you can put 'em up. But can you?"

"Ma'am?"

"Do you really how anything of importance, that might lead to the discovery of the people who murdered Sir Herbert Binney? I don't want any hemming and hawing, but a straight answer."

"Well, I can't give you a positive answer, because I don't know myself. But I do know somebody has been in the rooms since, several times, searching about for something."

"What did this person seem to be looking for?"

"Belike it was a paper, for I could tell as how the desk drawers and the boxes in the cupboard had been moved."

"That's the sort of thing I want to know, Molly." Zizi spoke quietly and earnestly. "You can tell when things are moved as no one else can. You mean, of course, before Mr Wise took the rooms?"

"And once since. Why, last evening, when Mr Wise was out, somebody got in there."

"Who could it be, Molly?"

The earnest, chummy attitude of the inquirer made Molly feel at ease, and also anxious to please.

"I'm not sayin'," the chambermaid replied, a cloud passing over her face, "for I've no wish to get in jail, but it's somebody from the floor below."

Zizi knew the Everetts' apartment was on the floor below, but she said, "H'm, seventh floor, then. Who's down there?"

"I don't know, ma'am," and Molly's vacant stare proved her a good actress, and one determined not to give away any information.

This attitude showed Zizi that the girl was shrewd and canny, and she changed her tactics.

"There you go, Molly!" she exclaimed. "How do you *know* some one came up from the seventh floor? You state these things, and if you're not able to prove them—well, you know what I told you."

"But I heard the—the person come up the stairs."

"Stairs! A likely story! Why not use the elevator?"

"That's just it,—the—the person didn't want to be seen. So——"

"The person?"

"Yes'm, the person sneaks up the stairs and into the sitting-room——"

"Opening the door with a key?"

"Well,—you see, ma'am, I was in the bathroom,—and——"

"And the person didn't know you were there, and you made no sign?"

"Yes," eagerly. "Yes, that's the way it was; I thought I'd find out something——"

"And did you?"

But that time Zizi's eagerness proved her undoing.

For some reason or other Molly took alarm and shut up like a clam.

"No," she averred. "I couldn't see who it was, and as I peeked out, the—person ran away."

Zizi knew from the sly and obstinate look in her eyes that Molly was lying and that she intended to stick to it. She was nobody's fool, this Molly, and though Zizi was sure that she would yet sell her secret to the highest bidder, it was not altogether wise to begin the bidding at once. Also, Zizi felt certain that what the girl knew was of serious importance and it was imperative that Pennington Wise should learn the truth. But Zizi's ways were devious and she chose now to treat the matter lightly.

"Molly, you're a fraud," she said, laughingly; "you've built up a person of mysterious appearance and unknown sex, but I can't fall for your plan. I don't blame you for wanting to make a little easy money,—who doesn't? But you didn't pick a winner when you selected *me* to try it on! Go to somebody else with your wares. Try Mr Bates or Miss Prall."

The girl's face fell and Zizi smiled in satisfaction. But Molly grew belligerent and exclaimed, "Oh, very well, miss, but you'll be sorry. I *will* go to some one else with my story, but it will be to——"

"I know! To the person herself! Well, go on, if you can get to her undiscovered!"

"I can! With no trouble at all!"

"Not forgetting the danger you run of being arrested?"

"Danger! Pooh! You can't scare me that way? Beside, you'll never know——"

"Who the person is? I know already. Kate Holland!"

This was a mere guess on Zizi's part, and she said it to learn from Molly's expression how near right it might be.

To her surprise, Molly looked mystified.

"Kate Holland!" she whispered. "You—you don't suspect her, do you?"

"Do you?" Zizi shot back.

"Yes, I do,—or I did, until——"

"Until you saw the person?"

"Yes, that's it."

Zizi was about to insist on the name of the person when there was a tap at the door, and the head chambermaid insisted on having the services of Molly at once. The girl went away and Zizi went straight to tell Penny Wise all about it.

She tried the door of Wise's rooms and as the knob turned she walked in. But to her surprise the man sitting at the table in the sitting-room, and reading the newspaper, was not Wise but Mr Vail.

"Good afternoon," he said, a little blankly, as he rose.

"How do you do?" Zizi returned, with one of her attractive smiles. "I'm Mr Wise's assistant. Can I do anything for you?"

"I'm waiting here in hope he'll come in. I'm Vail,—I've rooms on the tenth. You may have heard of me; I'm interested in the Binney case, and I'd like a little talk with Mr Wise,—that is, if he cares for it."

"He will," and Zizi nodded confidently. "Have you any knowledge, suspicion or evidence?"

"None of those important commodities,—merely straws that may or may not show the direction of the wind."

"There's no knowing when Mr Wise will show up," Zizi observed; "don't you want to tell me? It'll be all the same."

"All the same! Are you and Mr Wise partners?"

Zizi flashed her best smile as she returned, "Practically. I'm only assistant, but what is told to me goes to him just as I get it."

"Accurate and careful, eh? Well, my information is regarding a woman I saw skulking in the halls the night of the murder. You see, it chanced that I came into the house and up in the elevator just before the tragedy occurred. I stood a few minutes at my door, before leaving the car, because Bob Moore and I were discussing the book he was reading. He's a good sort, and often when I come in late I give him a jolly to help along his weary watch hours."

"All right," chirped Zizi, "what followed?"

"Only that as we came up I heard some one on the stairs. They surround the elevator, you know, and though indistinct, I know I heard a tread on the stairs as we were at or near the eighth floor. But we came on up and then, as I say, we stood a bit talking. Then Moore went down again, and I, feeling curious about the footsteps on the stairs, went around to the staircase and looked down."

"How far could you see?"

"Not far, because the stairs wind around the elevator well. But I went down farther and I caught sight of a woman with a shawl over her head——"

"What kind of a shawl?"

"Lord, I don't know! Grayish and softish, it looked, but the night lights are dim and I only caught a glimpse of this hooded figure moving stealthily along the hall. That's all, and if it's of any importance——"

"It doesn't seem to me to be of much,—what do you think?"

Vail stared at her. He was not accustomed to have his suggestions so lightly received. But he only shrugged his shoulders, and said:

"I don't think anything about it. I merely offer the information that there was a mysterious seeming woman lurking in the halls that night: If it means nothing to anybody, there's no harm done."

"No; certainly not. How tall was she?"

"Above average height, and gaunt of figure."

"About like Miss Prall?"

"Good heavens, I wouldn't say that!"

"Why not? Is it a crime to be of Miss Prall's appearance?"

"You're a funny little piece! Well, then, I may say the shape was somewhat like Miss Prall's, but I'm sure it was not she."

"How can you be sure it was not she unless you are sure who it was?"

"I can be sure anything is not anything else, without knowing positively what anything is!" and Vail glared at her an instant, and then both broke into laughter.

"It's all right," Zizi informed him; "I'm only pursuing my investigations according to orders."

"Oho! Am I being put through a third degree?"

"Sort of. But I think I've learned all you know. Or, wait, was the beshawled one of Kate Holland's style? You know to liken one woman to another in appearance doesn't necessarily accuse her of murder."

"No, that's true. Well, the woman I saw could be said to be like Kate Holland or Miss Prall either, in general outline, which is all I could discern of face or figure. But I can't see what either of those women would be doing prowling about the halls at two A. M."

"Unless it was in connection with the murder," Zizi said, straightforwardly. "They all have declared they were in bed and asleep but who's to witness that?"

"In the very nature of things, nobody," Vail said. "And now, I'll be going. I won't wait for Mr Wise just now, but I'll see him soon, if he cares to talk to me."

But just as Vail was leaving, Richard Bates appeared, and Vail tarried to speak with him.

"Any developments?" Vail asked.

"No," said Bates, despondently. "That is, nothing of importance. I say, Vail, what do you think about the Crippen deal? You know my uncle planned to see him that night regarding a sale of the business, and——"

"Did he see him?" Vail spoke eagerly.

"I don't know. Crippen's out of town——"

"He is! Don't you think you ought to keep tabs on him?"

"Why?"

"Only because he was interested in the Binney business."

"So were you."

"True, but Sir Herbert and I had our meeting and got over it long ago."

"He wanted to sell out to you?"

"You know all about it, Bates. Binney wanted to sell his Buns to anybody who would pay enough. Of course, in the event of your sticking to your refusal to Bun with him. If you'd agree to do that, he told me, he'd have no reason to sell. But he didn't want to carry it on alone, nor did he want to go in with anybody else. He wanted to sell outright to me, but his price was prohibitive and he wouldn't ease up on it a bit, so there was nothing doing. That's all our story."

"What did he want to sell you?"

"The good will, the bakery and fixtures,—in England,—why, the Buns, the Binney Buns, lock, stock and barrel."

"Didn't he have the recipe for sale?"

"I don't know. I assume that was included in the business, of course. As I couldn't dream of meeting his figures, we didn't go into details."

"Did Crippen?"

"Dunno. I never heard what kind of a discussion they had. But what are you getting at? Why drag in Crippen?"

"Oh, hang it all, Vail, I don't want to drag in anybody; and yet I'd be willing to drag in anybody, if I had a trace of suspicion against anybody. For, unless a new suspect turns up pretty quick, I'm afraid they'll pitch on my aunt."

"Ridiculous!"

"I know it seems so to you and me, for we know Aunt Letitia, but these strangers, this Wise and Miss Zizi, here," bowing in her direction, "they are already looking——"

"Now, Mr Bates, that's too bad!" cried Zizi, her black eyes shining with real sympathy, as she saw the young man's distress. "Please be sure Mr Wise and I never look seriously in any direction unless something definite points us that way. And by elimination not many suspects are left."

"Who are eliminated?" asked Vail, gravely.

"We have cut out all thought of the chorus girls, and the girls employed in this house," Zizi began.

"All the house girls?" asked Vail, quickly.

"I'm not sure about that, but I mean the elevator girls, the telephone girls, the news-stand girls and the pages. I don't know anything about the upstairs maids, chambermaids, cleaners, and such. But there's been no suggestion of those."

"Why should there be?" said Bates, impatiently. "I know myself, no stupid little servant killed my uncle. It was done by some one with brains, with power, with influence. He was not a man to be killed for some petty reason; he was a man of big interests in a business way, and of wide experience socially. His murderers—or murderesses—must be found, but I don't think we've got on the right track yet."

"And do you think Crippen is a promising way to look?" asked Vail, scrutinizing Bates' anxious face.

"I don't know. But he was mixed up in the Bun matter; he hadn't finished the deal, as you had, and as one or two other companies had, and it seems to me he ought to be looked up, at least, before we go on."

"I've looked him up," and Wise's form came into view around the corner of the hall. He joined the group that still stood by the door of the Binney apartment. "I've looked into the Crippen connection with the Bun deal, and there's nothing doing. Binney and Crippen were on the outs but not because of Buns. *They* were settled some time before the murder. Still, Crippen did want the recipe, and was willing to buy that without the bakery or any paraphernalia of the business."

"Is that so?" and Vail seemed interested. "Wouldn't Binney sell that?"

"I'm told not."

"Who told you?"

"Crippen's people,—down at his office. I talked with a secretary, and I've talked with some of the 'Crippen's Cakes' directors. They want the recipe and nothing else."

"Queer," mused Zizi, "that a recipe should be so valuable! Why can't they buy a bun and analyze it, and so find out how it's made?"

"That's been tried," Vail informed her. "But the secret can't be learned that way. There's an unknown ingredient, or the things are put together in some unknown order or way,—but no one has yet been able to imitate successfully the Binney Bun. I'm a bread man, and I know that."

"Well, if you've struck off Crippen's name, where do we stand?" Richard said, looking gloomily at Wise.

"We stand pat for the women," the detective declared. "And *I* have from the first. I can't doubt or disbelieve a dying statement,—can you, Mr Vail?"

"Surely not. That is, on general principles. But if this pursuit of women leads to——"

"No matter where it leads," Pennington Wise said, firmly, "the trail must be followed up. Murder demands a life for a life. The danger is that suspicion may be directed toward the wrong women. But that is our great care, and I can't think it will happen."

"It must not happen," said Vail, sharply, and, with a sympathetic glance at Richard Bates, he went away.

"Now, Mr Bates," said Wise as the others returned to the sitting-room and closed the door, "I've been pretty busy and I've some good news for you. I think we can say positively there is no danger of suspicion coming to rest on your aunt or her companion, Miss Gurney."

"Thank God," cried Richard fervently.

"The matter of the paper-knife is, I think, just as Miss Prall explained it; she did give it to Sir Herbert to be mended, and he did have it in his pocket the night he was killed."

"And the assailant did use it?" asked Zizi.

"Yes; or so it seems to me. But all this has nothing to do with the owner of the knife, for you see, Binney himself was the temporary owner to all intents and purposes."

"Then that makes the deed seem unpremeditated and impulsive," said Bates.

"Yes, it makes it seem so,—though it may not have been. But since my day's work, I've gathered suggestions and testimony,—though no material evidence, to turn my thoughts strongly toward the women on the seventh floor, Mrs Everett and her——"

"Her maid!" Bates interrupted, speaking with a desperate haste, as if afraid Wise would say some other word.

"No," said Wise. "Her daughter."

"You lie!" Bates cried, and Zizi, her face white and drawn, said "Oh, Penny, she *couldn't*!"

"Couldn't strike the blow, maybe, but she helped her mother, and did it by keeping watch. She was seen in the hall with a scarf over her head."

CHAPTER 16: TESTIMONY

"It's inconceivable, it's impossible, it's incredible!" Richard Bates declared. "I'll never believe it! Mrs Everett, even if she had the will, could never accomplish such a deed!"

"But that Kate person could," Zizi suggested, and Bates turned to her.

"But Mr Wise doesn't accuse the maid,—he accuses the daughter! A gentle, innocent young girl——"

"Now, wait a minute," put in Wise; "I don't say the daughter was at fault,—she might have been a tool without knowing it. I mean, she may have kept watch for her mother——"

"What do you mean,—kept watch? Miss Everett is not a numskull to be told to 'keep watch' and blindly obey."

"Nor is Mrs Everett ninny enough to expect that," Wise returned. "But the lady is clever enough to persuade her daughter to keep a lookout on some plausible pretense——"

"But I don't understand," Bates persisted; "just how do you reconstruct the crime,—on that theory?"

"Why, say Mrs Everett was in waiting, till Binney should come in——"

"Where was she?" Bates demanded.

"Perhaps behind one of the big pillars in the onyx lobby,—a dozen people could hide behind them——"

"Rubbish! But go on."

"Well, say she hid there with the knife, which she had procured from Binney earlier,—he admired her, you know——"

"He admired every pretty woman. Go on."

"And then, when Vail came in, and Moore took him up, the coast was clear, and just then Binney happened in——"

"Strange that he should happen in just then!"

"Well, but he *did*, didn't he? He *had* to, didn't he, to get there at all? You don't think he was hiding there *waiting* to be killed, do you? Well, then Binney came in, and the lady,—or her maid, Kate,—stepped out and stabbed him, and then ran up the stairs,—and in the halls Miss Everett was watching to see that there was no one looking on. She need not have known what her mother was up to,—but—she was seen in the halls that night by two separate witnesses."

"Are you sure it was Miss Everett they saw?" asked Bates in a tone of anxiety rather than surprise.

"Positive; they described her dress and ornaments exactly."

"But she might have been in the halls for any purpose——"

"At two o'clock in the morning?"

"She might have missed her mother from the apartment and stepped out to look for her."

"But then she would have been in negligee or with a wrap over her nightclothes. She was seen fully dressed, as she had been in the evening."

"Well," and Bates spoke defiantly, "what does it prove? You haven't fastened the crime on Mrs Everett yet. You haven't even any real evidence against her."

"Oh, yes we have,—but look here, Mr Bates. It won't do for you to take that antagonistic attitude toward me and my work. As you know, I told you I must follow wherever the trail leads, and this indicative direction must be followed up. It may be that the Everetts are not the 'women,' and if so, I'll find that out. But I may say, that so far, there are, to my mind, no women suspects but the Everetts or—your aunt."

"I'd rather you'd suspect my aunt! I'd rather the criminal should be my aunt——"

"But, Mr Bates, I can't consult your preferences as to the identity of the criminal!"

"Now, don't you worry, Mr Bates," Zizi said, gently, "I don't believe your sweetheart or her mother are mixed up in this thing at all."

"Why, Ziz?" and Wise turned a mild, questioning glance her way. He had great faith in the opinions of his little helper, and was always ready to revise his own judgment if hers contradicted it. For Zizi never spoke thoughtlessly or without reason. And this last remark of hers indicated some knowledge or indication that might turn the trend of suspicion.

"Because that little fluff of a Mrs Everett is too good-natured to kill or to direct the killing of anybody."

"She isn't so awfully good-natured!" exclaimed Bates, involuntarily. "You should hear her talk to my aunt!"

"Oh, yes, I know about that feud thing," and Zizi smiled tolerantly; "but that's a sort of obsession or idiosyncrasy of the two women. Really, Mrs Everett is a good-natured lady, and you needn't have any fights with your mother-in-law, unless you make them yourself."

"Don't be flippant, Zizi," warned Wise. "This isn't the time for banter."

"It's the time for action," said Zizi, springing from her seat. "I'm going straight to Miss Prall with the whole story, and I think we'll learn a lot. Are you men coming with me?"

Like sheep, Bates and Wise followed her.

Pennington Wise was really more at a loss than he had ever before found himself. The indisputable evidence of the dying man's message was all he really had to work on, and his work on that was not productive, so far, of success. The women accused *must* be found. But Wise, while he realized there were no other suspects, couldn't think the two ladies of Feud fame were the ones.

True enough, they could both be said to have had motive, and, in the house, anybody could be said to have had opportunity, yet both motive and opportunity were slight ones, and the latter largely dependent on a convenient chance.

It seemed absurd to think of Mrs Everett,—or Kate Holland,—waiting behind a pillar, and then seeing the victim walk in! And yet he had walked in; somebody had met him and stabbed him, so the other suppositions were, at least, plausible.

The three went to the Prall apartment, and, strange to say, found Miss Letitia in a quiet, placid mood.

She looked at them with a sort of wondering interest, and bade them be seated.

"You've been here several days, now, Mr Wise," she said; "have you made any real progress?"

"It's hard to say, Miss Prall," the detective replied; "but if you'll give me the benefit of your opinions I may derive help from them."

"Opinions on what?" and the sharp old face began to show its more usual expression of asperity.

"On whether the murder of Sir Herbert was the work of Mrs Everett or not."

"Of course it was! I don't say Adeline Everett held the knife, but she was the instigator and commander-in-chief."

"What makes you think so?"

"Because I know her. I know her soft, purring ways, and I know of the tiger's claws that are inside her velvet grasp."

"Well, it seems strange, does it not, that she says pretty much the same about you?"

"Me! Adeline Everett accuses me?"

"Yes; she says that perhaps you didn't actually strike the blow, but that you were aided and abetted by your companion——"

"That Eliza! She wouldn't kill a fly, and Adeline knows it!"

"She suggested that your nephew might have helped you in the actual crime——"

"Look here, Mr Wise, you're talking mighty queer talk. I suppose murders and killings are so much a part of your life that you think little of one more or less; but it isn't so with quiet, law-abiding citizens. And if you think I'm going to take this accusation of another woman calmly, you're very much mistaken. I'm going at once to see Adeline Everett, and if she did say that to you,—if you haven't misrepresented or exaggerated——"

"But wait a minute, Miss Prall. You are angry,—and perhaps justly so,—at her accusation of you. Remember that you've also accused her of the same crime!"

Letitia Prall looked at him. "That's true," she said; "now, as a detective, you can judge between us. I'll go to her rooms or you may bring her here, and let us accuse each other. We can't both be guilty, and I can judge from her manner whether she is or not, even if you can't do that."

"It would be a good test," agreed Wise. "But I'm pretty sure that if either of you really is the guilty person that you will be able to pretend you are not, so plausibly as to deceive Sherlock Holmes himself!"

"I could easily fool you if I wished to," said Miss Prall, with dignity, "but in this instance I've no occasion to do so."

Zizi looked up at this, and said, "You could fool a man, Miss Prall, but you couldn't fool me."

"Why not, child?" and the older lady looked at her curiously.

"Because one woman understands another. And I know that if you planned to or wanted to kill a man, you would choose to do it in some less conspicuous place than the onyx lobby."

"Nonsense, Zizi," Wise said, "no one would choose their own apartment——"

"No; but Miss Prall would have waited for a chance on some of these upper floors,—she never would have arranged the scene downstairs."

"You're right, girl," said Letitia Prall, "though it's uncanny for you to think that out. I've wondered many times why any one chose so public a place."

"But that showed cleverness," Wise insisted. "You see for yourself how difficult of solution it makes the mystery. It gives room for assumption that some one came in from the street."

"There's room for that assumption, if you like," Zizi declared, "but what've you got to back it up? Nothing."

"What have you got to back up any theory?" cried Bates. "Nothing."

"Then let's get something!" exclaimed Letitia, rising from her chair. "Come on with me to Mrs Everett's and we'll get something to back up some theory, I'll be bound!"

Glad of the chance,—for which he had maneuvered,—to see the two inimical women together, Wise followed the others to the Everett apartment.

The meeting between the two would have been comical, but for the underlying element of tragedy that pervaded the whole situation.

"Why are you here, Letitia Prall?" was Mrs Everett's greeting.

"To ask you why you accused me of murder," answered Miss Prall, her manner more the Grenadier than ever. "I'm told you sit in judgment on me and I ask an explanation."

"The facts explain themselves," returned the blonde little lady; "it's not hard to understand why I think you killed a man whom you had often expressed a desire to see dead!"

"Huh!" sniffed Miss Prall. "I've often expressed a desire to see you dead,—but I haven't killed you—yet! You know perfectly well, Adeline, that saying I wish a person dead, is merely a habit of mine,—as you say 'I nearly died when I heard it!' Now, you didn't nearly die at all, and death is not so trivial as we seem to think it, when we talk so at random. Lots of people, especially women, throw around phrases such as, 'I thought I'd die,' or 'I could kill you for that,' without any real meaning to the words at all. So, once and for all, Adeline Everett, stop using those silly phrases as evidence of my criminal tendencies! And suspicion thus being lifted from me, I denounce you as the one who killed Sir Herbert. And I have far more reason, for you were not only interested in his demise because of the affair between your daughter and my nephew but you had an ax of your own to grind. You wanted Sir Herbert for your husband. Yes, you may well blush——"

"Hush up, Letitia Prall! Am I to be insulted in my own house? Are the raving words, the wicked thoughts of a misguided, vicious woman to be believed by those who hear them? I protest! I,—shut up, Letitia!"

For Miss Prall was talking at the same time, and her biting, scathing words were only unheard because of the higher pitch and louder tone of Mrs Everett's voice.

The audience undertook to pour oil on the troubled waters but with no success.

"Keep still, Richard," Miss Prall ordered, when Bates began, "Please, Auntie——"

And Mrs Everett screamed "Shut up!" to Zizi, who, almost laughing at the strange scene, endeavored to placate one or both the combatants.

"You know you tried your best," declared the irate spinster, "you know you inveigled him in here, you wheedled and cajoled and fawned and flattered——"

"How well you know the process!" screamed Mrs Everett; "because you tried all your own pitiful, ineffectual cajoleries,—and all to no avail! I didn't have to make any effort to entice Sir Herbert to call on me,— indeed, he came so frequently, I was forced to dissuade him, lest people talk——"

"People always talk about you,—and rarely in flattering terms! You are well known through the house for what you are, and if you weren't already planning to leave, you would be put out,—that I happen to know."

"You don't know any such thing. You made that up——"

"I didn't!"

"You did!"

"Hush!" Wise's peremptory tone brought a momentary silence. "Now that you've reached the stage of silly vituperation, it's time to call a halt. This foolishness is uninteresting as well as unpleasant. You two ladies will answer a few questions,—in the name of the law!"

The last phrase, high sounding and threatening, had its desired effect. Like most women, they had a hearty and healthy fear of that mysterious thing called the law, and when it was held over their heads it acted as a rod.

"You have accused one another of the murder of Sir Herbert," Wise began, trying to sound formal and awe-inspiring. "Have you, Mrs Everett, any grounds for such accusation other than a foolish speech about wishing the man was dead?"

"No," was the sulky answer; "that is, I have no definite grounds, but I've known Letitia Prall for many years and I know her to be quite capable of murder or any other crime!"

"A belief in capability is not evidence," said Wise, sternly, and turned to Letitia.

"Have you, Miss Prall, definite evidence against Mrs Everett that you accuse her?"

"She wanted the man dead——"

"That's not evidence!" Wise fairly thundered; "answer my question."

"Well, then, I've no eye-witness proof of her crime, but I do know that her daughter was out in the hall, keeping watch——"

"Keeping watch over what—or whom?"

"Keeping watch to see that the way was clear; that her mother might return unseen from the ground floor to her own apartment by way of the stairs."

"You mean you think Mrs Everett walked up seven flights of stairs after the deed?"

"I couldn't do it," admitted plump Mrs Everett, drawing deep breaths at the mere thought of such a thing.

"Nonsense!" retorted Miss Prall. "There's only six flights, and they're easy steps. But, if not for that, what *was* Dorcas out in the hall for, all dressed, at that time of night?"

"She wasn't, so far as I know," replied the mother.

"It all hinges on that," declared Wise, with as much earnestness as if he believed himself what he was saying.

As a matter of fact he was striving, so far in vain, to gather some hint, some side light as to which way to look for the criminal, for he did not really think either of these women guilty, in deed or intent.

"What do you mean—all hinges on that?" Zizi asked, in rather a loud, clear tone.

Wise took her hint,—it was a standing arrangement with them,—and answered in an equally loud voice:

"I mean, that if the presence of Miss Everett in the hall that night can be innocently explained, it will save Mrs Everett from——"

"From arrest!" spoke up Letitia, grimly.

"Arrest!" Mrs Everett gasped, and burst into hysterical weeping.

Zizi's covert glance toward an inner door was rewarded and Dorcas flung it wide open and ran into the room.

"I can explain it!" she cried, "I've been listening, and I'll tell. I was in the hall late that night, but it wasn't as late as two o'clock. Whoever says it was tells an untruth. I was in the hall about midnight to,—to meet somebody."

"Me," said Bates, calmly. "This is no time for hiding any facts. I wanted to see Dorcas on a special and important matter. She had tried all the evening to get away from her mother but that lady was too watchful, so Dorcas sent me word by a maid that she would grant me a moment's interview in the hall after her people were asleep. This she did, and while we have no wish to exploit it, yet it was nothing wrong. Dorcas is my affianced wife, and as her mother is not in favor of our union it has been necessary for us to meet clandestinely."

"And this was about midnight?" asked Wise, apparently not interested in the clandestine part of it.

"Yes, not any later."

"It was twelve when I got back to my room," averred Dorcas. "Any one who tells a different story is making it up."

There was no doubting the statement of the clear young voice or the truth stamped on the sweet young face, and all present believed her.

Mrs Everett forebore to chide, so interested was she in learning if this confession would clear her from suspicion.

"We must look up the girl who told the story," said the detective. "The statement was about a veiled figure, and the assertion that it was Miss Everett was not from a dependable source. But I believe Miss Everett implicitly, and I want to see about some other details before I go further in the matter at all.

"I'll see that girl who told you the yarn, Penny," Zizi said, thoughtfully; "you go and look up those other people,—you know——"

"Very well, go ahead. It was Molly."

"Of course it was. She's a *News-Herald*. If you want to know *anything* ask Molly. I'm going to ask her now."

"I'll go with you," volunteered Dorcas, looking a little nervous and agitated.

"Come along," said Zizi, smiling at her, and Zizi's smile was full of comfort and cheer.

Mrs Everett began to say, "Oh, no, my child," but before she could protest Dorcas and Zizi had left the room.

"You see," Zizi began to the other girl as they went to Zizi's room, "Molly is crooked."

"Lame?"

"No," and Zizi smiled at such ignorance of crime slang. "No, that means she isn't honest or, rather, honorable.

She makes up yarns to suit herself, and often to suit some one else who pays well for being suited. Now, we'll get her in here and quiz her, and you say little or nothing at first, until we see what's doing."

Molly was summoned and Zizi began in a straightforward way:

"Molly, you saw some one in the halls the night of the Binney murder. You've said it was Miss Everett. Here's Miss Everett, do you still say so?"

"Lord, no, Miss. I've found out who it was, and it was a man."

"You said a woman."

"I know I did, but I—I made a mistake. It was sorta dark, you know."

"And you take back the statement that you saw a woman?"

"I do, miss."

"Who paid you to do that?"

"Nobody, miss." Molly's round, blue eyes seemed truthful, but Zizi was not sure.

"Well, now that you've decided you saw a man, who was the man?"

"That I don't know—for sure."

"Who do you think it was,—or, might have been?"

"I'm not saying,—for why should I make trouble for an innercent human bein'?"

"You're stalling until you see whether we'll pay you more for your information or he'll pay you more to suppress it! Now, you're foolish to act like that, for nine chances out of ten it was an innocent man, anyway."

"Oh, no, miss; oh, no!"

"What do you mean by that?"

"The man was up to no good. He was searching in Sir Binney's room."

"Oh, he was. Then tell us his name, or the Law will make you do so."

"You ain't the Law, miss. I'll be goin' now, and when the Law has anythin' to say to me, lemmeno."

"But wait a moment," said Dorcas; "just tell me this. Did the man get what he wanted from Sir Herbert's room?"

"Yes,—I mean, I don't know. How should I know?"

Angry at the slip she had carelessly made, Molly ran away and was down the hall and around a corner before the girls realized she had gone.

"I know what they're after," said Dorcas. "Suppose I tell you,—and perhaps we can do something to help along."

CHAPTER 17: A WOMAN SCORNED

"Whoever was searching in Sir Herbert's room," Dorcas began, "was after that recipe for the Binney Buns."

"What's that?" asked Zizi, to draw the girl on.

"Why, there's a special recipe for the buns, of course, and it's very valuable,—the buns can't be made without it,—and I can't help thinking that Mr Crippen or some messenger of his has been hunting around there for that recipe."

"Why not a messenger from some other of the bakeries interested? The Popular Popovers, or whatever it's called,—or Mr Vail's company?"

"Maybe. But I know that Mr Vail and Sir Herbert decided not to make a deal, and I think that Popular company also decided not to. Well, anyway, I'm sure whoever was prowling in the Binney apartment was in search of that recipe, which was hidden there."

"Well, but what good does it do to surmise that? Or even to know that?"

"I don't know, but I thought if Mr Wise knew somebody was hunting there for a definite purpose, he could find out who the somebody was, and it might be the murderer."

"A woman,—or women?"

"No—I suppose not—and yet, why not? A messenger from the bakery people,—any of them,—of course, *could* be a woman,—one of the maids, or some employee of the house."

"Suppose we go and search."

"Look here, Miss Everett, you are a sensible girl, and I'm going to speak frankly. You know that suspicion now is directed toward the aunt of Mr Bates or——"

"Or my mother! Yes, I do know it, but either supposition is so ridiculous——"

"Wait a minute; no matter how ridiculous a suspicion may seem to the people involved, it must be met and denied or it remains. Now, if suspicion in the two directions mentioned are so absurd, we must prove their absurdity."

"How?"

"Either by making it clear that the suspected women could not have been guilty or, better still, finding the guilty party."

"Let's do that, then! I know my mother had no hand in it,—and I'm equally sure that Miss Prall didn't——"

"But your surety and your certainty are of no evidential value."

"That's why I say let's find the real women! You are a detective just as much as Mr Wise is one,—I'm an interested principal, just as much as Richard Bates is,— can't we do something big?"

"Good! That's the talk! We'll try, at least. Let's go to the Binney rooms now, and see what we can see."

"Small chance of seeing anything in rooms that Mr Wise has already searched."

"Oh, I don't know. Set a woman to catch a woman! If women have sought and found that recipe, we'll find their traces. If it's still there, we must find the paper ourselves."

Zizi looked at Dorcas in surprise.

"You're a trump!" she exclaimed; "good for you! Come along, we'll see what we can do."

The two girls went to the Binney rooms and began their search. But it seemed useless to look through papers in the desk or books on the book shelves after Wise and the other detectives had gone over that ground.

"Was Sir Herbert sly and canny?" asked Zizi, thoughtfully.

"Oh, yes, indeed. He was never caught napping. If he hid that paper, he hid it in a good place. It won't be found easily. We must think of some inconspicuous place,—in the back of a picture, or tacked up above the inside of a drawer."

"Clever girl!" and Zizi's admiration increased. "Here goes, then."

They both looked in all such places as Dorcas had suggested, but with no success at all.

Wise came in while they were thus busy, and smiled approval at the work in progress.

"Hello," he said, suddenly, as Dorcas peered behind a picture that was hung low, "the wall paper isn't faded at all in this room. Must be new."

"It is," Dorcas told him. "Sir Herbert had this room repapered when he took the apartment."

"Why?"

"Said he didn't like the paper that was on."

"And yet he could stand that frightful Cubist nightmare on the wall of the bedroom! H'm! Well, well! Very interesting—ve-ry interesting! See, Ziz?"

The black eyes of his little assistant sparkled. "Of course I do! He had the room papered in order to hide his precious recipe."

"Right! Now, we may have to peel off the paper from the whole room,—for it's not probable he kindly left it folded, in order to help us along."

Dorcas listened with growing surprise. Here was a clever detective, indeed, to jump to this important conclusion,—if it was the true one.

"Let's feel around," Zizi said, and began passing her little brown paw over the walls.

"Not in plain sight, Ziz," said Wise, and he started moving out a bookcase to look behind it.

They felt nothing that seemed like a paper behind the wall paper, but if the recipe had been placed without folding at all it would doubtless cause no appreciable extra thickness.

"Maybe he left a memorandum," suggested Zizi, "or even a cryptogram in his desk telling where he hid it."

"Not likely," said Wise. "You see he wouldn't forget and he had no reason to make the thing clear to anybody else."

"Molly said somebody was in here prowling," Dorcas reminded, "so somebody knew there was a paper to look for."

"But all this paper business presupposes the bread or cake people, and they aren't women," objected Wise.

"That paper about the women may be misleading," Zizi said, thoughtfully. "They may have been back of the murder, or, on the other hand, they may have been the tools of men responsible for the murder."

"But you can't get away from women's connection with the crime. Whether directly or indirectly guilty, they are the people to look for,—they are our quarry, and they must be found."

Dorcas paled and her red lower lip quivered. "Oh, Mr Wise," she begged, "do be careful! It would be so awful if you suspected innocent women just because of the paper! Even granting it is a genuine dying message, it may mean so many things——"

She broke down and Zizi ran to her and threw her aims around the shaking form.

"Come, dear," she said; "you're all unstrung; don't look around here any more now. If there's a paper to be found, Penny will find it."

She led Dorcas away and took her back to her own home, and, urging her to lie down, she soothed the throbbing forehead with her magnetic finger-tips and soon Dorcas fell asleep.

Zizi tiptoed from the girl's bedroom, and encountered Mrs Everett on her way out.

"Do sit down, Miss Zizi," the lady urged. "I'm pining for some one to talk to. Tell me now, do you think Letitia Prall is at the back of all this? Not of course, the actual criminal, but in any way implicated?"

The plump little blonde lady fluttered about and finally settled herself among some cushions on a couch and turned an inquisitive gaze on her visitor.

"What would be her motive?" Zizi parried. "To say she did it for young Bates' sake sounds poppycock to me."

"Me, too," and Mrs Everett smiled. "If she did it, she had a deeper motive than that! A more disgraceful one."

"Meaning?"

"Well?—not to put too fine a point upon it,—breach of promise!"

"Was there such a breach?"

"Oh, I'm not saying,—but Letitia certainly wanted to marry Sir Herbert——"

"Why, I thought he was your admirer——"

"Oh, well," and the lady bridled, "I'm not saying anything about that—but if he did admire me, that doesn't mean I smiled on him. I'm no husband hunter,— and poor Letitia is and always has been—without success, poor thing!"

"And it went as far as an engagement?"

"I only surmise that from what Miss Prall has hinted—not, I must say, from anything poor Sir Herbert said! But you know what old maids are——"

"How comes it that, while you and Miss Prall are at such odds, you have the same admirers? I'm told Mr Crippen is a beau of both."

Zizi sensed the widow's willingness to exploit her conquests and utilized the knowledge.

"Oh, he didn't care for Letitia! He was rather polite to me, but I had to discourage him. One can't be too careful. And if you give a man a kindly smile, he thinks he may presume on it."

"Was Sir Herbert like that?"

"Yes, indeed! Although he was Richard's uncle, he was no kin to Richard's aunt Letitia, and he didn't hesitate to tell me how little he admired that Grenadier type of woman."

"Preferring more feminine natures?"

"Yes," Mrs Everett preened herself. "How you do understand, Miss Zizi! I expect you're a heart-breaker yourself."

"Oh, rather!" and Zizi's big dark eyes rolled roguishly. "But I say, Mrs Everett, if this breach of promise case is a true bill, it's a straw to show which way the wind might have blown,—at least."

"Well, don't quote me,—but I do know Letitia Prall's nature and you know it's said, 'Hell hath no fury like a woman scorned.'"

Zizi faced her squarely and with a sharp look said, "You know, Mrs Everett, you're making a very grave accusation. Do you really think Miss Prall is——"

"Yes, I do! That man was killed. He said women did it. There are no women sufficiently interested in his death to be suspected of it except Letitia and Eliza Gurney. So, much as I hate to think so dreadfully of any woman, I've no choice but to suspect them. Of course, it's a grave accusation, but you asked me and it's my duty to say what I think."

From all this Zizi gleaned one bit of satisfaction. She felt positive that Mrs Everett herself was innocent. She had never really suspected the little widow but her name had been mentioned as a possible suspect, and Zizi wondered. Now, she decided that, whatever might be true about Letitia Prall, Mrs Everett could not, were she guilty herself, talk the way she did about her enemy. Not so much the accusation as the way it was said. Had Mrs Everett killed the man, or assisted or directed the murder, she would have shown fear, secretiveness, or at least a harassed demeanor. Instead of which, she had apparently no interest in the matter save a vindictive desire to see her enemy in the clutches of the law.

Anyway, thought Zizi, I cross her off from my list of suspects, and now for the Prall side of the story.

Leaving the Everett apartment Zizi went up the stairs to the eighth floor, and though she was headed for Letitia Prall's, she paused at the Binney rooms.

"Come in," called Wise, as the sleek black little head peeped in at the door; "I've struck it!"

"Where?" asked Zizi, intuitively knowing that he had found the hiding place of the paper.

"Here," and Wise drew her attention to a fairly large mirror that was above the mantel in the sitting-room.

"Why, that thing was screwed fast," the girl said, "and we couldn't move it."

"I unscrewed it—and, behold."

Loosening the screws, which he had only partially readjusted, Wise lifted down the mirror, and disclosed a rectangular space where the wall paper had been cut away.

"The bakery men!" Zizi cried. "Why 'women,' then?"

"Now, look here, Ziz," and Wise replaced the mirror, "get it in your head that women may have been interested in getting this recipe. To suppose a woman may have been acting for a man, while possible, is not probable."

"Why not? Suppose a woman, say a working girl, so devoted to a man that she'd commit murder at his bidding——"

"No man could be such a coward as that!"

"Oh, Penny, what an exalted opinion you have of your sex! Of course he could! A man who would murder would use a woman to help him murder. Of course he offered a big inducement,—marriage maybe——"

"You're romancing——"

"No, I'm not; I'm reconstructing. I see a man wanting that recipe desperately. He sets a woman to get it. He may not have meant her to go to such lengths as murder, to get it, but——"

"All right, but stick to facts. The recipe has been stolen by someone in the know. Some one who realized why Sir Herbert had his room repapered——"

"Clever trick, wasn't it?"

"Yes, but unnecessary. He could have put the thing in safe deposit."

"Englishmen are queer that way. And he may have distrusted our American institutions——"

"Well, anyway, there's no doubt he did hide the paper behind the new wallpaper, and there's no doubt somebody has stolen it. I suppose you agree to that?"

"Yea, my lord! But it may have been taken after the murder."

"Of course it was. Why kill the man, else?"

"Why kill him at all?"

"To get him out of the way, in order to get the recipe and manufacture the buns."

"For whom?"

"That's just it. There are several bakeries interested,—others beside the principal ones, of which we know. Now we must find out which baker could have worked his deadly scheme through women."

"Does this let out the Prall or Everett suspects?"

"To my mind, yes. But I never suspected them, anyway."

"Nor I. And I've exonerated Mrs Everett to my satisfaction, and I'm going to find out for sure about the Grenadier. Now, there's that Molly,——"

"Yes, she's in it, up to the neck, I believe. And she's such a liar——"

"Oh, Penny, you can't let a lady liar fool you, can you? Get her up here, and put her through an inquisition. *I'll* tell you if she's telling truth or not."

"Yes, you're first class at that."

Molly was summoned and when she appeared Zizi saw at once something had happened. The girl's demeanor was entirely changed. She was more self-important and self-assertive, and Zizi wondered if she had learned something definite against some suspect.

"Molly," began Wise, "we've found that some one has been—prowling round in here, just as you said,—and you are to tell us who it was."

"That I don't know, sir," the girl replied, speaking with a flippancy that was careless and almost impertinent.

"Then tell us all you do know. Was it a man or a woman?"

"A woman, sir."

"Why, Molly!" Zizi cried, "you told me it was a man, and that he was up to no good. Those were your very words."

"Oh, no, you don't remember correctly. I said it was a woman."

"That is an untruth," Zizi stated, calmly. "So, now we know you are telling us falsehoods, we must find out why. Has some one paid you for it? We will pay you more for the truth. Might as well, Penny. This girl only sells her statements, true or false."

"All right, Molly. But we only want to buy the true ones. Now, what'll you take for all you really know about the matter, and guarantee to be the strict truth?"

"I don't want any pay. And the truth is that the person I saw was a lady—I mean a woman."

"Care to mention names?"

"I don't know who it was. I just saw a veiled figure——"

"Cut out the veiled figure!" cried Zizi. "You're making it up. There never was any veiled figure,—you saw a man hunting around here, while you were hidden in the bathroom. You know he was looking for something of value hidden in these rooms. And——" Zizi's black eyes fairly seemed to bore into Molly's own as she went on, "you know he got it. Also, you know who the man was,—and you won't tell, and you say it was a woman, because—because what, Molly?"

"I don't—I mean——" Molly blushed scarlet and dropped her eyes; then, with a revived bravado she cried, "It *was* a woman,—I tell you it was a woman!"

"Stop lying!" said Zizi sternly, "she's doing that, Pen, because the man she saw has ordered her to."

"No, he hasn't," Molly declared, but Zizi said:

"Yes, he has, and what's more, he has bribed you by——"

Zizi's penetrating glance overcame Molly's boldness and she trembled in silence as Zizi said, "by marriage!"

Even Wise looked up in amazement; "What *do* you mean, Zizi?"

"Just what I say. Molly is wearing a very bright, new wedding ring. She didn't have it yesterday. Molly knows the truth we're looking for, and she won't tell because it implicates a man who has married her to keep her quiet! Is it Bob Moore, Molly."

"Yes, ma'am," said the girl, in a low tone, and with a very apparent look of relief.

"Then it isn't," said Zizi triumphantly; "I know by the way you speak! Who is it?"

"It isn't anybody," Molly said, but she said it with a furtive glance at their faces in turn; with a hesitating air of uncertainty as to what course to take; with a futile attempt at her old impudent manner. "I'm not really married; lots of us girls wear a wedding ring to fool people."

"Rubbish!" said Zizi, contemptuously. "There's no sense in that! You are married,—or, you think you are— aha, I thought so!"

For Molly's scared glance betokened that Zizi had struck on the truth. Quite evidently she was apprehensive lest the aspersion should prove a correct one. "He married you in an extremity of fear,—fear that you would tell of his visit to the room,—now, who could it be, Penny? It's easy enough to judge if we guess right,— but I can't think of any one. It must be some employe of the house,—or——"

"Or some tool of some of the bakery people," said Wise.

"Look higher," jeered Molly, her self-confidence returning, as she realized their uncertainty.

"Good heavens!" cried Zizi, "you can't mean Richard Bates!"

"Yep," said Molly, and her eyes danced with a wicked glee.

"Oh, incredible!" wailed Zizi. "Yet I've been afraid of him all along. You see, he's shielding his aunt. I'm sure Miss Prall is——"

"You said you didn't believe her guilty," spoke up Wise.

"I know I did, but what other way can we turn? It can't be any less important person who married Molly to shut her up. There can't be any reason that would make Bates do so, but to shield his aunt from suspicion. Molly says now it was a woman searching the room,—of course, she didn't want the recipe,—that's a side issue; she wanted some letters or something in connection with the breach of promise——"

"Come, come, Zizi, you can't take that little yellow-topped widow's yarn of a breach of promise too seriously——"

"Why not? She is innocent herself, I know. She suspects Miss Prall, I know. She gave a perfectly good motive,—why, Pen, if women killed that man where's another motive that can hold a candle to the 'woman scorned' idea? Come, Molly, own up; was it Miss Prall searching the room?"

"Oh, no, miss!" and Molly's eyes bulged with such real surprise that there was no doubting her sincerity this time.

"But how could you tell, if the figure was a veiled one?" asked Wise.

"Oh, I could tell it wasn't Miss Prall,—gracious, no!"

"What was the—the person looking for,—I mean where was the search made?"

"All around."

"In the desk?"

"Yes, and in the table drawers and the cupboards,—and—and—everywhere." Molly waved a vague hand about the room.

"And behind the mirror?" Wise sprang this at her suddenly.

The girl's face blanched. "How—what made you think of that?" she gasped, her voice quaking with fear.

"Ah, that brings back the picture, does it? You saw the—the person, hunting about; you saw him go to the mirror, gaze at it thoughtfully, then unscrew it, and then—then he succeeded in his search? Eh?"

"Yes," Molly breathed, fairly hypnotized into the truth by Wise's suggestive air and tense, compelling voice.

CHAPTER 18: FITTED TO A T

"Now, look here, Molly," and Wise fixed her with his piercing gaze, "you say Richard Bates married you. I don't believe it for a minute, but I do believe somebody married you, or pretended to, to keep your mouth shut on an important matter. It may have been Bob Moore, or—— but I'm going to find out who it was, and I'm going to find out now. If, as you say, it was Richard Bates, why did he do it?"

Molly gulped in a scared, desperate fashion and her eyes rolled wildly about as she replied, "To shield somebody else."

"Who?" Zizi snapped at her.

"You know well enough," the girl sullenly answered.

"But you said it was *not* Mr Bates' aunt."

"Oh, no, it wasn't."

"Then,—it was——"

"Yes, it was."

"Dorcas Everett, she means," Zizi said, scornfully. "As well accuse me! You must know, Molly, you can't put over any such a bluff as that!"

"All right, you needn't believe it if you don't want to. But Miss Everett and her mother are the 'women' you are after."

"That child couldn't do such a thing!"

"Oh, *she* didn't do anything but obey her mother's orders blindly. Mrs Everett and her maid, Kate Holland, committed the murder and Dorcas kept watch in the hall without knowing why she was doing it. Now, Mr Bates knows all about it,—and he knows that I know. And I said I'd tell if he didn't marry me, so rather than have his girl accused, or his girl's——"

"Zizi, why do we listen to this pack of lies?" exclaimed Wise. "This girl is making up as fast as she can talk,——"

"Indeed I'm not!" cried Molly, seemingly in desperation; "I can prove all I'm saying! Here's my wedding ring——"

"Yes, but Mr Bates didn't give it to you," said Zizi, scornfully. "I know who did, though, and if you'll own up it will be better for you."

Now Zizi didn't know at all,—in fact, she wasn't sure that Molly hadn't bought the ring herself, but both Wise and Zizi were at a loss to know which way to turn next, and they were omitting no possible chance at a stray bit of information.

"How do you know?" demanded Molly, and again she looked frightened.

"Now, see here, Molly," Wise tried again, "if you'll tell us the truth you'll be rewarded. But if you don't, you'll not only lose your reward but you'll find yourself in the biggest pickle you've ever been in."

"I'm not afraid," was the pert reply. "My husband will look after me."

"Yes, if he *is* your husband," Zizi jeered, and saw again that Molly's greatest fear was that the wedding had not been a real one.

Therefore, Zizi argued, there had been a ceremony and why would it have taken place except to shut Molly's mouth? And who could have been the bridegroom except the one interested in suppressing Molly's secret, whatever it might be?

"Clear out, Molly," said Wise, suddenly. "Don't clear far, for if you try to leave this house you'll be arrested. Merely go about your work as usual, and say nothing to anybody. If you'll take my advice you'll run pretty straight, for I don't mind telling you you're in deep waters!"

"It's a bad lookout, Ziz," said Wise after Molly had gone; "any way you take it it comes back to either the Pralls or the Everetts. There's no other bunch of women implicated. I've been into everything thoroughly and if we go by that written message of Binney's,—and how can we ignore it?—we've got to get women, and the women are the——"

"The Everetts," said Zizi moodily.

"Oh, no, the Pralls!"

"When you say the Pralls, you mean Miss Letitia and Miss Gurney, I suppose."

"Rather Miss Gurney and Miss Letitia. If they did it, the Gurney woman struck the blow at the bidding of the other. If the Everetts did it, the Holland woman stabbed at the order of her mistress. But I incline to the Pralls, and that explains Bates' anxiety to shield his aunt."

"He'd be equally desirous of shielding his sweetheart's people, but in any case, I can't believe *he* married Molly, either really or by a fake ceremony."

"It isn't like the chap,—he's an all-round straight one; but he's young, and in a desperate emergency,—well, anyway, things must be brought to a head. I'm going for Bates now."

The detective found his quarry and asked him for an interview.

The two men went into a small reception-room on the ground floor and Wise closed the door.

"There's no use in my going on, Mr Bates," he began, "unless you want to see the thing through to a finish. I must tell you the evidences are pointing to women,—whom you would be sorry to see accused."

"I know—I know——" and Richard bowed his head in his hands and groaned. "It isn't my aunt, I'm positive of that. I've not only satisfied myself by confidential talks with her, but I've proved it by definite facts and testimony of servants and others. Now, I suppose you hold that the only other possibility is——"

"Yes, I'm obliged to think that. I know what you mean, and this is no time to be squeamish. We both mean Mrs Everett and her maid, Kate. If there were any doubt about the written paper,——"

"There isn't. It's my uncle's writing, undeniably. He was found with the pencil just falling from his nerveless hand. There's no escape from all that. I've been over and over it. There's no chance of the chorus girls or house girls,—oh, I've been over all the possibilities,—and there's only Mrs Everett left. Honestly, Wise, I'd rather it had been my aunt! That may sound dreadful to you, but after all, she's only my aunt, while Mrs Everett is Dorcas' *mother*! And I'd rather bear sorrow and disgrace myself than to have my little love bear it. Can we drop the whole thing?"

"Not very well now. Bates, are you in any coil with Molly?"

"Molly? The chambermaid? No. Why?"

"Good! I believe you. She says you married her."

"What does she say that for? Is she crazy? But it doesn't bother me; I've troubles of my own. I can't think anybody will believe her."

"No; she said it to shield someone else. And of course, a man. So, that's our one hope. Who is that man?"

"What matter? We're looking for a woman."

"But the man might be a help. Why could Melly make a man marry her, unless he were desperately afraid of what she could tell?"

"But it may all have no connection with our case."

"I've got a hunch it has. And I'm going to find out. And, first of all, I want to go over the ground again of scrutinizing the place where Sir Herbert died."

"No evidence there. The floors have been scrubbed many times."

"But the marks remain."

The marks that had been drawn round the blood spots at the scene of the crime were still faintly visible, and Wise knelt down to study them. It seemed utterly useless to Bates, for what could possibly be gained from scrutinizing the floor where the dead man had lain?

Yet Pennington Wise found something!

The body had fallen at the base of one of the great onyx columns, near the side wall of the lobby. In fact, the head and shoulders had fallen against the wall, as if the victim had been driven back by his pursuers till he could go no farther.

And, after scanning the floor, Wise's eyes traveled on to the onyx wall itself, to the heavy surbase of wide, smooth onyx blocks, and on the pinkish, mottled surface his trained eyes descried a pencil mark.

"Gee!" he cried, explosively, "oh, I say!"

Quickly he ran for the paper the dead man left, stripped from it the protecting glass panes, and with the utmost care he laid the paper itself against the onyx block that showed a pencil mark.

His eyes bulged with surprise, his face flushed with excitement, and he jumped up from the floor, where he had pursued his quest unnoticed save for a disinterested passer-by.

"Bates!" he cried, as he returned to the little reception-room and found the young man still there and still in deep dejection, "Oh, Bates!"

"What?" and Richard lifted his head to see the excited detective brandishing the paper in a wave of triumph.

"What do you think? Listen, man, put your whole mind on this! When Sir Herbert was stabbed he fell to the floor."

"Yes."

"He rolled over toward the wall,—or fell against the wall,—and he had just sufficient strength left to get a pencil and a scrap of paper out of his pocket and write that message."

"Yes,—good heavens, Wise, I know all that!"

"Sure you do. Well, now hark. He didn't place that paper on the floor to write on it; he held it up against the wall."

"Well?"

"Well, and part of the writing,—the first part, fell on the wall and not on the paper——"

"What!" shouted Bates. "What was it? Does it change the meaning?"

"*Does* it! Well, rather! The part on the wall is one letter,—the initial letter of what he wrote——"

"What was it? Tell me, Wise, don't keep me in suspense!"

"I don't mean to. It was a T,—a capital T."

"Well? I don't see——"

"Why, it makes the message read 'Two men did this,' instead of 'women did this.' The words are run together, for he couldn't lift the pencil——"

"He always did that,—his writing always shows connected words!"

"So, there's the message as clear as print! The T on the onyx just fits to the first mark on the paper,—any one can see that,—and we have the dying statement, 'Two men did this.' With what is undoubtedly the further instruction, 'get both'."

"What a revelation! Who can they be?"

"It ought to be easy to find out. They are, of course, some of the bakery men. And Sir Herbert's idea was that doubtless one would be apprehended, but for us to get both of them."

"And the women are out of it!"

"Ab—s—lute—ly! But we must go warily. You see, the guilty men have been glad to hide behind the idea of 'women' which came to their rescue by the merest chance. It's all so easily understood now. Sir Herbert, with dying effort and failing eyesight, wrote hurriedly, and efficient, though he was, his haste made him begin his writing off the paper instead of on it. His habit of connecting words, or his inability from weakness to lift his pencil, made the words 'Two men,' the capital missing, seem to be 'women.' Think how delighted the two men must have been at this! I doubt if they realized what did happen,—more likely they thought Sir Herbert denounced women for some reason of his own. Now, to catch them we must walk delicately, like Scriptural Agag, and spring on them unawares."

"Which way shall we look?"

"Take the Bakery men in turn. Crippen first, I should say."

"Vail?"

"Vail's out of it. You see, he was in the elevator with Moore when it happened."

"Unless Vail and Moore were the two men, and trumped up the whole story."

"I don't think that. Moore's no criminal; he had no motive, and the whole weight of evidence and testimony goes to prove Moore truly interested in the solution of the mystery. He's worked harder on it than you know. I've watched him. No, Bob Moore is not the man! And that lets Vail out."

"Well, then—but I won't suggest. You can dictate."

"First let's get Zizi and tell her."

The girl was summoned and when Wise told her what he had found her big, black eyes danced with delight.

"Who's the criminal, Zizi?" asked Wise.

"The man who married Molly," she returned, promptly. "Also the man who hunted and found the recipe. Molly saw him doing that, and made him marry her or she'd tell. If he could contrive a mock marriage of course he did. Or it may have been a real one. That doesn't matter. It's his identity that matters. Two men! That man, then, and another."

"Vail's out of it," Wise informed her, and told why. "Then, there's Crippen,——"

"No;" Zizi interrupted, "don't go further afield. It's—wait a minute,—get Bob Moore in here."

This was accomplished and Zizi did the interrogating.

Care was taken not to divulge the new evidence and when Zizi asked him to detail his actions at the exact time of the crime, the man wonderingly recounted his oft-told tale.

"Did Mr Vail seem about as usual when he was talking to you, going up in the elevator?" Zizi asked, casually.

"Yes, but very chummy and talkative, more so than I ever knew him to be before."

"Yes? And did he detain you at this floor,—or did *you* keep *him*, talking about the detective story you were reading?"

"Why, I don't know. Come to think of it,—I should say he detained me,—for he was so interested,—and, too, I never would have presumed to talk to him so familiarly if he hadn't egged me on."

"Think back, now. Did he really keep you from going back by talking to you? Could you say he did that purposely?"

"I can say that may have been the case," Moore averred, thinking hard. "But he seemed really interested——"

"As he never had been before," commented Zizi, and adding, "and as he never has been since?"

"No; he's never been so chummy with me since. I've tried to talk to him about the Binney murder case, but he almost snubbed me,—at least he shut me off mighty quick."

"That's all, Moore, and not a word to any one of anything that has been said in this room!"

"Now," said Zizi, after Moore had disappeared, "Vail's one; who's the other?"

"Why, Zizi, Vail was in the elevator——"

"Penny, I've known that 'Vail was in the elevator' all through this whole matter. I've been told a thousand times that Vail was in the elevator! It's been fairly rubbed into my noddle that Vail was in the elevator! Why, don't you see, that's Vail's alibi! His being in the elevator is his safeguard! Oh, Penny-poppy-show, sometimes I despair of *ever* making a detective out of you! Well, my dear child, Mr Vail is one,—as I remarked,—and I found him; now you may find the other, and then we'll have the 'two men' who 'did this.' Get busy."

"S'pose, since you're so smart, *you* find the other one," said Wise, with no trace of jealousy in his tone. He was as elated at Zizi's cleverness as if it had been his own, and he believed her implicitly.

"I can do it," she said, calmly. "Send for Molly."

"Yes, there's the key to the situation," Wise agreed.

Richard Bates sat still, wondering if the joyful news that no one he cared for was implicated could really be true! He awaited Molly's coming with impatience, longing to get the whole matter cleared up.

"And so, Molly," Zizi began, when the girl came into the room and Wise had closed the door behind her, "and so it was Mr Vail who married you!"

A suppressed shriek answered them, and Molly glared like an angry tiger. "No!" she screamed, "*no!*"

"Useless talk," said Zizi, "your fright and your excitement give the lie to your words! Though your words are oftener lies than not. Now, Molly, you don't dare go contrary to Mr Vail's orders, I know, but don't you think you'd better do that than to go to jail?"

"I don't know——Oh, I don't know *what* to do," and the girl broke down and wept so piteously that Zizi was sorry for her.

"There, there, Molly," she said, "I'll take care of you. You're only a tool in the hands of a villain; you stay by me, and I'll look after you. Penny, we want Vail."

They got Vail. At first he brazened it out, and finally, when he was cornered, he turned state's evidence to save what he could of his own skin.

It seemed, Vail was determined to make the deal for the Binney Buns, and, as a last resort, had waylaid Sir Herbert on his way home from the Hotel Magnifique after the dinner to the chorus girls.

With Vail on that occasion was a friend of his, one Doctor Weldon, who was a skillful surgeon, more careful in his surgical operations than in his mental or moral ones. He was Vail's tool, by reason of past historic incidents, and the scheme had been planned by the two conspirators.

Binney was invited to Dr Weldon's home, not far from The Campanile, and there, from midnight on, both Vail and Weldon tried to persuade the Englishman to consent to Vail's terms.

But Binney was obdurate and finally went home, accompanied by the two men. When near The Campanile, Vail darted on ahead, and managed adroitly to get into the elevator with Moore and be on the way up when Binney and Dr Weldon entered the onyx lobby.

The rest was easy. Binney had the Prall paper-knife with him and the Doctor knew it. With it, the skilled surgeon stabbed his victim and made away at once. Sir Herbert, dying, but with mind alert, wrote the fact that two men were responsible for his death; and whether he tried to continue with 'get both' or 'get Bob's evidence' or 'get bakery,' or what was in his fast clouding brain, they never knew.

But when to the surprise of the criminals, women were suspected, they felt so freed from suspicion that they took no care about it.

Vail, however, was keen for the recipe, which was, in part, why he had Binney killed, and he made many attempts to find it in its clever hiding place. When he did find it, Molly knew of it, and in order to keep the girl quiet he married her, with, however, a mock ceremony.

Discovering this, Molly was so angry that she told on Vail, and he, in turn, told on Doctor Weldon.

All of this was disclosed promptly, and justice took its course with the "Two men."

It would be pleasant to write further that the historic feud of the "women" who had been so keenly suspected was settled as satisfactorily. But not so. The two opposing forces seemed to take on new vim from the revelation of the truth about the murder, and each positively seemed angered that the other had not been found guilty.

This may not have been the real truth at the bottom of the hearts of Miss Prall and Mrs Everett, but certain it is that, though they might not have desired conviction for one another, they greatly enjoyed suspicion.

"At any rate," said Miss Prall, "Adeline did set her cap for Sir Herbert, and I think that's a crime in itself."

And Mrs Everett remarked, "Poor man! but he's better off than if Letitia Prall had caught him! Which she tried her best to do!"

The young lovers, relieved of all fears that their people or each other's people were implicated in crime, were so emancipated from fear of any sort, that they dared to plan their marriage without the consent of their elders.

Said Richard, "We're going to be married, anyway, Aunt Letitia; you can understand that! And your own conduct you may shape as you choose."

Quoth Dorcas: "I'm going to marry Ricky, mother. If you consent all right,—if you don't, I'll elope."

And the Feudists, though incensed to the point of exasperation, had a certain secret feeling of satisfaction that the wedding would add fuel to the flames of their somewhat smoldering fires of wrath.

"Bless 'em," said Bates, as the honeymoon began, "they ought to be grateful to us for giving them something new to fight about."

"They are," said Dorcas.

THE END

Resurrected Press Mysteries From Louis Tracy

The Albert Gate Mystery
Four men murdered and a fortune in diamonds belonging to the Turkish Sultan stolen, while the Foreign Office official in charge has gone missing. Was it a common jewelry theft or was it a case of international intrigue? This is the question that barrister detective Reginald Brett must solve.

The Bartlett Mystery
When Ronald Tower is murdered on his way to a bridge game on the yacht Sans Souci it at first appears a common crime. But as Rex Carshaw finds, a tragic case of mistaken identity leads to political scandal among the rich and powerful of New York.

The Strange Case of Mortimer Fenley
When the wealthy Mortimer Fenley is struck down by a shot from an express rifle on the steps of his mansion, detectives Winter and Furneaux of Scotland Yard must find the culprit. Was it the artist who claimed he was painting a picture at the time of the shot? The disaffected younger son? Or is there another suspect?

The Stowmarket Mystery
For five generations the Fergus-Hume family has been cursed. Each of the baronets has met a violent end. When the fifth baronet is found slain by a ceremonial Japanese dagger, suspicion falls on his cousin David. It falls to barrister detective Reginald Brett to prove his innocence and find the real murder in a case that spans two continents and as many centuries.

Resurrected Press Mysteries by J. S. Fletcher

The Orange-Yellow Diamond
When an elderly pawnbroker is murdered in the London parish of Paddington, a young, down on his luck writer is accused of the crime. But then it's found the pawnbroker had had in his possession an extraordinary South African diamond worth over eighty-thousand pounds — a diamond that's now missing. It falls to Melky Rubenstein to unravel the mystery and prove the young man's innocence.

The Middle Temple Murder
When an elderly man's body is found on the steps of chambers in the Midde Temple, one of the Inns of Court, it falls to newspaperman Frank Spargo and Detective-Sergeant Rathbury to solve the crime. The murdered man, for indeed it was murder, was found with no money or identification on his person except for a piece of paper with the name and address of a young barrister. Who is the victim? Why was he killed? Who is the murderer?

Scarhaven Keep
Bassett Oliver, the famed actor, has gone missing. When Oliver fails to show for a rehearsal, aspiring playwright Richard Copplestone finds himself sent to the small village of Scarhaven on the northern coast of England to track down the actors movements. What he finds is mystery. Find the answers as Copplestone unravels the mystery of Scarhaven Keep.

Visit www.resurrectedpress.com

Resurrected Press Mysteries by Fergus Hume

The Green Mummy

Professor Braddock hoped to compare the burial practices of the Egyptians with those of the ancient Peruvians with his latest acquisition, the mummy of the last Inca, Caxas. But on arrival, the packing case proved to hold not the mummy, but the body of his assistant Sidney Bolton. It falls to Archie Hope to discover the murderer if he is to marry the professors step-daughter, Lucy Kendal. Who killed Bolton and where is the mummy? Was it the sea captain Hervey? The mysterious Don Pedro? Cockatoo the Polynesian servant? The professor, himself? And what has become of the emeralds? These are the questions that Hope must answer amongst the secrets of the past in The Green Mummy.

The Mystery of a Hansom Cab

"Truth is said to be stranger than fiction, and certainly the extraordinary murder which took place in Melbourne Friday morning goes a long way towards verifying that saying." Thus opens The Mystery of a Hansom Cab, the best selling mystery of the nineteenth century. When a man is found dead in a hansom cab one of Melbourne's leading citizens is accused of the murder. He pleads his innocence, yet refuses to give an alibi. It falls to a determined lawyer and an intrepid detective to find the truth, revealing long kept secrets along the way. Fergus Hume's first and perhaps most famous mystery... The Mystery Of A Hansom Cab.

Visit www.resurrectedpress.com

Resurrected Press Mysteries from the Dr. John Thorndyke Series

Dr. John Thorndyke - Lecturer on Medical Jurisprudence and Forensic Medicine. Before Bones, before CSI, before Quincy, M.E– there was Dr. John Thorndyke solving the most baffling cases of Edwardian London using the latest tools of medical science. Read about his cases in:

The Eye of Osiris
John Bellingham, noted Egyptologist has vanished not once but twice in the same day. Now Dr, Thorndyke must unravel the tangled claims on his estate, solve the riddle of the missing man and find the "Eye of Osiris".

The Mystery of 31 New Inn
When Dr. Jervis is whisked away in a coach with no windows to an unknown location to treat a man in a coma from undivulged causes it is Dr. Thorndyke who must come up with the solution.

The Red Thumb Mark
The first of Dr. Thorndyke's cases finds him trying to prove the innocence of a young man accused of being a diamond thief despite the fact that his finger print was found at the scene of the crime.

John Thorndyke's Cases
More cases of medical mysteries as told by his trusted assistant Jervis, M.D. Eight stories of crime and deduction in Edwardian London.

Visit www.resurrectedpress.com

Resurrected Press Mysteries by John R. Watson & Arthur J. Rees

The Hampstead Mystery

High Court Justice Sir Horace Fewbanks found shot dead in his Hampstead home, a butler with a criminal past, a scorned lover and a hint of scandal. These are the elements of the Hampstead Mystery that Detective Inspector Chippenfield of Scotland Yard must unravel with the assistance of the ambitious Detective Rolfe. But will he be able to sort out the tangled threads of this case and arrest the culprit before he is upstaged by the celebrated gentleman detective Crewe. Follow the details of this amazing case at it plays out across Hampstead, London and Scotland until it reaches a stunning conclusion in the courts of the Old Bailey.

The Mystery of the Downs

When Harry Marsland was caught in a sudden down pour he sought shelter at Cliff Farm. Met at the door by a young woman clearly expecting someone else he is only too glad to get inside to wait out the storm. When they hear a noise upstairs in the deserted house they investigate only to discover the body of the farm's owner, Frank Lumsden, dead of a gunshot wound. Who then, killed Lumsden, and why? Who was the woman expecting and did she have any roll in the murder? These are the questions that private detective Crewe must answer in The Mystery of the Downs.

Visit www.resurrectedpress.com

Other Resurrected Press Mysteries

Mysteries on a Train

Before the Orient Express there was:

The Rome Express by Arthur Griffiths
A man is found dead in his first class sleeping compartment on the express from Rome to Paris. Who was his murderer? The Countess? The English General? His brother the clergy man? The maid who has disappeared? Is the French justice system up to solving the crime? Read about it in The Rome Express.

The Passenger from Calais by Arthur Griffiths
Colonel Basil Annesley finds he is the only passenger on the train from Calais to Lucerne. That is until a mysterious woman shows up at the last minute to book a compartment. Who is after her? What is her secret? Is she a criminal or a victim? Read about it in The Passenger from Calais

About Resurrected Press

A division of Intrepid Ink, LLC, Resurrected Press is dedicated to bringing high quality, vintage books back into publication. See our entire catalogue and find out more at www.ResurrectedPress.com.

About Intrepid Ink, LLC

Intrepid Ink, LLC provides full publishing services to authors of fiction and non-fiction books, eBooks and websites. From editing to formatting, from publishing to marketing, Intrepid Ink gets your creative works into the hands of the people who want to read them. Find out more at www.IntrepidInk.com.

www.ingramcontent.com/pod-product-compliance
Lightning Source LLC
Chambersburg PA
CBHW060913180626
46817CB00004B/1241